THE VEILED KINGDOM

USA *TODAY* BESTSELLING AUTHOR

HOLLY RENEE

PRONUNCIATION GUIDE

Marmoris: MAR-moris
Enveilarian: ON-veil-air-ian
Dacre: DAY-ker
Nyra: near-ah
Wren: ren
Verena: Vuh-rehn-ah
Kai: K ai h
Eiran: AIR-in

PRONUNCIATION GUIDE

CONTENT WARNING

This book contains depictions of sexually explicit scenes, violence, and assault. It contains mature language, themes, and content that may not be suitable for all readers. Reader discretion is advised.

For Amber Palmer—
Thank you for your endless support and friendship.

CHAPTER 1
NYRA

S weat ran down my spine beneath my thin cloak.
    There was still a slight chill clinging to the air, but the guard who stood near the end of the bridge with his meaty hand resting on the hilt of his sword made my heart race at the thought of my next move.

I took a deep breath and looked out over the bustling market alley. The smell of smoke and salty fish stung my nose, but it couldn't mask the scents of the slums or the sweaty bodies that pushed past me.

I let my dark hair fall over my shoulder as I moved through the crowd of people and as far away from the guard as I could get.

My eyes flicked up to the palace and the large iron gate that separated it from the busy bridge that was almost a city block wide.

The great bridge of the Marmoris Kingdom was a place of legend.

At least that was what the king would have liked for everyone to believe.

My traitorous gaze swept up the palace to where I knew my former room lay. The window was so high that I caught one of my father's flags flapping in the wind just above it.

It was high enough that no one could see in, that my safety could never be breached.

Or so I thought.

In reality, it was just high enough for no one to see the king's shame of a powerless heir.

I had spent far too many years mistaking his disgrace for vigilance. My parents lost hope that the heir to their throne would have power when I reached the age of ten without a spark. I could still remember the fear and concern in their eyes when they told me that we must keep the secret between us, but that concern died long before my mother. My father had become void of his care for me, and it was resentment that stared back.

It was hard to hear the muffled conversations around me with the sound of the rushing water from the massive falls as it fell from beneath the bridge. I strained to listen, but all I could make out was the exchange of coins and whispered deals that weren't meant to be overheard.

A breeze off the ocean had my hair whipping around my shoulders, and I inhaled until my lungs begged me to release it. Every time the gust of wind carried that familiar scent, it flooded me with bittersweet memories. I was torn between the nostalgia and resentment.

I looked out over the water at the dozen boats that were being boarded. My stomach ached with longing as I remembered how I used to watch them and daydream about taking sail until the wind carried me away from this place.

But my stomach always ached these days.

I forced myself to move and weaved through the worn carts until I passed by the merchant whose gaze always lingered on my body a little too long for my liking, but I smiled at him as he leered at me.

That was all I needed.

His gaze dropped to the swell of my breasts, and I let my hands fall behind me.

If he was watching the curves of my body, then he had no time to watch my hands.

"Good afternoon, you," he said before he ran his tongue over his bottom lip that was barely visible through his over-grown graying beard.

"Afternoon," I called back gently, ducking my head to make him see how shy I was, how flattered I was by his attention. All the while my hands wrapped around a single apple and a stale piece of bread.

I tucked the bread into the back of my trousers, keeping my hands hidden beneath my thin cloak.

With a practiced smile, I fluttered my eyelashes as the man ogled me with no concern about the worn ring on his hand.

"It's supposed to get cold tonight." As his gaze remained fixated on my body, I focused on maintaining the steady rhythm of my breathing, concealing the pounding of my heart.

I looked up at the sky, making a show of studying the clouds as I nodded. "Thank you for letting me know."

As if those of us who slept on the street weren't more

than aware of the changes the pressure in the air would bring.

"You know where to find me if that cloak of yours doesn't provide enough warmth."

I bit down on my tongue to stop the retort that was begging to slip past my lips. The apple was still nestled securely in my harsh grip, its weight providing a semblance of comfort amid his remarks even as the juice dripped down my fingers as my nails dug into its flesh.

"Thank you." I nodded once before I took a step back and got lost in the throng of patrons before he could get bored with my body and look elsewhere.

I couldn't afford for him to look elsewhere.

I had been living on these streets for almost a year, ever since the raid, and I had been careful to make sure that no one watched me too closely.

I didn't have enough money to buy my passage on one of the ships like I longed to and rumors of the danger beyond the coast had kept me rooted in place.

The rebellion had grown more ruthless, and I couldn't risk moving south until the tithe, until the rebellion was watching my father and the palace far too closely to notice me.

I moved swiftly through the people milling about the bridge and noticed a man wearing the finest fabrics as he walked up to one of the merchants whose eyes lit up at the sight of him. The man wore no cloak, his shirt more than thick enough to keep away the chill in the air, but that also meant that the pouch that was tied to the front of his belt was clearly visible.

And based on the way it hung just below his hip, I'd bet that there were at least ten coins inside.

I quickened my pace, my eyes fixated on the man as I moved. Desperation clawed at my insides, urging me forward. But greediness would only get me killed, or worse, caught.

And I had enough food to take the edge off my hunger for a couple days.

But the tithe was only a few days away, and I had to run before it happened.

Because everyone in the kingdom was expected to present themselves before the king and pay the tithe owed with whatever power they held.

And I couldn't.

Even if I did have the power to somehow pay what my father thought he was owed, the people who lived inside the palace would know me the moment they saw me. The guards who patrolled the bridge, the city streets, and the dungeons didn't have that privilege, but my father's closest guards did. And they would no doubt be there to protect their king when he stripped his people of what little he allowed them.

They murdered our people for not paying the tithe without a second thought, and it was the fear of what they would do to me that overpowered the fear of the rebellion.

I forced myself to move closer to the man as he ran his hands down his crisp shirt, completely oblivious to those around him.

It was a fool's move on this bridge.

The bridge had proven to be the easiest place to become a thief, but it was also the easiest place to get caught.

And if it weren't for the dread filling my gut at the lack of coins in my pockets and food to fill my belly, I probably would have turned away.

But I couldn't afford to.

Not this close to the tithe.

The man spoke to the merchant in front of him for only a few seconds before he passed over two gold coins.

It was two coins less than I would be able to take from him.

I swallowed the fear that threatened to paralyze me and continued to shadow the man as he moved away from the merchant.

His gait was confident, his steps purposeful, as he made his way down the bridge completely unaware of my presence.

The cloak I wore could easily blend into the sea of cloaks that adorned the market, offering me a small measure of anonymity.

I moved as quickly as I could, trying to get to the man before he got closer to the palace.

I picked up my pace, closing the distance between us, my heart pounding in my chest, matching the rhythm of my footsteps.

He paused, letting a small merchant cart wheel past him, the wooden wheels loud and rickety across the pavers, and I knew this was my only chance.

The cart barreled toward me, narrowly missing me, and I shot forward, clinging to the man as I used him to catch my fall.

I stumbled into him, my hands flailing as I desperately

clung to his shirt, pretending to lose my footing and forcing him to lose his.

He slammed into the man standing behind him, and the three of us barely managed to stay upright as we were jostled among the crowd.

I wasted no time as I pulled on the leather strings that held his pouch to his belt and caught the force of it in my hand.

"I'm so sorry," I stammered, my voice shaky as I steadied myself. "I wasn't watching where I was going."

His eyes scanned over me, assessing me. I could feel the weight of his scrutiny, and every nerve in my body screamed at me to run.

My right hand was buried in his shirt, clinging to him as I tried to straighten myself up, and my left hand held on to his coin pouch for dear life.

The man's confusion turned into concern as he extended a hand toward me. "Are you alright?"

I forced a small smile, doing my best to appear vulnerable.

"Yes. I just… I lost my balance. I'll be fine."

I prayed that he had yet to notice the loss of weight at his hip.

His hands were on my upper arms, holding me steady against him, and he hesitated for a moment before he nodded.

"Be careful out here. The bridge can be a dangerous place for a girl like you."

A girl like me.

He had no idea that this bridge was more dangerous for a girl like me than anyone else. This entire kingdom was.

I nodded back and gripped the pouch in my fist before taking a small step back.

I inclined my head, keeping my eyes downcast. "Thank you, sir. I will be." With that, I turned and effortlessly melted back into the crowd, my heart pounding with a mix of anxiety and guilt.

But neither were enough to make me regret what I had done.

As I made my way through the bustling market, I couldn't help but steal a glance at the pouch clutched tightly in my hand. It was more than enough to sustain me for a few weeks, perhaps even months if I were wise with my spending. The weight of the coins eased some of the urgency that had been gnawing at my insides as I tucked it away into my pocket.

The guards were still standing at the entrance of the bridge and I forced myself to move past them, even though my muscles ached with every step that drew me closer to them. Once I stepped over the threshold of the fine pavers and onto the dusty cobblestones that lined the streets, I allowed myself to glance over my shoulder only once to make sure that no one had noticed me.

That the man hadn't realized my thievery.

When the guards didn't spare me a glance, I picked up my pace and navigated through the narrow streets. The farther from the bridge I got, the less grand the homes and shops that lined the streets became.

And the people who lived in those houses? They became less and less important as well.

You only got to be that close to the king if you had something to offer him.

If your magic was something he might need.

The stench of garbage and decay filled the air, mingling with the distant scent of spices drifting from the run-down food stalls that were scattered along the streets.

It was a stark contrast to the opulence of the palace and its bridge, but the farther away I got from them both, the more I felt like I could breathe.

As I walked through the dilapidated streets, my eyes scanned the faces of those passing by. Many wore expressions of weariness and resignation, their spirits crushed by the weight of their daily struggles. The world outside the palace was a harsh reality, one that constantly reminded me of what I had left behind.

I mourned parts of the life I once lived while simultaneously praying to the gods that I never went back.

I kept my head down, blending seamlessly into the background of poverty and desperation. The ragged cloak that concealed my identity did its job well, lending me the illusion of obscurity among these forgotten streets. Survival has taught me to be invisible, to become a ghost drifting through the shadows.

And that has served me well.

I turned right down an old forgotten alleyway and passed the old house with vines creeping up along the crumbling red bricks. The old woman who lived there rarely left or had visitors, and she checked the small alcove near the back of her gardens even less.

I took a seat there, in the spot that had become my home, and pulled the bread and apple out from beneath my cloak. It was moments like this that I wished I had a blade, but Micah would be here soon enough.

As I savored the first bite of the stolen bread, I heard footsteps growing louder from the end of the alley. I stowed the food away at my side, just in case, and remained quiet as the footsteps slowed. Micah emerged from the shadows, his lean frame blending seamlessly with the darkness around him.

"Any luck today?" he asked in a low voice, his eyes scanning our surroundings for any potential danger before he leaned down and took a seat beside me with a groan.

"I did pretty good," I replied, pulling out the bread and tearing it in half. He took his piece greedily, and it would be impossible to miss the hunger in his eyes. "How about you?"

He nodded approvingly and handed me a small pouch that felt far too light to contain any coins. "I managed to snatch these from a nobleman's carriage near the palace."

I pulled the pouch open gently and saw several folded pieces of parchment all with the royal seal holding them closed.

"It's correspondence for the king."

My fingers trembled as I reached inside the leather pouch, but his words froze me in place. Fear pressed down on me, suffocating me as I dropped the pouch to the ground.

"We can't keep these," I said firmly, my voice barely above a whisper. "If they catch us with these letters, it'll be more than just our lives on the line."

I shook my head, my mind racing with the implications of what Micah had just said. Correspondence for the king meant that these were important documents, potentially containing information that could be used as leverage against those in power. It was a risk we couldn't afford to take lightly.

It was a risk that put me in far more danger than the coins I had just stolen.

If the king and his guards weren't already looking for me, they would come looking for this.

But that was the thing that unsettled me the most. If he had come looking for me, no one knew.

I was the lost princess who everyone still thought was locked away in her tower.

I was the flaw to the king's perfect reign, and he was still hiding me as much as I was hiding from him.

Micah looked at me, concern etched in the lines on his face. "You're right," he admitted, his voice tense. "I never would have taken them if you weren't leaving." He ran his calloused hands through his light hair that seemed to shimmer in the sunlight.

Micah was the only person I had confided in since leaving the palace, but he also only knew what I allowed him to. He had shown me kindness on the streets when no one else had, and I did not return the favor by keeping my identity from him. But my father would kill him if he ever found out he was helping me stay hidden.

To Micah, I was a girl with a past who was on the run, but to my father, I was a liability.

And anyone who knew about me and my lack of power fell into that same category.

"But look." He pulled open one of the parchments, one whose seal had already been broken, and he quickly unfolded it as his eyes scanned over the contents inside. He pointed down the page, and I looked over the edge of the paper to see what he was pointing at.

"We didn't get the rebellion mark just right." He took my left hand in his and pushed up the sleeve, revealing the simple black rebellion mark he had given me.

He ran his thumb across the sensitive skin of my wrist, where the mark had been carefully etched with his magic, and chill bumps broke out along my skin.

The mark was two simple arrows intersecting to form an X. We had both heard of it so many times before, but Micah was right, it was slightly off from the mark listed in the correspondence. The feathers on the fletching weren't the same, and anyone who was already a part of the rebellion would be able to spot the difference easily.

They would also be able to spot that I was nothing more than a traitor trying to impersonate one of them, and they would kill me as quickly as the king would.

But supporters of the king didn't leave the royal coast unless they were joining the rebellion. Not since the raid.

It was too dangerous otherwise.

If one of them were to find me when I ran from here, the only way I would be able to survive would be to make it clear that I was on their side.

They could never know the truth about who I was.

No one could.

"We need to fix this." His fingers moved gently over my mark, and my stomach clenched as I watched the movement. "They'll know you're a fake the moment they see it."

A fake.

Gods, I couldn't think of a better word to describe me.

"Do it." I nodded to the parchment still in front of him

and swallowed. I could still remember the way his magic had burned into my skin the last time, and I knew it would be no less painful now. But pain was a small price to pay in the grand scheme of things. My fate would depend on it.

Micah's face contorted with concentration as he channeled his magic into his fingertips. The air crackled with energy, a tangible anticipation that filled the narrow alleyway. I took a deep breath, steadying myself for what was to come.

Gently, Micah pressed his thumb against the mark on my wrist, careful not to disrupt the existing lines. His magic flowed from him into me, mingling with my flesh. Heat radiated from his touch, searing my skin and etching new details onto the mark.

I bit my lip, enduring the agony as he meticulously adjusted the feathers on the fletching. Each stroke of his thumb felt like fire, branding me with a new identity. It was a reinvention born out of necessity, a desperate attempt to survive in a world that demanded loyalty and allegiance.

As the pain intensified, I clenched my fists, my nails digging into my palms. Micah's touch grew lighter, his focus unwavering as he studied the parchment.

Finally, Micah withdrew his touch, and a wave of relief washed over me. I examined the altered mark on my wrist, the lines now crisp and rimmed with my red, irritated skin. The feathers on the fletching were perfectly aligned, each delicate detail etched into my skin as a permanent testament to who I had to become.

"You have to be careful with this," Micah warned, his voice laced with concern and the same disapproval he had the first time I asked him to give me the mark. "The rebellion is a dangerous game to play."

I nodded solemnly, fully aware of the risks I faced. It was rumored that the rebellion had been gathering strength in secret, driven by the injustices committed by the king and those in power. They fought for freedom, for a world where everyone had an equal chance at life, regardless of their magic.

But they also operated in shadows, their tactics as merciless as those they opposed.

And I had seen the proof of that when they raided the palace that had previously been thought of as impenetrable.

"I know it is," I replied, my voice steady. "But hopefully, I don't have to use it."

We both knew I would never be able to afford passage onto one of the ships in the kingdom's harbor, but if I could travel far enough south, then I might have a chance.

The southern coast was a long journey, especially for a girl who hadn't been more than a mile from the palace, but I didn't have any other options.

"I don't want anything to happen to you." Micah lifted his hand toward my cheek and guilt flooded me.

There was so much weight to his concern and the reasons that compelled him to worry for me. Micah had become my anchor since leaving the palace, my confidant and closest friend.

But the way he was studying my face was...*more.*

A loud and piercing cry echoed in the distance. Micah's hand, which was half an inch from my face, stopped abruptly in midair. We both stilled, our bodies tense as we listened, and suddenly the sound of boots hitting the cobblestones were far too close for either of us to feel safe.

Micah's eyes widened with alarm as he turned his head toward the direction of the approaching footsteps. His hand dropped and his fingers brushed against the hilt of a concealed dagger at his belt. The desperation in his voice was palpable as he whispered urgently, "We have to go, now."

My heart raced in my chest as panic coursed through my veins. I grabbed Micah's arm, my grip tight and unyielding. "Here," I said, my voice filled with both fear and determination as I reached into my pocket and pulled out half the coins from the pouch.

"Where the hell did you get these?" Micah grabbed my hand in his and closed my fingers around the coins as he looked back over his shoulder.

"I stole them," I whispered urgently, my eyes flickering toward the approaching footsteps. "Take them and go. Find a safe place to hide, somewhere they won't find you. We'll meet back here tonight."

"You need these."

"We both do," I urged, and we both knew it to be true.

Micah hesitated for a moment, torn between his concern for me and the need to escape. But we both knew that we were far harder to catch alone than when we were together. I dropped the coins into his hand, and he nodded, his grip tightening around them, before squeezing my hand one last time.

"Be safe," he murmured, his voice filled with a mixture of worry and determination. And then he was gone, disappearing into the shadows as if he were never there.

Left alone in the dimly lit alley, my heart pounded in my chest like a war drum. The approaching footsteps grew louder, drawing closer with each passing second. Fear and adrenaline surged through my veins, fueling my instincts as I turned and sprinted in the opposite direction.

I darted through the narrow alleyway, jumping over a discarded crate and dodging a man who was scurrying in the opposite direction. My lungs burned with every breath, but I pushed through.

My mind raced, trying to formulate a plan as I ran. I needed to find a place to hide, blend in with the crowd, and disappear from the eyes of those who were moving through the streets. It didn't matter who they were after, the King's Guard didn't discriminate against those who got in their way.

The streets were teeming with people, and everyone was on edge. My eyes darted around, as did everyone else's, and there were dozens of guards moving through the crowds.

I slowed my pace, keeping my head down as I moved through the bodies.

"There!" I heard a man call out behind me, but I didn't dare turn around to see who it was. "That's her."

My heart skipped a beat as the voice pierced through the bustling street. Panic surged within me, urging me to run, but I forced myself to remain calm. I weaved through the crowd, my body slipping effortlessly between bodies, desperate to get lost among them.

But fate was not kind to me.

Before I could react, strong hands closed around my arms, yanking me back with a force that sent a jolt of pain shooting up my shoulder. I stumbled, fighting to maintain my balance against the sudden onslaught.

A burly figure loomed over me, clad in the dark navy uniform that marked him as a sentry of the King's Guard. His eyes bore into mine, and my fear fought with my defiance as I forced myself to drop his gaze as I pretended to be someone I wasn't.

Someone who respected the king and his men.

"I've got her," he called over his shoulder, and I winced as I heard more loud footsteps approaching.

He reached forward, lifting my chin with one calloused finger as he studied my face.

"Is it her?" another guard asked from behind him, and I swallowed hard.

No. Please. Please. Please.

If they took me back to the palace, I wouldn't survive. My father wouldn't allow it. I had betrayed him and his kingdom when I ran during the raid, and he wouldn't let me forget it.

"It's her."

He lifted my wrist in his hand, tugging me closer to him as people scattered as far away from us as they could.

I was nothing to them, nobody that they would be willing to risk their own lives for, and Micah had disappeared just as I told him to.

The princess.

I was ready for his next words to escape his lips, prepared for the gasps when everyone heard, but I was shocked when he ran his thumb over my still sore rebellion mark.

"And it looks like the little thief is a traitor."

CHAPTER 2
DACRE

I gritted my teeth as I listened to my father berate me.

As if it was my fault that my sister had been captured.

As if I wasn't already dying inside trying to figure out exactly how we were going to get her out.

This was nothing new.

Members of the rebellion were caught almost daily by the palace guards.

Some rebels, they killed on the spot for their treachery while others were forced to pray to the god of fortune for death to claim them. A prisoner of the king was a prisoner of torture, and the rebellion had many secrets worth spilling.

And my sister was far too young and far too pretty for them to kill off so quickly.

Those guards would have far worse plans for her than discovering her secrets.

But I would bleed and fight until my last breath to get her out.

We were squatting near the edge of the woods, waiting for the last touch of the sun to fall behind the coast.

The tithe was just two days away, and I had to free her before then.

I let my gaze roam through the tree line, searching our surroundings, as my father driveled on.

I didn't have the energy to expend on him.

He may have been the leader of the rebellion, but he was also responsible for getting my mother killed.

He was responsible for getting a vast number of the rebellion killed when he planned a raid that we weren't prepared for.

A raid that changed our lives.

A raid that caused me to lose the respect I had for him.

"Did you hear what I said?" His deep voice grumbled, and I finally met his gaze.

"What?"

"You're not even fucking listening to me, Dacre." The skin on his forehead creased, forming two deep lines as his brows furrowed in frustration. His green eyes narrowed and flickered with a flash of annoyance.

His hair was a deep, dark black, like the endless expanse of a night sky. It fell in soft waves that framed his face and contrasted with his sharp, angular jaw that still carried a scar from the raid.

If it weren't for my mother's dark eyes, I would have been a spitting image of him.

"We know where they keep the prisoners." I ran my hand through my hair as I stared up at the palace and the market bridge we tried to avoid at all costs. "Kai and I are going in alone. If we're unable to find her within a half hour, we retreat."

Over my dead fucking body.

"Half an hour," he reiterated the time frame. "If you can't find her before then you get out. You're too important."

I scoffed at my father's words, but he wasn't paying me any attention.

"We should be sending Mal in with Kai."

"I'm going in, with or without your approval," I stated firmly, meeting my father's gaze with determination. "She's my sister, and I won't leave her at their mercy."

He relaxed his jaw, his head tilting a fraction as he regarded me. He should have been demanding that it was him that went in after his daughter. "You have thirty minutes."

It didn't matter what he said. My mind was already made up. I had no intention of retreating if I couldn't find her within half an hour. No matter the consequences.

Without waiting for further orders from my father, I turned to face the darkening shadows of the capital city.

Kai and I had studied every inch of the palace, every guard's routine, and every possible entry point. We had been studying them for years. But now, as we prepared to enter the palace grounds again for the first time since the raid, the veins in my neck hammered as my chest heaved with each beat of my racing heart.

"Are you ready?" Kai asked, his voice barely audible in the silence.

"As I'll ever be." My palms were slick with sweat and my voice wavered as I forced out a response.

We moved through the shadows, our footsteps barely making a sound against the moss-covered ground as we left my father and the others behind. We didn't head straight for the bridge. Instead, we moved to the right, toward the sound of the few street merchants that still milled about the streets.

"This is where the fun begins," Kai whispered, his voice tinged with dread.

I nodded, the same trepidation filling me as I looked around. We moved in sync, like two coils of the same snake, one step at a time, navigating through the maze of people and goods.

The market was still alive with the sounds of bargaining and laughter. Ahead of us, the palace towered above the city, its grandeur and power a stark contrast to the plight of the king's subjects.

Kai nodded to the right, and I followed him down a narrow alleyway that led between two tall buildings. I looked over my shoulder, seeing the familiar house that was so covered with ivy it was almost unrecognizable, before looking back ahead.

I couldn't think about that house. Not right now.

The hairs on the back of my neck stood up, and I clenched my fists, trying to squelch my nerves.

Kai led us through another alleyway, deeper into the city's houses and farther away from the crowds. The smell of the ocean was unmistakable here, and I could almost taste the salt on my tongue.

The sound of waves crashing against the rocks echoed

in the distance, and I allowed myself to take a moment to catch my breath.

We emerged from the alleyway, and the bustling crowds gave way to the quieter streets of the old city. The palace was still a ways away, its shadowed form a beacon in the gathering dusk.

"This way." Kai motioned forward, and I followed behind him.

We moved swiftly, our footsteps echoing against the damp cobblestones. We crossed the empty streets, avoiding the rare pedestrian or stray cat that roamed looking for food. The palace loomed closer, its dark silhouette standing like a fortress against the backdrop of the stars that were starting to twinkle to life.

As we approached the palace walls, two guards were pacing back and forth before the front gates, their eyes constantly scanning the area. Kai and I exchanged a silent look, then we split up, each of us taking a different route to get past the wall undetected.

I crept along the wall, farther away from the gates, and I couldn't shake the feeling that something wasn't right. The hairs on the back of my neck stood up, and I hesitated for a moment, looking around warily.

But there was nothing there.

I moved farther down the wall until I reached the spot that Kai and I had discussed, and I began to climb, using my fighting leathers to grip the uneven stones when I couldn't find footing. As I silently dropped down to the other side, onto the palace grounds, I heard a rustling coming from my left.

I froze, trying not to make a sound, my heart pounding in my chest as unease washed over me.

There was a sudden movement, and I pulled my dagger from its sheath along my chest. I was just about to launch it when I finally spotted Kai, his face a mask of worry. "We have a problem."

I looked back over my shoulder, at the direction of the gates, and I could hear it then, the quiet chaos of the guards knowing something was wrong.

We used to believe that the palace was impenetrable but getting in had never been the issue. It was getting back out.

But there was no turning back.

There was no threat in this world that would make me leave my sister behind.

"Rebels!" one of the guards shouted, and mine and Kai's gazes slammed into one another.

"We need to find her." My voice was barely above a whisper. "Quickly."

Kai narrowed his eyes as he searched the gates. "My magic?"

"Use it." I nodded toward the guards. "They already know we're here."

Kai's eyes flickered to the palace then back to me. "We need to be quick," he said as he closed his eyes, and I felt a tremor in the air.

He dug his fingers into the loose soil beneath him, his grip tightening for a moment before loosening again. As he slackened his fingers, tendrils of thick black smoke seeped out of his fingertips and slithered along the dirt before vanishing into the ground.

The earth quivered, and the sound of the guards' panicked voices grew louder.

"We need to move." My heart pounded as Kai's eyes shot open. They were almost solid black, somehow even darker than they were normally.

"Around the back of the palace. The dungeon."

We both stood, moving as swiftly as we could as we tried to remain in the shadows. When we reached the back of the palace, there were two guards standing watch, both of them with their swords drawn and their gazes vigilantly darting around looking for danger.

Smoke shot from Kai's fingers, slamming into one of their chests, while my dagger lodged into the other.

Sweat dripped down my temples, and I quickly wiped it away as a heaviness pressed down on my chest. The weight of taking a life was not lost on me; yet, I couldn't dwell on it now.

I would kill every one of them for her.

Guilt and remorse could gnaw away at me later.

Kai and I moved over their bodies, one of them still shaking as the last bit of life drained from his body with the blood that now seeped into the pristine palace grounds.

My hand gripped the handle of the door they laid before, and the loud chime of the clock tower rang overhead. I didn't dare look behind me, but I heard Kai grumble under his breath.

"Looks like we missed your father's deadline."

I scoffed and would've smiled if my sister wasn't waiting for us inside the palace. Kai respected my father's orders almost less than I did.

"In and out," I reminded us both of what we already knew. "We get Wren, and we leave."

There were horrors in the palace. Marmoris Kingdom was vast, and it was soiled by a king who had more bloodlust than care for the people he was meant to serve.

But we were only here to save my sister.

Kai signaled for me to take the lead, and I pulled another dagger from my vest before we stepped inside.

The temperature seemed to drop as the door closed behind us, and the only light through the narrow corridors came from the sparse lanterns that hung from the wall.

The palace was designed like a labyrinth, with twists and turns leading to dead ends and secret chambers. It had been a complete mystery to us until the raid happened, and even then, we had no real idea what we were doing.

Kai and I had studied what we did know, but even with that knowledge, we knew we had to be careful.

We made our way deeper into the palace, the air growing colder with each step. The sound of our footsteps echoed through the silent halls, the only sound breaking the eerie silence.

Then, just ahead, we heard faint whispers, and it took everything inside me not to run toward the sound.

With each cautious step, we could hear the soft echoes of footsteps and hushed murmurs. As we edged closer, I caught a glimpse of several guards huddled together, each of them looking more on edge than the next.

They were standing before a cluster of cells, and the stench of rotting flesh that came from behind the steel bars made my stomach churn.

My gaze darted from one cell to another, searching for

any sign of my sister through the people who were kept there.

I looked back at Kai, but he shook his head, his face grim as he looked back at the guards.

There was no way I was leaving her here in this hell.

I stepped forward, my dagger hanging loosely in my hand, and each of the guards whipped their heads around in my direction.

"Good evening, gentlemen." I held my hands out as I smiled at them in a way that I was sure made me look as insane as I felt at that moment. "I believe you all have something that doesn't belong to you."

"Dacre." I heard my name whispered on a gasp, and I allowed myself a glance past the guards until I finally saw her.

My dark gaze met her bright-green eyes that were so much like my father's, and even though she was kneeling, her hands clinging to the bars of the cage they had her trapped inside, I breathed a sigh of relief.

"That one yours?" the tall, lanky guard asked with a fucking sneer on his face as he glanced from me and back down to my sister. "What a lucky bastard you are. She and her friend have been a nice change of scenery from the usual shit we normally drag in here."

I bared my teeth as my hand clenched around my blade, but the fool wasn't finished.

"Who knew a filthy rebel could be so pleasing?" He squatted down so he was closer to her, his face far too near to hers, and I had enough.

So had Kai.

I threw my dagger, the tip lodging into the man's neck, and chaos erupted around us.

Kai's black smoke poured from him and clouded the room in a mist so dark that I knew it would make it hard for them to see us. I reached inside myself, embracing my own powers, and I coaxed them forward.

I felt for the elements around me, tasting the ash on my tongue from the lanterns burning near the guards, and drew it in.

My lungs filled with their smoke, and I let it consume me until I could hardly breathe.

Only then did I draw back my arm, and the air around me hummed with energy.

One of the guard's swords whirred past my ear as he lunged at me, but I didn't falter. The air around me crackled, and I grabbed his blade in my hand, the metal beginning to turn to liquid in my hold before I jerked it from his grasp and slammed the hilt into his stomach.

The guard fell to the ground, his dazed eyes looking up at me, but I was already moving on to the next.

Kai's magic seemed to hum against my own, the darkness in both of us easily recognizing the other, and I didn't have to look at him to taste the death he was leaving behind as he moved through the guards.

Another guard, dressed immaculately in the king's royal colors, charged toward me with his hands raised. Bright blue sparks danced between his fingers, crackling with electricity that coiled around his blade.

I caught him by the throat as he slammed his dagger into my thigh. I didn't let myself think of the pain, about the shock magic his skin delivered against mine; instead, I focused on my hold and the way my skin was burning his as easily as if I had pressed the flames that were lighting up the room against him.

His gargled screams echoed throughout the room before they finally cut off, as did his magic. I dropped him to the ground before pulling his blade from my thigh, my blood pouring from the wound, and using it to slice into another guard who was attempting to run.

I pressed my burning hand against the wound, searing my skin until the bleeding stopped.

These men were responsible for keeping my sister in that cage, and there would not be a single one of them that would survive.

The fire inside me was clouding my thoughts and screamed for me to burn them all. My own anger fed it, making the flames stretch and lick to every part of me.

I reached for the guard who dared to speak about my sister, my dagger still buried in the side of his neck, and his eyes were wide with panic as I gripped the collar of his uniform and lifted him until the tip of his nose touched mine.

"What was it you were saying to me?" I spat the words through my teeth, but he couldn't answer me. Blood was dripping from his mouth, but it wasn't enough.

His gaze rapidly searched around us, but when he looked in Wren's direction, I jerked him back to look at me.

"Don't you dare look at her." My grip on his uniform was so tight that my knuckles were turning white. "You are not worthy to look upon her. It will be me you watch until the last spark of life leaves your eyes."

Kai, sensing my loss of control, moved through the chaos, his smoke wrapping around the remaining guards, blinding them. He sent out tendrils of darkness, wrapping around their necks, and he squeezed until I heard the soft pop of their broken bones.

Even with their own magic, they weren't enough to fight against him.

With every thud and crack, I breathed and tried to release the flames that had become alive inside me.

The uniform in my hand was turning to ash under my touch.

"Dacre, we have to move."

I knew he was right, but I felt desperate to watch his bones char under the fire in my hands. I reached for my dagger, quickly pulling it from his neck, and blood flooded from the wound as he attempted to fight against me.

The fight only lasted for a few seconds before there was nothing left of the man as I dropped him back to the ground.

"Keys." Kai pointed to the guard that was slumped at my feet, and I reached down, my hands singeing his clothing as I dug for the keys.

"Fuck." I tried to release more of the power that was now devouring me.

Power was meant to be controlled, but far too often it became blinding and instead became the master.

I had seen it happen far too many times before. Our kingdom was built on men who were slaves to power.

But as my grip on reality seemed to slip away, I felt Kai's hand on my arm, grounding me, snapping me back to why we were here. I gulped down the air around me and forced my power to bend to my will. Heat dissipated from my fingers and crept through my veins until it snaked back into my gut where I could control it.

My hands shook as I finally found the keys and pried them off the belt of the lifeless guard.

I passed them to Kai, and he quickly unlocked the cell that held my sister. I pushed inside, lifting her from the floor, and cradled her in my arms.

"Are you okay?" I asked, the smoke and fire still etching my voice. Relief flooded me now that I was touching her, now that I knew she was still alive.

"We have to go." Kai spoke, but his worried gaze never left Wren.

He was right. There would only be more guards heading our way. I pulled my sister behind me, but she pulled back.

"Wait."

She looked behind her, but I tugged harder against her.

"We have to leave, Wren."

"I know, but I'm not leaving without her." She nodded to a girl who sat on the ground with her knees tucked against her chest.

"We're not taking anyone else." I wrapped my hand around Wren's arm gently as I held her close to me.

"She has the rebellion mark, Dacre." Wren's voice was scratchy as if she hadn't had water since they captured her.

"I don't give a fuck what she has." My eyes landed on the girl, but her face was hidden by the hood of her cloak. Dirt and grime caked her tattered clothes, and her hands were encrusted in dirt and dried blood. She must have struggled fiercely before they finally managed to shove her into this cage.

"I'm not leaving her." Wren jerked her arm out of my hold and took a small step back toward the girl. "You should have heard what those guards were saying."

I turned my head away from her, trying to block out her words, trying to block out what I could only imagine those guards were spewing before I stormed back out there and became the kind of monster that our entire rebellion stood against.

"Fine." I glanced at Kai. "You take Wren."

He nodded once, but I didn't need his reassurance. I knew Kai would protect her with his life.

I stepped past my sister, toward the girl, and I reached down for her thin arm and hauled her up until she was on her feet.

"Let go of me!" she hissed as she tried to pull out of my hold, but she felt so fragile in my clutch.

"I don't have time for this." I pulled her to my side, causing her hood to fall back, and when my gaze met hers, it was like looking into the depths of the ocean. The same color as the sky when the sun disappeared behind the clouds and a storm brewed on the horizon.

A gorgeous storm that I could see staring back at me now.

I could feel her rapid heartbeat beneath my fingers as her frantic eyes darted around the dimly lit cell. Her dark brown hair fell into her face, but she didn't bother to push it back.

"I know you," I spoke, even though I couldn't figure out from where.

"No. You don't." As she spoke, her teeth clenched together with a sharp click, and a glint of defiance flashed in her bright blue eyes. She shifted her weight nervously from one foot to the other, tugging at her sleeves. Every muscle in her body was tense as if she didn't want me to know who she was.

"I remember you from somewhere."

There was a bang from a door in the distance, and I tore my gaze away from hers and tugged her toward me as I looked back at my sister. I was just about to open my mouth to tell them to go when her small fist connected with my jaw.

I stumbled back, the force of the blow catching me off guard, but I quickly regained my footing. My hand moved to my sore jaw, and I glared at her, my eyes burning with the same fire that had been consuming me only moments before.

"I told you to let me go," she spat, just as the rush of footsteps echoed off the walls from one of the corridors.

"Let's go," Kai growled as he pulled Wren behind him, but I was still staring down at the damned girl before me.

"You can rot in here, for all I care." I ran my hand over my jaw as I took a step back from her, but there was something. Something I couldn't quite put my finger on.

Something that demanded I not leave her behind.

I remembered her.

"Fuck." I felt Kai's power without even looking behind me, and I knew that we were out of time.

"Let me see your mark," I demanded. If she was one of us, I could justify it to myself why I wasn't willing to leave her behind.

"Fuck off." She clutched her sleeves against her palms so I couldn't see her wrists. Her eyes darted around the room, never settling on one spot for too long. "I'll rot just the same whether I have a mark or not."

She was right, of course, but I couldn't force myself to care about that fact.

I leaned down, pressing my shoulder into her stomach, and I lifted her far too easily. I could feel her sharp hip bones digging into my shoulder, and I silently wondered when the last time was she had eaten.

She cursed, but I looked to Kai and followed him out of the cell without paying her any mind.

Kai's black smoke crept before us as we pushed back down the same corridors we had entered through. My grip anchored down around her thighs.

She struggled against me, and if she weren't so light, I probably would have dropped her. "You're going to regret this," she promised, even though her voice barely carried over the sound of her ragged breaths.

Even if she was right, I didn't leave her behind.

CHAPTER 3
NYRA

My gaze rose up past the towering trees, my entire body aching as the man lowered me to the ground. I could hear the familiar rushing of the waterfall, though the sound was distant and calming.

Which meant we were farther from the palace than I had ever been before.

We had been walking for what felt like forever.

"We need to get underground," the man who stood next to Wren spoke, but I couldn't look at him. I was too busy staring up at the man who had carried me out like I was a damned child.

His inky black hair was messy, curling into his face, and matched his eyes that were still bearing down on me. They were so dark that they reminded me of a stormy night when the sky was so black that it swallowed the light of the stars.

He was tall, the line of his jaw was strong and clean-shaven, and his full lips pursed as he searched over my face.

He was beautiful, although harsh, and I hated the way he was looking at me.

I remember you from somewhere.

His words from before echoed in my mind, and they made being with the rebellion far more dangerous than even I believed it could be.

If he knew who I was…

I didn't know which was more dangerous—being a prisoner in my father's palace or being with the rebellion if they were to figure out who I was.

He squatted down beside me, and his hand shot out and grabbed my forearm, pulling me closer to him. The muscles of his arms tensed as he raised the sleeve of my shirt, revealing the forgery of a brand.

His thumb slowly traced the length of the mark, and a chill ran down my spine. I tried to pull away from him, but he held firm, his grip digging into my skin. "You wear the mark of a traitor so well." His voice was low and intoxicating, and I found myself watching his lips as he spoke. "Next time, get someone better to fake your mark."

"What?" Wren asked from behind him, and there was a part of me that felt bad for lying to her. She had been kind to me.

"Get up." He stood, pulling me with him, and I had no choice but to climb to my feet.

The night air was cold, and my torn clothing did little to ward it off.

"It's a fake." He held my arm out to the others, not caring at all that his fingers were still digging into me.

"I saw it in the cell, Dacre. It didn't look fake to me."

Dacre. I had heard her call his name in the cell, but hearing it now, when I could see him, when his skin felt like it was searing mine, I remembered where I had heard that name before.

"You're the commander's son."

I had overheard my father and his advisers talking about him and his father time and again. They spoke of their ruthlessness, of how they heartlessly killed in the name of a rebellion.

His fingers flexed around my arm, but he didn't respond to what I had just said.

"Look closer," he said to Wren, and both she and the other man stepped forward and looked at my arm before glancing up at me.

Her green eyes were laced with disappointment, but I couldn't let that affect me. Not when I needed to get away.

"Why?" Wren asked, but she looked away from me and toward Dacre as she spoke.

"Because she's a fucking traitor. The only reason someone would forge one of our marks is because she's betraying her kingdom while being too fucking cowardice to fight against it. What was your plan? To use this mark to escape the tithe you know is cruel without ever lifting a finger to earn it?" Dacre slipped his fingers into my hair, yanking my head back until I was forced to look up at him, and he scrutinized my face.

"Who are you?" His touch was painful against my scalp, but I locked my jaw, refusing to answer him as he narrowed his eyes.

"Kai, stop him," Wren begged, but Dacre wasn't paying

her any attention. He was far too busy inspecting my face as if he could decode my every secret.

I squeezed my hands into fists as I tried to stop them from trembling.

"I saw you in the raid," he said so effortlessly, leaving no room for doubt or confusion.

And my heart sank with his words.

"That's not true." My words quivered and betrayed my false confidence, the pitch of my voice rising with each syllable. I took a deep breath and tried to steel my nerves. "I've never seen you before in my life."

I hadn't. That part wasn't a lie. I would have remembered him.

"Were you in the palace that day?" I could feel his anger radiating from him, could practically taste it on my tongue.

And I knew that I needed to be careful with my answer.

"Dacre, let her go." Wren placed her hand on Dacre's arm, but his hold held firm. "We need to go. You can finish this when we get home."

Home.

I had heard stories of their hidden city, and I knew that once they got me there, there would be no chance of escaping.

And Dacre was far too close to the truth for me to ever be safe there.

"Were you in the palace?" he repeated, his voice low and threatening.

I hesitated for a moment before answering, searching for the right words to say.

"I was." I nodded. "My mother lived and worked there."

My mother. Gods, I didn't have the energy to think about her today. Not if I didn't want to falter under his scrutiny.

"I don't believe you." I could feel the roughness of his calloused palm against my skin as he spat out the words.

He finally looked away from me and dropped his hold, causing me to stumble forward. "Let's get home. We can deal with her lies there."

Kai nodded before leading the way, and Wren moved to my side. Her arm pressed against mine momentarily, and I could feel her watching me, but I stared ahead. Too riddled with guilt to meet her gaze.

And I knew I would feel even more guilt for what I did next.

We moved through the trees, the forest becoming more dense with every step we took, and I followed behind them. Dacre kept glancing over his shoulder at me, but I refused to look at him. I was too busy in my own head trying to figure out my next move.

The darkness pressed in on me, suffocating and unyielding. Every muscle in my body ached from exhaustion, and I had no sense of direction, lost in the maze of the trees.

Lost in the overwhelming fear that every option that lay before me would end in my death.

Hunger clawed at my stomach, and I clamped down on it. I tried not to think about the last time I had eaten, didn't dare count the days.

How long was I in that cell?

Kai raised his hand in the air, and both Dacre and Wren slowed immediately. I tried to listen for something there, but I didn't hear or see anything.

Which meant they were preparing to take us to the hidden city.

If I was going to run, I had to do it now.

I would never be free in my father's kingdom or the rebellion, and it was the only thing I longed for.

I took a deep breath and mustered every ounce of strength I had left. My heart pounded in my chest as I took a small step back, careful not to make a sound.

No one turned to look at me.

Without warning, I darted off into the dark forest. I moved as quickly as I could, my breath coming in ragged gasps.

The crunch and snap of leaves and twigs echoed behind me as I sprinted farther into the darkness, and I ducked behind a thick oak tree, hoping to shield me from view.

I swallowed down a deep breath as I looked back over my shoulder and didn't see any of them following me.

"Little traitor." Dacre startled me, his voice low and menacing, each word laced with venom.

"Shit," I cursed under my breath and quickly looked in the other direction, but still there was no sign of him.

I crept out from behind the tree, my heart pounding in my chest as I searched for him in the darkness. I filled my lungs before running again, my weak legs pumping furiously as I tried to put as much distance between us as possible.

The night air was cool and damp in the forest, and I could feel my clothes sticking to my skin. The sound of footsteps behind me spurred me on, and I pushed harder, my thighs aching as I did so.

A hand gripped my shoulder with such force that I was whipped around until I collided with Dacre. My heart raced in terror as I tried to catch my breath and regain my bearings. The grip on my shoulder was firm and unyielding, like a vise closing in on me.

He smirked down at me, his fingers digging into my shoulder. "What's this? You're running from me?"

"Just let me go."

"That's not going to happen, little traitor."

I flinched as his fingers dug into my shoulder, the pressure sharp. I struggled to break free from his grasp, panic rising in my chest.

"Don't call me that." I swallowed hard as I tilted my chin and looked up to take in his harsh features that were in startling contrast to the way he smirked at my words.

"But you are a fucking traitor." His voice was low and intoxicating, and I found myself watching his lips as he spoke. He lifted my wrist in front of him as if he were inspecting the mark once more. "It's almost as if you have something to hide."

"You got her, Dacre?" I could hear Kai coming toward us, and panic clawed at me.

I thrust a heavy boot forward with all my strength, aiming it at the healing wound on Dacre's thigh I had noticed earlier.

"Fuck!" With an agonizing groan, he doubled over in pain and dropped his hold on me.

I wasted no time before bolting away from him again, running as fast as I could.

But I didn't make it more than a few steps before I felt an impact strike me from the back that sent me tumbling to the ground.

The force of my body hitting the ground reverberated through my chest, leaving me gasping for air. I felt his oppressive weight on my back and frantically clawed at the soil and moss beneath me, desperate for leverage to push against it.

"Get off me!" I shouted, twisting onto my back, desperate to free myself. But Dacre was relentless, his fingers digging into my flesh as he forced me into the hard, damp ground. I bucked wildly, trying to kick him off, but he pinned down both of my legs with his own until all I could do was writhe beneath him.

I tried to buck my body against his, to knock him off me, but it did nothing but press him harder against me. "You're only making this harder for yourself." His body was unmovable, and I could feel the heat radiating from him. He leaned in close, until his face was just inches from mine, and spoke in a low voice. "Just give up now, and I won't hurt you any more than necessary." The threat in his words sent a chill down my spine and my heart hammered wildly in my chest. I knew if they took me back to their city, it could mean more than just death—there were far worse things waiting for me there.

If they were to find out who I was.

I fought against his hold, my eyes blazing. "I'd rather die than go back with you," I snarled through gritted teeth.

It was a lie. I didn't want to die, but more than anything, I didn't want to become a pawn in my father's game.

Dacre's lips curved into a smile and his dangerous gaze seemed to bore right into me. My heart raced as a strange sensation crept up my spine—fear intertwined with something unfamiliar that caused a deep ache in my belly.

"Then I'll make you wish for death." As he spoke, his voice was barely audible, barely a whisper, and it sent shivers down my spine.

I tensed my thigh muscles to launch a kick into his groin, but I did nothing but slam it into his hard thigh. "You're going to regret that." He moved closer until his breath brushed my ear, low and raspy.

Before I could react, his calloused hand pressed firmly against my throat, and I saw fiery rage in his eyes.

His thumb slowly brushed over the pulse in my neck, and I felt like a current had been fired through my veins. "You have no idea what I'm capable of." He leaned back slowly until he was sitting astride my hips.

He grasped me firmly, his hands rough against me. I tried to still the shaking in my fingers as the finality of the situation sank in, leaving me no hope for escape.

From the corner of my eyes, I could see Kai in the moonlight standing above us glowering at me, eyes narrowed with anger. But all I could focus on was the way Dacre's pupils dilated as they locked with mine.

"Let's get her underground." Kai's voice was dark and soft, but demanded attention. "We need to get there before the guards become brave enough to search these woods for us."

But Dacre's eyes were like fire, blazing against my skin as I held his gaze, despite the fear that threatened to consume me. I clenched my jaw, refusing to give in.

"I won't go back to the capital city," I said defiantly, though it came out little more than a whisper. "I refuse to go back there."

The tan skin around Dacre's eyes crinkled as he studied me. His hands clamped around my wrists like iron shackles as he pulled me to stand.

Fear flooded my veins as I thought of the tales that had been whispered about what the rebels did to their captives. Images of torture and pain flashed through my mind.

They were going to take me to the hidden city. The city we had heard stories about for years, but the monarch had never been able to find.

The monarch whose bloodline ended with me.

CHAPTER 4
NYRA

They moved as a unit, each of them watching the backs of the others with precision, and they didn't slow down in the slightest bit to accommodate me. Wren's light hair fell in front of her face as she turned to look at me. Her eyes were filled with sadness as she gave me a small, sympathetic smile.

Thick branches clawed at my clothing as I stumbled forward in the route they directed me. Dacre had tied my hands together, and the rough rope dug into my wrists as Kai pulled me forward.

Kai held me firmly as if he worried I was going to run again. His arms bulged under the leather uniform as he pulled me along the dense forest. I stumbled over a thick root and gritted my teeth against the pain of my knees slamming into the ground.

Kai helped me back to my feet, but he didn't utter a word.

We trudged on in silence for what felt like an eternity.

My feet ached and my stomach still grumbled from lack of food. I sneaked glances at Dacre, watching his broad shoulders carry us in an unfamiliar direction. He hadn't spoken a word to me since he bound my hands and handed me off to Kai.

He hadn't looked in my direction either.

But I stared at him as the moonlight danced off his jet-black hair until the lush trees gave way to a small glade.

The full moon cast a silver glow over the clearing, highlighting the massive tree at its center. Its trunk was wider than any I had ever seen before, and its branches reached high into the sky as if trying to embrace the moon itself. The intricate web of gnarled roots spread out from the base, anchoring the tree to the ground.

"Stand there," Kai rumbled, his eyes spearing me in place as he pulled one of his daggers from its sheath and sliced through the rope at my hands. It snapped apart effortlessly with a single swipe. I quickly rubbed at my wrists and tried to bring life back into them.

I felt the rough bark of the tree press cool against my back as I stood still. Dacre moved just ahead of me and spread his hands in front of him, palms outspread as he whispered words I could not understand in a tongue that sounded ancient. A fine sheen of sweat broke out across my brow as I watched magic slip from his fingers in glowing golden threads.

The ground beneath our feet began to vibrate and small cracks formed in the earth. The dirt buckled, sending trees swaying and leaves fluttering to the ground as I stumbled backward, clinging to the trunk for support.

Magic had been used in my life daily, but it felt mundane compared to this.

"What are you doing?" I whispered, my voice giving away every bit of my fear.

Dacre didn't answer me, his focus solely on the ground before him as if he could reach out and physically control the elements. A low rumble filled the air, and the ground began to heave beneath our feet. Energy seemed to dance across my skin as the tremors grew stronger.

The tree quivered violently, its trunk creaking ominously as I heard the sound of wood splintering as it swayed.

The grassy earth suddenly disappeared in an avalanche of dirt and stones plummeting into darkness.

My scream echoed sharply around me as I dropped, my arms wildly flailing in a desperate attempt to find something, anything, to stop my fall. But it was too late. I fell down into the darkness and plunged into the icy water below that stole the breath from my lungs.

As I gasped for air, my mouth opened wide, but instead of air, salty liquid filled my lungs. I thrashed wildly, grasping to find the surface. Desperate for oxygen, my chest tightened and my vision blurred with inky blackness. Panic consumed me as my arms swung, searching for something to hold on to. But the water offered no salvation. It was relentless as it pushed me farther into the depths.

My cloak, already loosened from the struggle of staying afloat, suddenly tightened around my body. I thrashed and kicked, expecting to be dragged down deeper, but instead, something pulled me upward toward the surface. My lungs burned for air as I emerged from the water, gasping and sputtering.

A strong hand gripped the back of my cloak, yanking me upward with ease so that my upper body was pressed firmly against the ground. My chest heaved against the hard earth.

"Are you okay?" Wren asked as she made her way down the last step of a dark set of stairs with Kai behind her. Her eyes searched over my face, but I simply nodded.

Lying had become so easy lately.

Dacre pulled me toward the base of the wooden stairs, and I scampered fully onto the landing. The water was a black abyss, like a midnight sea, without a hint of light or movement.

Sunlight was still pouring in from the chasm in the earth above us, and I blinked up at the stairs reaching all the way to the top and ending at the base of the cave floor.

They could have prepared me for what was happening, let me use the stairs the same way they descended, but they let me fall.

"This way." Dacre's voice was like coarse sandpaper as he nodded toward the thin strip of ground that was surrounded by water.

As we moved farther into the cavern, the walls came alive with a warm glow from dozens of floating torches. Firelight danced and flickered along the rough stone, casting shadows that seemed to dance alongside them.

I followed closely behind Wren, my heart pounding in my chest as fear and curiosity warred within me.

As we rounded a sharp corner made of jagged rock, I stopped in my tracks. Before me lay an ethereal city from another world, an immense expanse of ancient architecture half submerged in the eerie water and veiled by the lack of sunlight. The rough silhouettes of broken stained-glass windows caught the flickering firelight of the hundreds of lanterns that seemed to hang from the sky like stars and crumbling stones laid at the base of the snaking river.

The buildings and small patches of land were connected by hundreds of small hanging bridges and pathways. Up above, thick moss and vines clung to the roofs of the buildings and coiled down the sides until they kissed the edge of the water as if they were thirsting for a drink.

My nerves were on edge, but I couldn't deny the sense of wonder that washed over me as I gazed at this place for the first time. A part of me wanted to savor this moment forever, while another part was already trying to rationalize why I shouldn't be in this place.

The city my father had spent a lifetime searching for.

Everywhere I looked, people were milling about, most of them dressed in fighting leathers like Dacre, but some were wearing normal clothes instead of a uniform.

There were at least a hundred people walking across the bridges and down the narrow dirt paths. Some were moving in and out of buildings while I could see others through windows settling down for the day.

"This is impossible." I inhaled a shaky breath, my voice barely above a murmur.

Dacre shifted his hard gaze to me. "Impossible for you, maybe. But for us, it's the only home we've ever known."

"I don't understand." My voice quavered as I spoke, my body wrought with tension. "How could you keep something like this hidden?"

Dacre's face grew stern, his voice was low and grave, like a thunderstorm rolling in from the horizon. "As if we would tell you that. You can't even figure out who it is you're betraying. I don't trust you."

I snapped my gaze away from him, taking in the sights and sounds of the hidden city while trying to block out his harsh words. It was far from the legends my father had told me. He had spoken of horror stories and ruthless rebels, but this felt...different somehow.

When I looked around, this felt like a city of people just trying to survive, trying to rebuild something my father had taken away.

Yet, I couldn't shake the fear that crawled up my spine.

My father's words of hatred and contempt for this unseen world echoed in my mind, but as I peered out at the sprawling network of bridges and tunnels that seemed to be carved from the earth, I couldn't find the same disdain. The glimmering torches glowed like stars scattered across an infinite sky, and I couldn't imagine anyone destroying it.

"Move." A woman's forceful hand shoved me forward, breaking me from my thoughts, and I spun around to look at her.

She was roughly my age, dressed head to toe in fighting leathers, and she had more weapons strapped to her body than I had ever seen. Her eyes bore into me with an intensity that made me shift uncomfortably under her gaze.

I had been too busy taking everything in that I hadn't noticed her approach.

"Your father's been waiting for you." She looked away from me to meet Dacre's gaze as she nodded to the left.

"I'm sure he has, Mal." Dacre moved past her, barely paying her any attention.

"They brought in a load of recruits." She said the word with a sneer on her face, and my stomach tightened. "He wants you to deal with them."

Dacre let out an exhausted sigh before moving across a weathered bridge. The rest of us followed him, and the boards creaked beneath us as I peeked down at the ebony water. I breathed in a short-lived sigh of relief when we reached the other side, where an imposing structure loomed before us. The tall walls were made of thick gray stone, and at its peak was a worn wooden sign that read *Revolt* in flaking black letters.

We stepped inside, and there were a few people huddled together in a small group. But it was the seven individuals lined up together against the far wall that I couldn't take my eyes off of.

Each of their clothes were marred with dirt and filth, but it was the hunger in their eyes that I couldn't look away from. The hunger that told me they were trying to escape my father's cruelty.

"Line up." Mal nodded toward the others who stood before me, and I foolishly looked behind me before taking another step.

Wren's eyes darted away from me, her hands fidgeting with the hem of her shirt as she stood near the door. Dacre and Kai sauntered over to the small group, their heads leaned toward one another's as they spoke. I squared my shoulders and strode toward the line, ignoring the glances and whispers from those around us.

I looked over the faces of the seven people lined up, but

I didn't recognize any of them. They had to be from Marmoris to be lined up here, but the people of my kingdom didn't know me.

They knew a name, a character that stories were told about.

But I was nothing more than the princess my father kept hidden, the one he refused to concede as his heir.

My gaze met the man who was closest to me, and his eyes widened as he looked upon me. My stomach clenched as I slowly stepped toward him.

I didn't recognize him, but I could feel the intensity of his stare radiating from him like heat. It made me pause as I tried not to reveal how nervous I was.

"Princess?"

My heart raced as his voice reached me, barely more than a whisper. I slowly turned my head toward him, scarcely daring to believe this was happening; he seemed to understand the raw fear in my expression.

"I'm not who you think I am."

He locked his eyes on mine, a fierce determination burning within them. But when Dacre stepped forward, the man's gaze flicked away from me, revealing a hint of fear that was coursing through me. Mal moved to Dacre's side and offered him a parchment, which he scanned quickly before returning his attention back to us.

"Welcome to the rebellion," Dacre said, his voice commanding the attention of everyone in the room. There was no trace of the *welcome* in his hard gaze.

The man next to me shifted his feet, but I kept my gaze glued forward.

"Some of you are here by your own free will, but for

those of you who aren't, allow me to enlighten you. The Marmoris Kingdom's protection ends the moment you step down from that mountain they're perched on. You're in Enveilorian land now. You either stand with us or die by our blades."

Dacre's voice rumbled like thunder, shaking the air around us. His eyes were cold as steel, his broad shoulders squared in a determined stance.

"We don't allow King Roan's snakes to move through our land to the southern coast. You either fight with us against his tyranny or you become a traitor to us all."

My heart thudded in my chest and sweat prickled on my brow. He couldn't be serious, could he?

The man beside me spoke, and I tensed. "We will never join you filthy traitors. King Roan is the only true ruler."

"Yet, you run from his tithe?" Dacre cocked his head, and the move reminded me of a predator.

"I will return to the capital city, but I have no magic to spare for my king."

The man had barely finished speaking when Dacre flung his arm forward and released a dagger I hadn't even noticed him grab. It flew through the air with a sharp whistle before embedding itself into the man's neck.

The sudden noise made me flinch, and something warm and wet hit my cheek. I glanced down at my cloak and saw blood mixing into the still-wet fabric. My fingers trembled as I tried to wipe it away, but it only smeared and spread wider.

A ragged cry came from someone off to my left, followed by muffled sobs as the man's body slumped to the ground.

My breaths came in shallow, ragged pants as I stared down at the lifeless body. I jerked my gaze away and Dacre's eyes locked onto mine, and I could see something veiled flickered in their depths.

He clenched his jaw and glared, his eyes like burning embers. "We have no tolerance for supporters of the crown," he growled. His words seemed to echo in the room as the air grew thick with tension. "You join us or you share his fate."

My vision blurred as I looked down the line of those who stood with me. Everyone had grown eerily quiet and stood as if frozen in place.

My heart raced, pounding against my rib cage as I looked back to Dacre. His jaw clenched tight, and his eyebrows furrowed, creating a stoic mask on his face. Every inch of my body shook with fear and rage as I watched his cold, calculating eyes, witnessing the nonchalance with which he took the life of another.

How many lives had he taken just tonight?

My thoughts drifted to my father and the atrocities he had committed in his pursuit of power. The innocent people he hurt, the lies he spread.

Our world was filled with cruelty, and guilt gnawed at me knowing that it was because of him that brutality and anguish thrived in our kingdom.

He had afflicted our people with such suffering that they were forced to create this rebellion that I now stood before, then punished them for not celebrating his tyranny.

He had turned them into monsters.

"Name?" Dacre nodded to the first person in the line, the one farthest from me.

"Irina." The woman's chin trembled as she spoke. "I am the wife of...was the wife of a farmer."

Dacre kept his composure, but his eyes betrayed him. They darted over her face, taking in every detail with a mixture of sadness and yearning. "And your choice?" He said it so simply as if the woman's life wasn't on the line.

"King Roan killed my husband." She raised her chin, and there wasn't a trace of that trembling left as anger filled her eyes. "He couldn't pay the tithe, and he murdered him for it."

My throat tightened as Dacre clenched his jaw, but he didn't say a word.

"I want to join." The determination in Irina's voice was so clear, it seemed to echo off the walls and draw everyone's attention. Her mouth was set in a thin line, her hands balled into fists at her sides, and the light in her eyes burned with passion.

"Your magic." Dacre studied her intently as she raised her brows in confusion. "We need to know what magic you possess so we can know where you will be most useful here."

My hands formed into fists at my sides.

Irina's eyes roamed the room for a moment before they settled back on Dacre. Taking a deep breath, she slowly exhaled and murmured almost inaudibly, "I have earth magic."

"Good," Dacre replied, his face softening slightly. "We could use more of that." He looked over his shoulder toward an older man with dark skin and hair as white as freshly fallen snow. "You'll go with Calix. He's the head of devising."

Irina moved toward the man without a trace of hesitation in her steps.

Dacre quickly turned to the next person in line, a boy with sandy hair and large eyes the color of the sea, who looked barely old enough to grow a beard, let alone join a rebellion. "Name and station."

The boy's throat bobbed as he nervously swallowed, his eyes wide and frantic as he searched the room. "Cedric Fallon, sir."

Dacre raised an eyebrow, his gaze piercing.

"Where are you from, Cedric?"

Cedric's wild-eyed gaze swept the room repeatedly as if trying to find something invisible to everyone else. He stood silent and still for a moment, his thoughts obviously elsewhere, before he said softly, "My father. He was taken by the rebellion over a year ago now."

Dacre's Adam's apple bobbed as he spoke, and a heavy feeling of dread filled me. "What's your father's name?"

"Ammon," Cedric answered quickly.

Dacre looked over at Kai, and he came to Dacre's side instantly before they spoke in hushed tones that I couldn't make out.

"Follow Kai." Dacre nodded in his direction. "He'll take you."

Anger lit in my veins. Was Cedric's father alive, or had they simply thrown a dagger at that man's neck because he hadn't wanted to betray his kingdom?

But Cedric didn't ask these questions. He moved quickly behind Kai and followed him out the door I just entered through moments before. I watched his every step as he left. Not paying a bit of attention to Dacre or the next person he questioned.

My stomach churned and my skin prickled with dread as I watched the boy disappear from my sight. Dacre continued down the line, questioning and assigning people where he deemed appropriate. There were healers, another whose magic relied on the earth, and one who could manipulate the elements. It was only a matter of time before Dacre reached me, and even as I tried to focus on the words he was saying to them, there was only one thought that kept running through my mind.

I was going to die.

I had no magic to offer their cause. Even if they never found out who I truly was, I served them no purpose.

"And you?" Dacre gingerly stepped around the man's body that was still lying on the ground beside me and moved directly in front of me, blocking my view.

His dark eyes were cold as he glowered down at me, and his jaw was clenched so tightly I could see the muscles moving beneath his skin. I held my chin high, hoping the resolve on my face matched the disdain in his.

"What about me?" I gritted my teeth as I answered him.

"Name?" His face was a mask of suspicion as he cocked his head to the side and waited for my response.

I could almost taste the syllables of my name on my tongue, but as soon as they came close enough to say, I bit them back until I could taste the metallic tinge of blood in my mouth.

"Nyra." My voice trembled as I spoke my mother's name, a name that had been forgotten the moment they called her queen. A name no one seemed to remember when they laid her beneath the cold dirt and stripped her title away to give to another.

It took my father a mere few days to find another woman to have at his side.

A woman to bear him a true heir.

A woman who would never be my queen.

I could still feel the lashings my father had delivered across my back when I had refused to bow before her in the wake of my mother's death.

"And why did the King's Guard have you locked in that cell?" Dacre's eyes were dark and unwavering, his gaze locking on to mine with intensity. I shifted my weight from one foot to the other, fighting the urge to turn away as I held his stare.

"Because I stole ten coins from a man I shouldn't have." My voice quavered ever so slightly. It was the truth, and it was one of the first lessons that Micah had taught me on the streets. *Keep your story as close to the truth as you can.*

"Because he was a man of the king?" Dacre asked with contempt in his voice.

"Because he got me caught."

Dacre's lips curled up into a smirk as his eyes scanned me from head to toe. His eyes gleamed with amusement, and I couldn't help but feel a pang of annoyance at his smugness.

"Your magic didn't help you get away?" Dacre's eyes narrowed as he focused on my hands, which were clenched so tightly my knuckles had turned white.

His question was one that quietly and persistently

echoed in my mind. I was the firstborn child of King Roan, heir to the Marmoris throne.

But heirs to a kingdom couldn't be powerless.

My father knew that all too well, and his words were etched into my mind, a constant reminder of his disappointment.

I was powerless, and that made me worthless to a kingdom that thrived on power.

"I don't have to tell you what power I have." I squared my shoulders and lifted my chin, determined not to let him see any sign of wavering in me. His lips pulled back in a smug expression, and he took a step closer.

His gaze trailed over me, and his voice was low and cold when he spoke. "Would you rather be like your friend over there?" He motioned toward the man who still lay at our feet, and revulsion and fear flared within me before I schooled my face into a mask of composure.

"So you're asking me to join a fight against an oppressive ruler, only to show me more brutality than I've ever seen from him?"

Dacre's smirk evaporated, his jaw tightening. Glances were exchanged among the people around us, and I could hear their whispers, but I was too focused on Dacre to take in any of it.

"If you think this is"—he flicked his hand toward the man beside us—"more cruelty than your king is capable of, then you are one of the biggest fools we've ever brought in."

He slowly shook his head from side to side, and my stomach clenched with a mix of rage and terror. My palms became clammy and sweat trickled down my spine even though I was still cold from the dark water I had plunged into only moments before.

"It's such a shame." He started to turn from me.

"One cruelty doesn't deserve another." I crossed my arms and stared at the tense muscles of his back. "You're angry with the king, yet you punish the men and women of his kingdom?"

Dacre's feet halted mid-step, his body frozen in place. His gaze was fixed on a distant point, and he spoke without turning to me. "We punish those who are foolish enough to still follow a king who would rather hide in his castle and watch his people die than do a damn thing to save them. A loyalist to the king is an enemy to us."

He paused and slowly turned his head, revealing eyes so dark they seemed to reflect no light. His gaze was like two pieces of solid onyx, ever still and watching.

"Where is your loyalty, little traitor?"

"Don't call me that." My voice was filled with venom as the name he had given me hit far too close to the truth.

"I'll call you whatever I want." Dacre slowly rotated his body toward me, eyes narrowed and voice stern. "I'll ask you one more time: where is your loyalty?"

"I have no loyalty to my…" It was right on the tip of my tongue to say father, but I stumbled over my words. "The king."

He looked at me intently, his gaze lingering on my lips as if he could sense a hidden truth lurking beneath them. "And your power?"

My vocal cords felt as if they were seizing up, but I forced the words from my lips. "I have no power."

The whispering around me grew more audible as if the

crowd was a gathering force in their disapproval. My cheeks burned and my heart raced as I inhaled sharply. Being a fae without magic was unheard of in this realm, and yet, here I stood with no proof that I would ever have any sort of power to control. Despite years of training under my father's watchful eye, all my efforts had been for naught: never a spark, never a wave of energy to let me know I had even an ounce of potential.

Dacre stared at me, his dark eyes boring into mine and searching for answers. His brows pulled together as he clenched his jaw, and a heavy silence filled the air as if he were trying to decide whether or not I could be trusted. "What do you mean, no power?"

I cocked my head as if I was the one studying him now, and I couldn't control the irritation in my voice. "No meaning none," I reiterated. "Have you ever heard of it?"

He shook his head absently as if I hadn't spoken. "How is that even possible?"

I gritted my teeth at his question. "I've been trying to figure that out my whole life. But if you can call up to the gods and ask them, I'd really appreciate an answer."

He stood like a statue and surveyed me, unflinching despite the quick, sharp burst of laughter that came from the corner of the room. His eyes narrowed until I could feel his suspicion emanating from him. "You'll be with the warriors."

"What?" I blurted out in disbelief.

"Warriors. Ever heard of them? They wield a sword and fight for what's right."

I rolled my eyes as the heat of frustration rushed through me. "I never said I wanted to join your rebellion."

"You'd prefer to die?"

I didn't want to die, but I wasn't keen on being held captive in another prison either. Trapped by my circumstances. I had barely just begun to find my breath since running from my father's palace, and already, I could feel it being stolen from my lungs again.

When I didn't answer, Dacre nodded his head once. "Warrior it is."

"I'm not a warrior."

"Trust me, that's more than noted. But if you can't wield magic, you will learn to wield a sword."

He shifted his weight to turn away, but before he took two steps, my heart raced, and dread spread through my veins like gushing water.

"Who am I following? Who's the head of the warriors?"

This time, his smirk turned into a full-blown smile. "Me."

CHAPTER 5
DACRE

One of the new recruits moved out of my way as soon as they saw me enter the training grounds, and I was glad. I had no interest in dealing with them this late at night.

"Your father's with Reed," Kai said quietly from beside me as we walked together, and I grunted in reply as we rounded the corner to where my father stood.

I didn't feel like dealing with him either. Although, I rarely felt like being around him anymore.

"I heard you brought someone back with your sister." My father barely spared me a glance as he spoke. He didn't ask about Wren at all.

Fuck, I was starting to hate him.

"We did. I sorted through the rest of the recruits as well." The word recruits sounded sour on my tongue. "Only one chose not to join us."

My father nodded as if I hadn't just told him that I had

been forced to kill a man. But the blood on my hands always seemed insignificant to him.

"And you?" I shifted and looked around the grounds at the warriors who were still training. "Were you able to find anything from the intel?"

"Not enough." He huffed as he finally looked up to me. "But there has been word that the king was spotted on the palace grounds. If he's still there, then the princess has to be there too."

The princess.

She was his current obsession, and he believed that she would be the key to winning this entire revolution.

A girl barely old enough to be considered an adult, and everything we were doing was dependent on finding her.

The king had kept her hidden since she was a child, and my father was convinced there was a reason why.

"If she's still there, then we don't stand a chance of finding her."

Getting into the dungeon was one thing, but taking a guarded princess who was heir to the throne was something else completely.

She had been the thing my parents were looking for when the first raid happened. When my mother had…

I shook my head. I couldn't think about that right now.

"We have to." His gaze slammed into me, and I flinched at the agony I saw there. "There's only one reason the king would keep her hidden the way he has her whole life. The king craves power above all else, and he's hiding her magic until he needs it."

I knew my father was probably right. The king had always been secretive about the princess, but after the raid, he had become even more paranoid. I couldn't help but wonder what kind of magic the princess possessed that made her so valuable.

She was his heir, but this was more.

She was more.

And there had been no sighting of the king or the princess since the raid. Though there hadn't been a sighting of the princess in years.

"There's no reason to hide unless he knows we can use her."

I opened my mouth, preparing to tell my father about the girl I had brought in, about Nyra, but I stopped. She claimed she had no magic, and I had never met anyone who didn't possess power before. I didn't believe her.

She was hiding something.

There was no reason for her to hide unless she knew we would use her.

And the moment I told my father, he would do just that. He would try to use her in any way he could.

But she wasn't just any normal recruit. She had grown up in the palace, which meant her loyalties were to the people who murdered my mother, to the people who had massacred thousands of our people while draining the magic from the rest through the king's tithe.

My fists clenched at my sides as I thought of the fire in her eyes as she tried to fight against me.

I should have been more than happy to allow my father to break her, to figure out her secrets and exploit them to benefit us in any way they could.

But still, I kept my mouth shut.

"Do you think any of the recruits today will have information?" My father was searching my face, and even though there was a nagging urge inside me not to tell him about Nyra, I knew he would find out about her soon enough.

He would know that I lied for her.

"I don't know." I shook my head. "The girl we brought in was raised in the palace."

He fixed his gaze on me, lip curled in a sneer and brows drawn together in a menacing scowl. His eyes were cold, radiating an unspoken hostility that was almost palpable in the air.

"Bring her to me."

"She has no magic." I shifted on my feet and my gaze met Kai's for a moment before I looked back to my father. "She worked alongside her mother, and she claims to have not a touch of power."

My father snorted. "That's impossible."

I nodded. "I thought so too, but I couldn't sense any magic from her."

"None?" His eyes narrowed further.

"None."

"She still needs to be questioned. She couldn't have lived at the palace her whole life without knowing something. She'll have information on the princess."

"She'll begin training in the morning." I crossed my arms and met my father's stare head-on. "I will get her to talk."

My father's eyes flickered with approval before he turned. "Get me answers, Dacre, and get some rest."

I frowned, watching as my father disappeared into the shadows of the training grounds.

I turned to Kai, my mind thinking of nothing but that damned girl.

"I want you to keep an eye on her," I said to him. "I don't trust her, and I need to know if she tries to make a move."

Kai nodded, his gaze sharp and unwavering as he watched me. "Of course. Although, I'm not sure what she'd be capable of."

I grunted in response, my thoughts churning. There was something about her, something that unnerved me. I rubbed at my temples in frustration. "Just keep her in your sights. We can't afford for anyone to go rogue."

"You're really going to train her?" He smirked as he crossed his arms.

I rarely trained anyone anymore, not more than correcting stances or criticizing for lack of awareness when they were bested by an inferior fighter. I didn't have the time.

"I don't trust her." I reiterated my earlier statement.

His lips curled into a smug smile, revealing a small dimple on his left cheek. "You never trust anyone," he taunted. "But you never bother to train them either."

I grunted in response, not bothering to defend my actions. "She's different," I said, my voice low and guarded. "She grew up in the palace."

Kai's eyes flickered with amusement, but he didn't say anything else.

"I'll start her training tomorrow."

CHAPTER 6
NYRA

The massive cave was illuminated by small lanterns of firelight, some strung up on rafters overhead and others seemingly suspended in midair. Wisps of gray smoke swirled around them as if conjured by some forgotten magic. The soft light cast a gentle glow over the walls, reflecting off the glistening stalactites that hung from the ceiling like icicles.

"Keep up." Mal moved ahead of me, her figure illuminated by the soft glow of the firelight.

I trailed behind her onto a narrow wooden bridge, its weathered planks creaking under my feet. The bridge connected to a jagged rock that jutted out of the cave wall, and I looked down at the dark river snaking below. I tiptoed my way across, clutching the wooden railing as if it were my lifeline, and tried to ignore the icy chill that seemed to seep through the crevices in the wood.

I had no interest in getting back in that water.

We followed along a meandering path, the only source

of light coming from the infrequent firelight that intermittently illuminated our way. The darkness followed us like smoke, and the sound of water trickling echoed off the moist walls as we descended farther into the depths.

"Where are we exactly?" I looked around me, but I had barely ever left the castle. Everything I knew about our kingdom, I knew from studying maps. And the hidden city definitely wasn't on any map I had ever seen.

Mal turned her head slowly toward me, a smirk curling the corner of her lips. "That information is far too classified for a rat like you."

I jolted backward as if she had slapped me. "So, I'm good enough to fight for you all but not good enough to know where we are?"

"You're not good enough to fight for us either." As she spoke, her lips twisted into a sneer, and she shot me a withering glance as if I was the most repulsive thing she had ever seen. "You will have to prove yourself and your loyalty before you'll ever be given that honor."

I scoffed, but she had already turned away and was making her way down the path. She ducked beneath a jutting rock that dipped lower than the rest. I followed suit, bending my frame to fit beneath the low ceiling before emerging on the other side, and blinked in surprise at what I saw.

Before us stood a massive stone building that was crumbling along the edges. Ivy grew up over the sides of the building, bounding it in a green net and covering its darker stones with brown leaves. We walked down steps into an arched tunnel that led to the side of the building, which looked to be carved right out of the cave wall.

The ivy curled around columns that were embedded in the rock itself.

The vastness of it all was overwhelming, and I couldn't help but wonder what secrets were lurking within the hidden city's walls.

As we approached, a group of men and women gathered outside the entrance, eyeing me warily. Mal walked past them with an air of confidence, and I followed after her quickly.

I knew that none of these people could possibly recognize me unless they had once worked in the castle, but I still kept my head low as fear crawled along my spine.

"You're going to be on the second floor," Mal said as we stepped through the massive doorway and into the building.

I followed her up the shaky steps of the winding staircase, my hands trembling on the cold, metal railing. She turned down a corridor blanketed in shadows before stopping at a door of chipped wood that seemed to blend with the faded stone walls.

"This is your room." She turned the dull gold handle and pushed the door open.

The room was cramped, with two single beds leaning heavily against the walls and a small desk tucked between them. Above it hung a window through which nothing but faint firelight could penetrate, providing the only source of illumination in this otherwise dark space.

One of the beds was made neatly while the other was rumpled and housed two pairs of black boots beneath.

"Get some rest," Mal said, turning to leave. "Tomorrow, you will begin your training."

I wanted to open my mouth and ask her a million different questions, but there was no chance she'd be willing to give me any of the answers I demanded. So I simply nodded, watching as she closed the door behind her, and I sat down carefully on the edge of the bed, my mind racing.

My muscles screamed as I stretched out onto the mattress, and even though the bed was a nice change from the hard stone ground I had become accustomed to sleeping on lately, part of me missed the slums I had called home.

Because I missed Micah.

As I closed my eyes, I couldn't help but think of him. We both knew the unspoken rule—if we didn't return, it meant we were caught or dead.

And I prayed he thought it was the latter.

Because there was nothing he could do to save me.

I tried to shut out thoughts of him and listened to the sounds around me. The drips of water, the faint echoes of whispers and footsteps that filtered through the tiny cracks in the door.

I desperately wanted to lie down and sleep, but I didn't trust these people.

Part of me hated them. Hated everything they had ever done, hated that my father had pushed my mother for another heir because he feared them taking his power from him.

He had always known the rebellion was coming for him and his crown, and he couldn't protect it with an heir that he would never allow to take his throne.

And my mother couldn't give him more. She had given her life trying.

She had given her life and the life of her child, my sibling, when she had tried to bear another heir after the healers had warned her against it.

Deep down, I knew it was wrong to hate them. After all, they had suffered far more at the hands of my father than I ever could. But the anger and resentment still burned inside me.

The rusty hinges of the door complained loudly as it swung open. Startled, I jumped up from the bed and felt my head spin as I grabbed on to the edge of the desk for support. My heart raced with fear as I braced myself.

Wren stood in the doorway, a towel still draped over her shoulders and damp hair forming a loose braid down her back. Her eyes appeared tired, and she cautiously entered the room, carefully surveying my presence before closing the door.

"I guess we get to share more than a cell." She moved across the room before pulling a dagger from her boot.

I tensed, but she simply laid the dagger on the desk before dropping her towel over the back of the chair.

"I guess so," I answered with an unenthusiastic shrug, my shoulders lifting slightly before I took a careful step back, creating the slightest of gaps between us. "Mal just told me this was my room and left me here."

"Of course she did." She crossed her arms before turning to me.

She stared at me for a long moment, and I opened my mouth to speak before snapping it closed again.

"Why did you run?"

Shit. I guess I did owe her an explanation. "Because I was scared."

"Were you telling the truth about living in the palace?" She nodded out the window as if we could see it from where we were.

"I was."

"Then why were you in that cell?" She narrowed her eyes slightly, but I could feel the intensity of her stare. She had refused to leave me behind in that cell, and I had let her down.

"I've been on the streets for almost a year. Since the raid." I crossed my arms and looked away from her as I tried not to think about it. "I got caught stealing, and the King's Guard doesn't take kindly to thieves."

"You were there?"

"Yes." I nodded, my gaze fixed on the floor between us. "It's almost impossible to escape the palace if they don't want you to, and the raid created such chaos that no one noticed me when I ran."

Her gaze darted around the room. When she finally spoke, her voice was strained and raspy, like it had been dragged through a graveyard filled with ghosts. "My mother died in that raid."

I didn't know what to say, but I knew the very same demons that haunted her were lying in wait for me as well. My mother was all I could seem to think about when I closed my eyes, when I couldn't distract myself enough to try not to think of her. "I'm sorry."

"Yeah." She nodded as if she was trying to brush off the sudden emotion. "She knew the risks. She died fighting for something she believed in."

I bit down on my lip because I didn't know what to say to that. Her mother died raiding my home. She died fighting against my father and the power he held over this kingdom.

The silence lay thick between us like a heavy fog. My mind raced with guilt, even though I knew deep down it wasn't my fault.

"I lost my mother a few years ago." I swallowed and looked away from her. I never spoke about my mother. Ever. "Even if she knew the risks, that doesn't make it easier."

"No." She shook her head as she stared down at the floor. "It doesn't."

My arms were limp as I cradled them against my chest, curling in on myself as if I were trying to hold something between them.

"We need to get you some clean clothes." She pushed away from the desk before grabbing the dagger that lay there and tucking it back into her boot. "Come on. Mal should have her ass kicked for leaving you like this."

A smile graced my lips for the first time since the guards caught me in the alley.

I followed her out the door and back down the spiral staircase to the main area, where a few people were still milling about. I couldn't help but feel their eyes on me as we passed.

I wondered how many of them were like Wren, whose parent died fighting against mine.

"Is everyone here in the warrior unit?" I asked quietly, and Wren slowed her steps until I was right beside her.

"Shit. Mal really didn't tell you anything, did she?"

"No." I trembled a bit as I thought about her. "I think she might be even more of an asshole than Dacre."

The chuckle that escaped Wren's lips caught me off guard.

"You know he saved you from that cell, right?" The smile on her lips was soft.

"Of course I do, and I am grateful for that. But…"

"But?" She motioned her hand for me to continue.

"I can be grateful and still think he's an unbearable asshole, right?"

"Oh. For sure." She laughed again as she turned to face me, walking backward through the hall as if she had spent a lifetime here. "Trust me, I should know. I've only spent a lifetime with him."

My smile dropped instantly as I stared at her. "He's your brother?"

"The one and only."

"I'm so sorry."

She grinned so hard, matching dimples appeared on her cheeks. "For calling him an asshole?"

"No." I shook my head. "He is an asshole, but I shouldn't have said it to you."

Wren burst out laughing and moved to my side before sliding her arm around mine. "I think you and I are going to get along just fine, Nyra. At least I'll have someone on my side who doesn't worship the ground Dacre walks on."

"Trust me, that will never happen."

She tightened her hold on me as she turned us down a long hallway. "I'll hold you to that."

CHAPTER 7

NYRA

"These are too tight." I tugged at the unforgiving fabric as Wren stood back and assessed me.

"That's how they're supposed to be. Fighting in loose clothing is a disadvantage, and I don't think you can afford any of those."

I rolled my eyes, exaggerating the gesture as I crossed my arms to block out the sting of pain in my muscles. After tossing and turning for what felt like hours the night before, I'd finally managed to drift off into a deep sleep that lasted until Wren made so much noise that I had no choice but to wake.

The bed had been nothing like the one I was used to at the palace. It was hard, and the sheets were scratchy, but it was still a blissful divergence from the cold, hard cobble-stones I had been sleeping on.

"Here." She reached forward and pulled a dagger from her vest, the silver blade glinting in the firelight. She then carefully slid it into an empty sheath on my chest, and I could feel the weight of the metal on my skin.

"Thank you." I swallowed hard because I had given her no reason to be so kind to me.

I wondered if she would still show me that kindness if she knew who I really was. If she knew it was my father who was responsible for the death of her mother.

"Alright, we need to leave, or you're going to be late." She rolled her socks up to her ankles and then grabbed the dark leather boots from under the bed. She used both hands to quickly pull them on and swiftly tugged at the laces, creating tight knots with each loop. I glanced over my shoulder for only a moment as she finished and met my reflection in the small mirror mounted above the desk.

I could hardly recognize myself.

I ran my hands down the length of my body, tracing the curves of the leather uniform that clung to my skin. I was dressed head to toe in black fighting leathers, leathers that used to instill so much fear into me, and yet, here I stood, looking as if I was one of them.

But I would never be.

Wren patted her body, making sure she had all her weapons before she led me from the room. We strode down the dimly lit hallway, the faded paintings on the walls peeling in places. When we reached the main entrance, she pushed open the heavy door and a wave of cold, damp air washed over us.

We stepped outside, and I hesitated as I took in the darkness. Firelight strained to fill the void, but its warmth couldn't make up for the starless sky or the lack of the rising sun.

"What is this place exactly?"

Wren looked around as if she wasn't sure how to answer me. "The hidden city."

"I know that much." I laughed softly. "But how?"

Her expression changed with her thoughts, as her normally bright eyes narrowed almost imperceptibly and her jaw clenched in a subtle show of irritation before she spoke. "Most of the stone buildings you see are ruins." She waved toward the building we just left. "They are from King Nevan's rule."

"What?" I looked around me again. I had heard tales of King Nevan's time as a ruler, but it was so long ago that those stories had felt like fables. "That had to be…"

"Over three centuries ago." Wren nodded as we moved over a small bridge, and I carefully watched the dark water as we passed. "A time when our kingdom was at peace. A time that has long since been forgotten."

A sinking feeling filled my stomach, and a chill raced up my spine as I looked around. There was guilt there that I would never be able to let go of. "How did you all find this?"

"Desperate people will find a way." Wren shrugged as we made our way through the city, the sound of trickling water and passing boots the only noise on the dirt paths. "Everything else you see was built by the rebellion. There are small houses built along the sides of the caves. We have our own markets and healers."

"You don't have a house here?" I asked stupidly when I knew that she roomed with me.

Her throat worked hard before she answered. "We do,

but Dacre and I haven't lived there since my mother was killed. We prefer to stay in the warrior quarters."

I nodded in understanding because after my mother died, I had wanted to be anywhere other than that damned castle. It was haunted by all the happy memories of her that I would never get again, cursed with her screams from the day she died.

"And your father?" I had no business asking questions when I was unwilling to share any of my own answers.

Her brows were drawn as she looked back at me. "My father's love is this rebellion. He doesn't mind living on his own."

There was a long swinging bridge in front of us that crossed over the entire width of the river. My fingers felt raw from holding on to the ropes so tightly, but this was the largest part of the river I had seen since I arrived.

The gaping hole in the ground was a dark abyss that stretched as far as I could see. Its depths made my stomach tighten, and I took an instinctive step back, my heart pounding with fear.

Find your magic. I could practically hear my father's commands echoing in my mind. *The water can't beat you if you use your power.*

The ocean had been dark that night, just like the water beneath me.

"We're almost there." Wren seemed to notice my uneasiness as she turned toward me and slowed her steps.

The bank on the opposite side was covered in a layer of thick green moss, and I tried to focus on it and it alone as I forced myself across.

I let out a deep breath as my feet hit solid ground and

quickly followed Wren away from the water and through a small tunnel that I had to turn sideways to squeeze through. The chill from the rock walls pressing against my uniform seemed to bleed into me, and I shivered.

When we reached the other side, there was a large open space before us. The ground was still covered in dirt and patches of moss, and there was a small beam of sunlight that peeked through the ceiling somewhere far above us.

There were also several floating lanterns that helped illuminate the space, but it was all the people who caught my attention.

We made our way through the crowd, and I noticed all of the different weapons that adorned their bodies. Some had longswords hanging from ornate scabbards, while others carried short daggers like Wren's that tucked into their waistbelts and vests. I spotted a few with arrows jutting out from the quivers on their backs.

Wren tugged me forward, and I scanned the clearing. In the far corner, a cluster of warriors stood in a loose circle, arms crossed and eyes alert. As we stepped closer, their attention shifted to us. Some bobbed their heads in acknowledgment of Wren's presence.

"Morning, Wren," one of the men spoke, and I couldn't help but notice the way his gaze swept over her curves.

"Morning, Tavian," Wren replied, a smile on her face as she gestured to me. "This is Nyra. She'll be joining us today."

Tavian sized me up before nodding. "Welcome."

"Where's Dacre?" She looked across the clearing as she spoke, and I felt an uncomfortable heat rising to my cheeks. Despite the fact that Dacre was an ass, it was impossible not to notice how infuriatingly handsome he was.

"Scouting. There was movement noted at the base of the falls early this morning. He should be back soon." Tavian said it so absently, but I cataloged every one of his words.

What kind of movement?

"Morning." An older man with dark hair that was graying at the temples stood before the group and cleared his throat. "We had three groups out scouting last night, and we will send three more today. The rest of you will remain back to help train the new recruits. There are twenty in total that have arrived in the last three weeks."

His voice was commanding, drowning out the rest of the room. I flinched and my gaze shifted to Wren who was standing perfectly still, her eyes riveted on him.

"Are you scouting?"

She finally turned back to me, her gaze softening slightly. "Not today. Today, I'm with you."

I couldn't hide my relief. I didn't even know her, but I felt more comfortable with her than anyone else here.

"Come on." She waved me forward, and I followed her toward a white circle on the ground that appeared to be drawn in some sort of powder.

We both stepped inside, and she shook out her arms before she drew all the weapons away from her body and dropped them just outside the circle.

I hesitantly pulled out the one dagger she had given me and did the same.

"This is a sparring circle." She motioned around the

perimeter. "This is where we'll train, but we won't use any magic to start."

My throat constricted as she spoke, and I gave her a single, stiff nod. I should have told her that I didn't have any power, but I didn't.

Two people moved into the circle next to us, and I watched them intently as they started to dance around one another. They both still had their weapons, but neither had drawn them.

One of the fighters charged forward and managed to land a kick along the torso of the other, and I winced.

"What kind of training do you have?"

I brought my attention back to Wren as she bent at the waist and touched her toes.

"I'm sorry?"

"Training? Fighting? Weapons? What do you have experience with, and where do you need the most help?" She stood fully, and I jumped at the sound of clashing metal.

"I don't have any experience." I said the words quietly for only her to hear.

Her eyes rounded. "At all?"

"No." I shook my head and balled my hands into fists to stop myself from fidgeting under her assessment.

"Okay." She nodded as if I wasn't the most insignificant warrior she had ever trained. "We'll start simple then." Wren took a few steps back and gestured for me to follow. "Let's start with some basic footwork and evasion techniques."

I followed her lead, trying to mirror the elegant, effortless way she moved. She circled me as I awkwardly attempted to arrange my feet in the same way she did. With each misstep, Wren offered words of encouragement, and after a few tries, I had managed to balance my weight between both feet.

She began to circle me, her eyes scanning my body up and down, and I could feel sweat already beading across my brow. "Your stance is the most important thing you can learn. Your feet should be shoulder-width apart, with your knees slightly bent. Keep your weight evenly distributed between both feet and position your dominant foot slightly behind the other."

I followed her instructions, adjusting my stance until it felt comfortable. Wren nodded in approval and stepped closer.

"Now, let's work on your strikes." She tucked her chin, stepped forward, and threw a wide jab at the imaginary opponent in front of her. I copied her motion, feeling my shoulder strain as I tried to imitate the power of her punch. My knuckles were clutched tight and my footwork was clumsy.

Wren glanced at me with a critical eye and slowly began to correct my form, gently guiding my hands and feet into the correct positions. We drilled various strikes and footwork for what felt like an eternity. My muscles grew sore and sweat dripped down my forehead until I was forced to wipe it away.

But she wasn't done.

She paced in front of me, and my eyes never left her face. "Now we need to put what you've learned to use."

She advanced at an alarming pace, her body poised and lithe as she weaved around me with ease. No matter how hard I tried to follow her every move or anticipate a strike, she managed to catch me off guard. Her foot connected with my leg in an expertly calculated angle, sending me tumbling backward. The impact of the ground beneath my back sent a shockwave through my abdomen, leaving me gasping for breath.

"You were supposed to block me." Wren's warm laughter was like a balm that soothed my embarrassment. I reluctantly accepted her outstretched hand as she pulled me up with surprising strength, and I stumbled slightly before regaining my balance. "Are you okay?" she asked, her eyes wide.

I nodded, trying to steady my breathing. "Yeah, I'm alright."

She gave me a small smile before gesturing back to the circle. "Let's go again."

I took a deep breath, then steadied myself with feet planted wide apart and hands up in a blocking position. I focused on every detail—her footwork, the tension of her muscles, the intensity in her eyes. As she lunged forward, I managed to block her strike; the pain reverberated through my body. I gritted my teeth and tried to land my own punch, but before my fist could make contact, she grabbed me by the wrist and yanked me off balance. In an instant, I was on my knees, gasping for air.

"That's kind of pathetic."

At the sound of Dacre's deep, gruff voice, I jumped, and my shoulders tensed. He looked at me disdainfully as I scrambled to my feet.

"Don't be an ass, Dacre." Wren crossed her arms and stood between us.

I could feel my heart racing as I looked at him, his eyes locked on mine. He was beautiful, his sharp jawline and piercing eyes seeming to cut through me like a knife. But his words and the way he sneered at me made my skin crawl.

"I'm not being an ass. It's the truth. She's deadweight." He nodded toward me as if I couldn't hear his words.

Wren's back straightened. "Tone it down a notch. What did you find?"

I dusted the dirt off my pants and tried to appear like I wasn't hanging on to every word they said.

Dacre grunted. "It was nothing."

There was a tense silence between the two of them, and I wondered if he was being honest or if he was hiding the truth because I was standing there. Because he considered me a traitor.

Dark circles hung beneath his exhausted eyes, and he stood motionless with tense shoulders.

"Did she tell you about her magic?" Dacre cocked his head as if studying me, and my heart raced as anger bubbled up inside me.

Wren looked over her shoulder at me, but I was still staring daggers at her brother. "No. Why do I need to know about her magic?"

Dacre's jaw twitched as he stared at me. "Because she has none."

Wren's head whipped around so quickly back to her brother that it was almost comical. "That's impossible."

"I agree." He nodded as he stepped into the circle. His hands were balled into fists as he assessed me. "Which means your new little friend is hiding something."

"I'm not hiding anything," I said through gritted teeth.

"Let's see about that." He moved closer to me, and I countered his movements with a step backward.

"I don't want to train with you." I chanced a glance in Wren's direction, but she was still watching her brother.

"That's not really an option for you."

The way he studied me was so unnerving that I could hardly remember the way Wren had just taught me to stand. I stumbled over my feet as I took another step back, and Dacre made his move.

He was fast, much faster than Wren, and he knocked me on my ass before I could realize what was happening.

He reached his hand out as if he was going to help me up, but my anger surged inside me. I didn't take his hand; instead, I kicked my leg forward, something Wren most definitely didn't teach me, and I slammed my foot into his hard abdomen.

The impact sent him stumbling back, and I scrambled to my feet, ready to defend myself. His lips curled into a smirk, and he moved toward me again, his eyes glinting in the low light.

"There's that backbone," he said with a smile as he launched himself at me.

I ducked and weaved, using the basic footwork Wren had taught me to try and avoid his attacks. I managed to dodge the punch he swung toward my head, but he was too fast.

His other hand came down hard against my thigh in a slap, and I hissed in pain.

"Use your power to help you deflect." He kicked his foot out as he spoke, sweeping his leg out in a move that was eerily similar to his sister's earlier, and knocked me on my ass again.

I gasped for breath as he towered over me. He was breathing normally while my chest heaved with exertion.

"I told you I don't have any power." I lifted a trembling hand and wiped away the loose hair that fell in my face.

"You're really going to cling to that lie, huh?" He cocked his head as he studied me.

I didn't offer him an answer because it didn't matter what I said. He wasn't going to believe me either way. He thought he could break me, but there was nothing left for him to break.

"Tomorrow, you train with me." He stood to his full height, and I scoffed as I watched Wren take a step forward.

"Lay off, Dacre."

"No." He turned away from me, and I pushed up until I was sitting. "I don't trust her, and she trains with me until we find out more about her power."

"And if she's not lying?" Wren crossed her arms and cocked her hip. She seemed to have no fear when it came to her brother, and I envied her.

Dacre turned his head toward me, his expression unreadable. His dark eyes seemed to drill into my soul as if he was trying to uncover a secret. It felt like the slightest movement would shatter the intense moment that seemed to stretch on forever. "She's lying. I'm just not sure about what."

CHAPTER 8

NYRA

I felt like I could barely walk when Wren finally led me away from the training area. The muscles in my thighs trembled with every step I took, but I simply bit down on my lip to stop myself from wincing.

Wren's voice broke the silence, soft and hesitant. "I'm sorry about Dacre. He can be...difficult sometimes."

I raised an eyebrow and gave her a pointed look. "Difficult?"

She chuckled softly. "I promise he's not always like that."

I looked at her, really looked at her, and I felt desperate for her to know that I was telling the truth. At least about this.

"I'm not lying about my power." I looked down at my hands and how useless they had been when my father made my trainer strike them until I could muster some sort of magic from my fingertips. "I have never been able to conjure any sort of magic."

Wren's lips curved into a gentle smile, and she beck-
oned me to follow her across the quaint wooden bridge.
With every step we took, I couldn't help but feel
completely disoriented—every path looked the same, yet I
was almost certain I hadn't been this way before.

"I believe you. It's just we've never heard of a fae who
didn't carry at least some magic. It seems impossible."

My shoulders drew back, and my posture stiffened.

"There are occasions where there will be a delay in
someone's magic. Some people don't really know how to
manifest it until they are older."

Tiny flickers of hope lit up inside me, and I gazed up at
her. "Really?"

She nodded. "Yes, but usually they have traces of it that
they can feel or use. But they don't understand the extent of
it until they are older. But I've never heard of someone
coming into adulthood without it."

I felt my body sag as her words hit me, all the air
leaving my lungs. I was nineteen years old. If I were to
have magic, it should have more than manifested by
now.

"Come on." She nodded toward a tall wooden building
that looked as if it could collapse at any moment. It stood
on the far edge of the cave floor, and dark water flowed by
slowly. It seemed to moan with the movement of the river.
"Let's get something to eat."

I followed Wren into the building, which turned out to
be a small pub. The interior was cozy, with mismatched
tables and chairs. The walls were adorned with old, rusty
weapons and flaking paintings of mythical creatures that
had been all but forgotten. The smell of freshly baked bread

and roasted meat filled the air, making my stomach grumble.

Wren led us to a small table in the corner.

There were several people sitting at other tables, but I was caught off guard by the woman who came over to our table. I startled in my chair, the sound of it dragging against the floor jarring, and the woman narrowed her crystal blue eyes.

"Hello, Wren." Her voice was sharp and musical. "Who's your new friend?"

"Hey, Kit. This is Nyra. She's a new recruit."

"It's nice to meet you, Nyra."

I nodded in greeting. "It's nice to meet you as well."

"What can I get for you today?" Kit asked, and my gaze drifted from her face to the delicate iridescent wings that sprouted from her back. They fluttered softly in the warm glow of the lanterns, but I noticed they were frayed and worn around the delicate edges.

"The usual for both of us."

"Give me just a few minutes." With each step she took away from our table, her wings fluttered gently as if they had a life of their own.

"Does she have wings?" I whispered to Wren so no one else heard me.

"How long did you work in that palace?" She chuckled and leaned back in her chair. "They really had you sheltered, huh?"

I looked back in Kit's direction, but she was already gone. "I spent my whole life there and my mother before me."

It was another half-truth, half-lie.

"That's unfortunate." Wren cleared her throat. "Winged fae are a rarity, and most don't live anywhere near the palace if they can help it. The only way King Roan can tax their power is if he can find them, and he spent years clipping their wings at every tithe so they couldn't fly."

He clipped their wings.

There was a small pop in the air, and the food Wren ordered appeared on our table, steam billowing off. I felt like I was going to be sick.

"Hell yes." Wren grabbed her fork and quickly dove in, and I lifted my own fork in my hand as I searched the pub for another sighting of Kit.

She was standing behind the bar, laughing at something someone was saying, and this time when I looked at her wings, I paid more attention to the frayed edges I had noticed before. I couldn't tell now if her wings were fluttering or quivering.

Had my father done that?

She looked up, noticing my staring, and I quickly looked away and down at my food. It was some sort of fish surrounded by root vegetables, and even though I still felt nauseous at the thought of my father's cruelty, I took a bite.

"You know," Wren said as she absently rapped her knuckles against the table, "I don't think Dacre hates you."

A loud laughter bubbled out of my throat, and the two men sitting closest to us turned in our direction. I shoveled another bite of food into my mouth.

"I'm serious." Wren smiled. "He's just protective."

I scoffed. "Protective?"

"Yes. Of all this." She waved her hand around. "Our parents spent their lives building this rebellion, my mother gave her life trying to protect it, and he feels the burden of that responsibility now more than ever."

I wanted to ask her about her father; I also had a million questions about Dacre, but asking her to answer questions meant that I had to be willing to do the same.

"Was he protecting the rebellion when he kicked my ass in the sparring circle?"

"He didn't kick your ass." Wren rolled her eyes playfully. "He was pushing you."

I raised an eyebrow. "Pushing me? I'm pretty sure my tailbone might be bruised where he dropped me."

Wren's expression turned serious. "I know. But believe me, he's not like that with everyone. He's just trying to weed out anyone who might be a threat to the rebellion."

I chewed on my lip, even as I nodded. "I can't wait for tomorrow then." I laughed without humor. "Hopefully, he takes out some of his aggression tonight, so he's nicer tomorrow."

Wren scrunched up her nose and made a gagging noise. "I do not want to think about my brother taking out his aggression." She said the last few words dramatically, and a flush crept up my chest.

"Oh, gods. That's not what I meant." I stumbled over my words.

"I would much rather think about me taking out my own aggression." Wren rested her chin on her fist. "Especially by someone who knows what they're doing."

A laugh bubbled out of me, and I couldn't hide how uncomfortable this conversation made me. I hadn't so much as kissed a man, let alone done anything more. And here I was at the dinner table thinking about her brother and whether or not he would know what he was doing.

Wren gave me a knowing grin, and I tried to divert her attention from me. "That one guy today looked like he was interested in you."

"Tavian?" Her eyes widened, and she shook her head. "Absolutely not."

"Why not?" He was handsome, and he looked at her like she was the best thing he had ever seen.

She waved her hand dismissively. "He's just a friend."

"So, who are you interested in?" I took another bite of my food and almost groaned as the flavors hit my tongue.

A blush rushed up Wren's cheeks, and she darted her eyes away from me. "I can't tell you all my secrets."

Guilt panged in my chest, but I quickly pushed it away and took the last bite of my food.

"Let's go hit the hot springs." Wren stood and stretched. "Your body is probably going to be killing you tomorrow."

She wasn't wrong. I could already feel the ache in my muscles as I stood and followed her out the door.

We weaved through more trails and bridges, and this place felt more like a maze with every step we took.

"Where are the hot springs?" I asked as Wren seemed to be leading us in circles.

"Just a little farther." She ducked under a large hanging stone, and I did the same.

The smell of sulfur in the air hit me instantly, but it was the dozens of pools of dark water in front of us that made me stop in my tracks.

The pools were surrounded by small rocks that kept the water from bleeding into one another. Steam rolled off the surface of the water like smoke, and drops of water splashed into them from the rocks above as if it were raining.

Amid the steam rising from the hot springs, I noticed a man with blistered and peeling skin on his arm gingerly dipping it into the water. He winced in pain and let out a small exhale. Sitting beside him was a woman in a cream-colored shirt and trousers, gently cupping the water into her hand and pouring it over his damaged skin. Her soft words of encouragement floated through the quiet space.

"I've never seen anything like this," I admitted out loud to Wren as she moved us to a small pool on the far side of the open-mouthed cave.

She caught my gaze that was still on the man who was wincing as he lowered into the pool until his shoulder was now covered by the water.

"The hot springs have many healing properties." She pulled at the straps that held her vest to her body before lifting the weapon-filled vest and setting it on the ground at her feet. "I'll admit, we warriors probably use them way more than anyone else."

I followed suit, removing my own vest and placing it next to Wren's. The hot springs were even more beautiful up close, and the heat was almost suffocatingly intense.

Wren kicked off her boots and started removing more clothing, and I followed her lead until I realized she was climbing into the water wearing nothing but her under-garments.

She lowered herself into the pool before she looked up at me expectantly. I was still covered in my uniform, and I wiggled my bare toes against the rocks.

"Come on." She nodded toward my clothes, and I crossed my arms.

"There are a lot of people in here."

She chuckled softly and looked over her shoulder. "This is quiet. Plus, no one is going to look. They are all far too interested in their own sore bodies. I promise."

I looked around, and she was right. No one was looking at us. They were too busy dealing with their own aches and pains.

I glanced around one more time before slowly lowering my trousers to the ground. My shirt was long enough that it covered most of my body, and I pulled it up around my hips as I stepped into the water.

I hissed as the heat hit my skin, but as I sank deeper into the water, the warmth began to feel soothing. I let out a sigh as I dropped farther into the water, and I groaned as the heat bled over my shoulders.

You're safe.

"I told you." Wren leaned back against the rocks, closing her eyes. "These hot springs are miraculous."

The heat radiated from my neck down to my toes, and I settled into the soothing sensation. My eyes fluttered closed as I nodded in agreement, letting out a comfortable sigh of satisfaction.

I felt like I was almost asleep when the sound of men's voices drew me out of my trance.

I cautiously opened one eye and saw Dacre and Kai striding confidently side by side. They hadn't noticed me yet; my back was angled toward them, but it was clear they were headed our way. My stomach tightened to the point of pain as they approached.

"Really, Wren?" Kai chuckled, and I sank down deeper into the water and forced my attention back on my roommate. "I heard that you barely got any sort of workout today. Yet here you are in the springs?"

Wren's body went taut as she peeked one eye open. "Fuck you, Kai." She stretched her arms over her head lazily, and I looked in his direction just in time to see the way he watched her body. "I get in a workout every day. But thanks for the concern."

Dacre was quietly removing his boots, and the expression on his face was lethal.

I didn't dare say a word to draw his attention toward me.

"You most certainly didn't get a workout today." Dacre peeled off his shirt, revealing a lean torso sculpted by hours and hours of training. His biceps bulged as he tossed the fabric carelessly to the ground. I couldn't help but stare, my eyes tracing the lines of his defined muscles with fascination.

He still hadn't noticed me, and I forced myself to look away as his thumbs hooked into the sides of his trousers.

Wren was grinning at me from across the spring, and I shook my head at her so she would quit giving me a knowing look.

"I'm pretty sure you'd be better off with a training partner who had lost his legs in battle than her." Dacre chuckled, and my chest hollowed at his words.

"Oh, yeah?" Wren cocked her head as she studied her brother. "Please tell me more."

Kai stepped into the water beside me, and he let out a harsh chuckle when his gaze landed on me.

"Yeah, Dacre. What is it about this girl that has you so riled up?" Kai took a seat to my left, right between Wren and me, and winked at me.

He had led me here with my hands tied behind my back only a day ago, and now he had the nerve to wink at me.

"She doesn't rile me up. I just don't like her."

I sat up straighter as Dacre stepped into the water and winced as the water moved up his calf. There were scars along his skin and fading bruises.

I wondered if those were simply from training or if the cocky bastard actually saw battle.

"Don't worry. I don't like you either."

At the sound of my voice, Dacre's attention snapped to me, and he paused for a moment. Our eyes met, and I felt a shiver run down my spine under his scrutiny. His eyes fell away from mine quickly, but they lingered on my breasts before traveling down to the dark water.

I felt a flush rise up my neck and quickly sank deeper into the water, trying to hide my body from his gaze.

"I didn't realize you were here." Dacre's voice was low and dangerous and lacked the playfulness he had only moments before.

"No, really?" I looked up at him as if he hadn't just been so cruel. "You'd think I might have picked up on that when you were talking badly about me so freely."

I gritted my teeth and tried to ignore him as he moved farther into the water. He sat as close as he could to his sister, as far as he could get from me, although I could reach out and touch him with my foot beneath the water if I wanted to.

"Trust me, I wouldn't have come if I had known you were here."

"Likewise." I crossed my arms just as Wren rammed her elbow into Dacre's side.

"Don't be such a jerk." Wren moved across the small pool until she was sitting right beside me. "You were right."

Dacre cocked an eyebrow at me even as his mouth stayed in a harsh line. "It looks like I wasn't the only one talking badly about the other."

"I called you an ass. It's the truth."

The corner of his mouth curved into a half smile. "And I called you weak. It looks like we're both just telling the truth today."

I clenched my fists under the water, willing myself not to react to his words.

"I don't care what you think about me." My voice was low and forceful as I met his gaze once again.

He held my stare for a moment before nodding almost imperceptibly. "We'll see about that."

I rolled my eyes because this guy was so damn full of himself. Wren's brother or not, he was an ass, and I had no interest in spending any more time with him than was necessary.

I closed my eyes and tried to focus on the warmth of the water, the way the heat soaked into my muscles, but I could feel his gaze on me even as the three of them began talking.

"There were three more recruits brought in today," Kai spoke, and I finally opened my eyes to look at him.

"And?" Dacre leaned his head back against the jagged

rocks, his neck muscles straining beneath taut skin. I couldn't help but notice the lines of tension running through his body as he exhaled heavily.

"Two of them were devout followers of the king and chose not to join."

He said it so simply, but I knew exactly what it meant. They chose to die.

"Did you even give them a choice?" I asked before I could stop myself, and Dacre's eyes shot in my direction.

"We always give you traitors a choice. They knew exactly who they were fighting for, what they were fighting for, and that's what they chose."

"Have you ever stopped to think that the people of Marmoris aren't fighting for anything other than their own safety, for their hunger?" I sat up higher in the water as my anger fueled me. "Not everyone is worried about the war between a king and this rebellion. They are worried about putting food in their bellies, about not being killed."

Dacre's gaze was as dark as the water that surrounded us, and neither Kai nor Wren spoke a word.

"In this world, you don't have the option of not choosing sides. King Roan has been draining this kingdom dry for years, and no one can survive under his rule. Those who don't join us are a danger to us because they are still paying that man the tithe. They are making him stronger just by him sitting in his palace while we kill ourselves every day to make this kingdom a better place." The muscles of his neck and shoulders bunched as he clenched his jaw. "Don't speak about things that you have no knowledge of. You spent your life in that palace. You can't possibly know anything that was happening outside of it."

Panic clawed at my chest until I remembered that he only knew what I told him.

But there was a part of me that wanted to tell him the truth. I wanted to spew it in his face, consequences be damned, until he realized that he couldn't possibly know what life was like in that palace, in that cage.

But I couldn't.

"You shouldn't speak of things you don't know of either. You have no idea what growing up in that palace was like. You think the king is a monster, yet have you ever met him? Have you had to face him every day of your life?"

The next words that left his mouth shocked me. "Maybe you're right."

His gaze dropped away from my eyes, and I could have sworn he was staring at my mouth. I bit down on my bottom lip and forced myself to sink beneath the water before I did or said something stupid. The water moved over my face as I slipped below the surface, and I clamped my eyes closed.

I stayed below the water for as long as I could handle before my lungs begged for me to surface again.

My body *begged* me to get out of the dark water.

But there was something about me that felt stronger than before—now that I was out of my father's kingdom and out of his reach. Dacre was a force, but I would not cower as he demanded.

I sat back up, coming out of the water until the tops of my shoulders were exposed, and as soon as I opened my eyes, all I could see were Dacre's eyes still on me.

Wren was grinning as she looked back and forth between me and her brother. "Are you ready?"

"Yes." I nodded and pulled my attention away from him. I climbed out of the spring, forcing myself not to cover an inch of my body as I did so.

I reached for my discarded clothes before glancing back at Dacre. His eyes were lingering on my almost bare body, and they slid down until they landed on my ass.

Chill bumps formed on my skin as I grabbed my clothes and boots in my dripping wet hands.

I wanted to get as far away from him as I could.

"I'll see you in the morning for training. Don't be late," Dacre said gruffly.

I turned toward him and saluted him with the hand holding my trousers. "I'll be the weak one. You can't miss me."

CHAPTER 9

NYRA

I couldn't see the sun, but I knew it had yet to rise when Wren shook me from my sleep. I had groaned and tried to pull my blanket over my head, but she had simply laughed and jerked it away.

I was exhausted.

But I had dressed and followed Wren to the training area, just like I had the day before. I stopped mid-step when I saw a very irritated-looking Dacre waiting for me in one of the sparring circles. His face was flushed, and beads of sweat dotted his brow as if he had already been here for hours. His arms were folded across his chest, and his eyes narrowed as I approached.

As I stepped into the ring, he stood at the opposite end, his muscles tense and eyes fixed on me. He didn't speak a word, but his intense gaze followed my every movement, as if he was studying me for weaknesses.

We circled each other warily, both of us waiting for the other to make a move. His muscles were taut, and his eyes were fixed on mine with an intensity that made me uncomfortable.

Following Wren's instructions, I inhaled deeply and focused every small movement of my body. But every time I caught a glimpse of him out of the corner of my eye, my balance wavered. Those stolen glances were like magnets, pulling me toward him and away from my concentration.

And just like that, for the fourth time since arriving, I found myself sprawled on the ground, courtesy of his distracting presence.

"Your stance is all wrong," he grumbled and extended his arm out for me to take, but I stiffened and pushed myself off the ground. My legs trembled as I stood, feeling a deep ache in my overworked thighs.

"I'm standing exactly like you told me to." I dusted the dirt from my trousers and crossed my arms in an attempt to look as annoyed as he did.

"You aren't." He moved around me, his fingertips lightly brushing against my right thigh before giving it a soft tap until I shifted it out of the way. His breath was warm on the back of my neck as he passed.

I gritted my teeth as I moved my foot forward, but he wasn't satisfied.

"More."

I made a move to take a step, and he quickly shifted his weight, kicking out his foot between mine and causing mine to slide to the right.

"You could use your words, you know?" I quipped when he almost knocked me off balance completely.

"I could, but I've found that you're not a very good listener."

I fought the urge to growl as he walked around me and deliberately stepped back into my direct line of sight. I rolled my eyes before letting out a heavy sigh.

"Feel how your weight is distributed more evenly. Do you feel more sound on your feet?"

I did, but I didn't want to give him the satisfaction of knowing that. "Not really."

He pressed his lips together and the corner of my mouth curved up in a smirk.

"Your arms should be in front of you, ready to block whatever is coming your way." His strong grasp wrapped itself around my wrist like a snake before he forced it up in front of me. I could feel his powerful grip searing my skin, as if branding me.

"You know the only time I've ever been attacked in my life was by you."

Dacre's eyes gleamed dangerously as he slowly and firmly moved my hands to where he wanted them. His grip was sure, confident, and unyielding. "You were caught by the King's Guard, and if you had been trained better, you would have been able to get away, but here you are."

He took a step away from me, studying my posture with cautious eyes. His gaze traveled slowly down my body, pausing at my hands before slowly dipping to my feet. "Did your parents never teach you any sort of self-defense?"

"No." I raised my chin even as a chill ran over my skin. "I don't think they ever thought I would need it."

He took another step back and his eyes narrowed as he rotated around me. I stood motionless, my cheeks flushed pink, my hands held exactly where he had put them as he assessed his handiwork.

"Where are your parents now?"

My throat felt so tight and constricted as his words hit me; yet I forced myself to take a deep breath. "I don't know where my father is."

It wasn't a lie. I hadn't seen him since the raid. There had been an increase in guard presence in the capital city ever since the raid. Everyone thought they were looking for a rebel sympathizer, but I knew they were looking for me. It was the reason I didn't do my first thieving job with Micah until months after we found each other.

But my father wouldn't dare show his own face outside of his palace.

There had been rumors that he was still tucked away safely beyond the palace walls, but there had been other rumors that he had fled.

But I knew my father better than that.

"And your mother?" He moved back around to the front of me and studied my feet.

"My mother is dead."

He raised his eyes to meet mine, and I saw a shadow pass through them. His expression softened briefly in what looked like guilt before hardening again. "I'm sorry."

"Don't worry. It wasn't your precious rebellion that was responsible for her death."

His knuckles whitened as he balled his fists, the veins in his forearms bulging. His eyes shifted away from me, and I hated that I felt guilt over my words as I watched his nostrils flare. "Your right foot should always be in the back. You have more control that way." He stepped back and moved into his own stance that matched the one he had just placed me in. "We should train you to be prepared to kick with your left."

"You already saw that I can't kick," I grumbled.

"Then we're going to train you until you can." He lunged forward so quickly that I didn't have time to think. I felt my breath catch in my throat as I desperately tried to backpedal away from him, but I struggled to keep my balance.

"Kick out," he growled at me, and I lifted my hands as I tried to remember what he had shown me. "At least try to block me."

I launched my foot forward with all the strength I could muster, but it was futile. In a split second, he had seized my ankle and held it in midair in his hand.

He jerked my foot forward until my body slammed into his. His body was warm against mine, and my cheeks grew hot as I desperately tried to turn away from his gaze.

But he didn't let me go. He gripped the back of my neck, his touch firm and steady, as he forced me to look up at him, and he ran his hand slowly up my leg until his fingers rested gently on the back of my knee. His dark eyes looked into mine, unblinking and intense.

"A child could have blocked that kick." His voice was scathing, and I could feel his warm breath against my cheek.

I swallowed hard, my heart pounding in my chest.

My breath caught in my throat as panic began to swell within me. His fingers dug into my calf, his grip tightening with each passing second. I tried to yank my leg out of his grip, but he held on tightly with a fierce determination that enraged me.

"Pathetic." His voice was low, but the word shot through me as if he had screamed it.

I let my leg go heavy in his hand, and I slammed the rest of my weight into his chest. He wasn't expecting it, and both of us lost our balance.

Dacre's eyes widened as he fell backward onto the ground, and I landed on top of him with a groan as my knees collided with the hard dirt floor. Our bodies were pressed together, his hand now gripping my thigh, and I could feel every inch of him through our leathers.

For a moment, neither of us moved, our bodies so close that I could feel his exhales roll through me like a warm breeze.

"Son."

The sound of a man's voice sliced through the air like a knife, and Dacre pushed me off him with an iron grip. I stumbled backward, my heart racing, as he leaped to his feet. Sweat dripped from his brow as the air in my lungs fled.

"I think that's enough for today," Dacre said sternly, his eyes avoiding mine, as he turned to the man standing just outside the sparring circle.

The man squinted his eyes, narrowing his gaze as he studied me. He looked so much like Dacre, except for his bright-green eyes that matched Wren's and the gray hair that was sprinkled throughout the black. His lips parted, and he spoke again, the intensity of his scrutiny making me shift uncomfortably. "I need you on patrol this afternoon."

Dacre's back straightened, and he nodded. "Of course," he replied in a tight voice.

The man finally shifted his gaze away from me to

Dacre. "Finish what you're doing and meet me," he said before turning on his heel and moving away from us.

I shifted my weight from one foot to the other. My hands nervously clasped together in front of me as I stood a few steps behind Dacre. His eyes were fixed on the direction the man had just gone, and I cleared my throat before cautiously speaking.

"I'll find Wren."

"No." He slowly faced me, his expression drawn and unreadable. His jaw was tight, and his eyes were narrowed as if he was trying to figure something out. "She'll go too soft on you. You need someone who will push you."

I rolled my eyes and rubbed my sore muscles that were proof that Wren had pushed me. By the time we climbed into bed last night, I thought I would cry from the way my muscles ached.

"I'll find Kai." He scanned the large cavern, his brow furrowed with concentration. I watched him, craning my neck to try and catch a glimpse of Kai, though I hadn't seen him all morning. But that didn't matter—all I could focus on was the way Dacre moved, the movement of the muscles in his back as he looked for his friend.

He was...*distracting*.

"Shit," he cursed under his breath when he didn't find him.

"Don't worry. You go do your little patrol, and I'll find him. Any special instructions other than to try to kill me?"

The corner of Dacre's mouth lifted, so slight I almost missed it. His dark eyes seemed to bore into mine as my stomach flipped, and I felt warmth spread through my body. "That should do it," he murmured in a low voice.

I felt his eyes on me, scanning me as I remained stoic, trying to hide the shivers running down my spine. "On it," I said, hoping he didn't notice how uneasy I felt around him.

He met my gaze with a single nod before turning on his heel and stalking off, his leather-clad muscles flexing with each step. As he disappeared from sight, I shook my head to clear the fog that had settled over me and took a breath, steeling myself to search for Kai.

I paused and thought about turning around, the thought of my warm bed beckoning me, but my feet kept carrying me forward. There was a part of me that was desperate to prove Dacre wrong. To prove I wasn't as weak as he believed me to be.

It didn't take long to find Kai. Within moments, his broad shoulders were visible from across the room as he circled a much smaller opponent in his sparring circle.

"Hey." I cleared my throat and shuffled on my feet, glancing around uncertainly. "Dacre said he wants me to train with you today."

Kai slowly pivoted his body toward me, and his eyes shifted as they locked onto mine. He paused briefly before he turned back to confront his opponent, his features set in a determined expression. "Sure thing. Just as soon as I'm done kicking his ass."

The man across from him grinned, revealing a flash of yellow teeth. I cautiously leaned back against a jagged rock, my palms sweaty as I watched the two of them continue to circle one another.

"I'm free." I heard a husky voice and turned to find the source. A man stood beside me, his light-brown curls tousled in every direction atop his head. His bright blue eyes shone with warmth as he smiled at me. His gaze ran over me curiously, and my cheeks grew warm from his scrutiny.

There was something about him that reminded me of Micah.

"Not happening, Eiran," Kai called out, even as the man across from him charged, and I flinched at the sound of his kick against Kai's thigh.

"Okay." I nodded as I stood.

"Don't you fucking dare, Nyra. You're training with me," Kai grunted as the man landed a hit.

"I'm sitting here watching you lose."

"He'll be fine." Eiran made a subtle gesture with his head, a barely perceptible nod to the left.

"It's your death wish, Eiran," Kai warned, and I quickly followed behind Eiran before Kai could stop me.

We moved through the cavern in silence as we passed others training until we reached a corner where the shadows were thick and heavy enough to conceal us from any prying eyes or ears.

"So, what exactly is Dacre wanting you to be trained on today?" Eiran moved inside a large sparring circle, and I followed suit.

"I'm pretty sure he was just trying to humiliate me, but we were working on stance and blocking."

His lips curled into an amused grin as his eyes moved from my face down my chest and then slowly dipped lower. I could feel a flush rising on my cheeks as I shifted uncomfortably beneath his gaze.

"Let's see what you can do then." He moved into a

stance, his arms outstretched and his feet planted firmly on the ground, just like Dacre had done.

I inhaled a deep, steadying breath and tried to recall Dacre's stance instructions as best I could. My gaze wouldn't stay fixed on Eiran; his piercing blue eyes made me nervous.

"Relax," he said with a low chuckle. "You're not going to be able to block anything if you aren't breathing."

I closed my eyes and inhaled deeply, forcing myself to dig deep and focus on Eiran as he came at me. He was fast, but he wasn't as fast as Dacre.

Each time his fist or foot flew toward me, I felt my muscles strain as I tensed to block the attack. Eiran looked completely at ease while sweat trickled down my back and I struggled to catch my breath.

He was holding back and not throwing his full force at me, which I both loathed and appreciated. As we kept going, my body adjusted to the movements, no longer feeling as stiff or as strained. I could sense when he was about to strike and reacted quickly, reading his movements before they were made.

"Good job." He took a step back and folded his arms, offering me one of those easygoing smiles I'd already come to expect from him. "Looks like you're a natural." His words were like warm honey, coating me from head to toe.

"I don't know about that." I shook my head as I braced my hands on my hips and tried to catch my breath. "I think Dacre's just knocked me on my ass enough times that my fight or flight is starting to kick in."

Eiran laughed and rubbed his hand along his jaw.

"Maybe if I train you well enough, you can knock Dacre on his own ass for a change."

A chuckle escaped me as I tried to imagine it.

"It would probably take a miracle for that to happen."

"I don't know."

I met his gaze and my stomach fluttered. His blue eyes were intense and his jaw tightened ever so slightly.

"Wilder things have happened," he said softly. "Let's try again."

He motioned me forward with a flick of his fingertips, and I let myself imagine that it was Dacre standing in front of me. I raised my guard just in time to deflect a swinging punch. Taking advantage of an opening, I threw all my weight into a kick that connected with his rib cage, and I smiled.

CHAPTER 10

DACRE

As our weary feet trudged over the rough, uneven streets, I struggled to keep my eyes open.

My body ached with every step, but my father strode confidently ahead of me, the weight of his longsword barely noticeable as it hung from his back. He never complained about the fatigue, no matter how long he had been out on patrol; only a slight hunch in his shoulders betrayed any sign of weariness.

"Get some rest." He extended his arm, palm open and fingers splayed, the movement fluid and familiar. As he traced a circular motion, the soft light of the glowing lanterns flickered and swirled before they dulled and smoke crept around them. "We don't know what's to come."

It was the thing he always said when he left me. It used to fill me with the thrill of adventure we would face, but now it felt ominous. Everything about the rebellion had become uncertain since losing my mother.

"Night." I turned away, my stomach in knots, and

trudged in the opposite direction. I glanced over to the home he was heading to—the one that held so many memories of what we used to be. The ghosts of those days seemed to linger in the shadows that surrounded it.

I moved over the long bridge, heading for the warrior quarters, and I couldn't wait to hit my bed. I could have used a long session in the springs, but now when I thought about them, all I could think of was Nyra.

And that pissed me off.

She pissed me off.

Trust was a rare commodity for me, but with her, it was nonexistent.

I hesitantly pushed open the heavy wooden door, wincing at the loud creak as it opened, and the sound of loud laughter washed over me. In the corner of the room, Kai's figure was outlined against the flickering glow of the fireplace.

His eyes were trained on me as I approached, his arms crossed tightly across his chest. "Anything?"

I shook my head because tonight's scouting had been worthless. My father kept picking up surges of power near the base of the waterfall below where the palace rose high above, but we hadn't been able to track it to anything.

But he was relentless.

He always had been.

"How did training go?" I winced as I tried to shift my weight off my aching feet and onto the cool, hard surface of the wall behind me.

"Training with who?" He chuckled softly. "Your girl told me that you wanted me to train her, but as soon as I asked her to give me a second, Eiran stepped in."

My jaw clenched as I forced my gaze away from my best friend and toward the people seated around the hearth.

Eiran was so smug and arrogant, the thought of him assisting Nyra in her training made me want to put my fist through a wall. I pictured her sharing secrets with him that I was dying to know, and I couldn't stop the frustrated growl that escaped from deep within me.

"She's not my girl." I swept my gaze over the crowded room and finally caught sight of her. She sat cozily beside Eiran. Their heads bent close together as they chatted and laughed, completely unaware of my presence. A sickening sensation churned in my stomach, and I gritted my teeth until they ached.

Eiran leaned closer, his lips inches from her ear, and his hands moved dramatically in the air, emphasizing his words. My vision tunneled as waves of anger surged through me.

I pushed away from the wall, my heart pounding as I crossed the room. The group of them sat in a tight circle, all of their eyes trained on Nyra as she laughed.

Wren looked up at me and grinned, her smirk irritating as she saw through me. "Hello, brother."

Nyra straightened, her eyes meeting mine. I took a breath as I tried not to fall into their depths, annoyed with my desire to be on the other end of her smile.

"Can you not follow simple instructions?"

Wren let out an annoyed laugh.

"What?" Nyra asked as her eyes flicked between mine.

"I told you that you were to train with Kai after I left, and you couldn't do that one simple thing." I huffed.

"Calm down, Dacre." Eiran's lips parted in a slow, infuriating smirk, and the corners of his eyes crinkled with amusement. He subtly shifted his body closer to hers. "She trained with me."

My gaze met Eiran's, and I could feel the small amount of patience I had snapping.

"She's not yours to train," I growled, my voice low but heavy with anger. "And she's not here to be entertained."

Nyra choked on an unamused laugh.

"Excuse me?" Her eyes narrowed into slits as she glared at me. A flush crept up her cheeks, and I could almost feel the heat radiating from her skin.

I should have stopped pushing her and gone to bed.

But I wanted to keep pushing.

People made errors when they were angry. They made mistakes that would reveal whatever the hell it was they were trying to hide.

And I was desperate for her to make one.

"What part are you confused about?" I cocked my head slightly, and the flush on her cheeks spread down her smooth neck.

"I trained with Eiran because Kai was busy. It isn't a big deal."

The possessiveness that rushed through me surprised me, even as I struggled to keep it in check.

"It *is* a big deal," I said, my voice barely sounding like my own. "You train with who I tell you, or you don't train at all."

Nyra buried her teeth into her bottom lip as if she were trying to hold back the words she wanted to say, and I found myself captivated with watching the movement. "I learned more with Eiran than I did with you."

My sister had the nerve to snicker at that, but I didn't pay her any attention.

"Let's go." I nodded toward the stairwell.

"What?" Her voice was a thin, trembling thread of sound. Her eyes widened as she looked back at my sister as if she could protect her from me.

"If you learned so much from Eiran, then let's go. You can show me exactly what he taught you."

"It's late, Dacre."

I clenched my fists and gritted my teeth as Eiran's arrogant voice filled the room. My chest tightened, and I felt a burning need to show them all that nothing Eiran could give her would ever be better than me.

"No one asked you, Eiran." I didn't spare him a glance as I spoke. "Let's go, Nyra."

She swore under her breath as she pushed to stand, and I couldn't hide the smirk on my face. She hated me as much as I hated her.

She trailed behind me as we left the building, the cool, damp night air hitting us as we moved outside. I led her down the path to the training grounds, and even though I hadn't been able to detect a trace of power from her, I knew if she had it now, she would burn me to ash.

She didn't say a word as we reached the clearing, and a wave of anticipation rushed between us as we moved into the sparring circle.

Her dark hair was loose and fell in thick waves along her shoulders, and her full hips swayed as she paced in front of me.

"Are you always this pleasant when you return from patrolling?" she asked, breaking the silence that surrounded us.

I ignored her question. "Show me what you learned."

Her expression was hard to read, but the way her gaze flicked over my body appeared calculated. *Good.*

She moved into the fighting stance I had shown her this morning, and I was surprised by how few adjustments she needed.

"I showed you that." I crossed my arms as I assessed her.

"Did you?" She raised an eyebrow and cocked her head to the side, mirroring the way I had assessed her earlier. "I'm pretty sure it was Eiran."

"And what else did Eiran teach you?" I practically spit out his name.

Nyra's eyes narrowed at my harsh tone, and it appeared we were both looking for a fight. "Why do you care?" she asked, her voice laced with anger. "You wanted me trained, didn't you?"

"I want you to train with someone who knows what the hell they're doing. I trust Kai."

She relaxed out of her stance. "And you don't trust Eiran?"

"I don't trust most people," I answered her honestly.

"That is more than obvious." She waved her hand in my direction. "What exactly did I do to piss you off so much?"

"Do you want me to count them off?"

"If that would help."

I circled around her slowly, and she brought her hands up, loosely stepping into the stance I taught her as if it were already becoming second nature. "First of all, you're a fucking traitor."

She jerked her head around and looked at me over her shoulder. "Because I'm from Marmoris?"

"Because you lived in that damned palace, watched what those bastards did every day, and still you had the nerve to put our mark on you as if it was a ticket to freedom and not a death sentence for most of us."

She gently shook her head. "That's not what…"

"I recognized you from the raid." My jaw twitched as I moved back around the front of her. "We were there to free our people your king had locked away. We were there to try to stop a monster who ate at our power until the rest of us starved to death."

"He's not my king."

"My mother died for this mark." I lifted my sleeve and pointed to the mark I had earned. "She died, and you make a mockery of everyone who died for this by putting this mark on you when you haven't done a damned thing to earn it."

She cupped her hand over her wrist almost protectively, but the forgery wasn't even visible through her sleeve. "I'm sorry," she stammered.

"Show me what he taught you."

She searched my face, and I gave her nothing. The only thing she would find there was the rage I was allowing to fuel me.

I expected her to wait for me to make the first move, but she surged forward and swept her leg out in my direction.

I averted it easily, but she recovered far faster than she had this morning.

Maybe Eiran had taught her something, after all.

She threw her left elbow out toward my ribs, and I blocked it with my forearm and quickly countered by slapping my hand against her stomach. She grunted and stumbled back but quickly regained her footing.

There was a fire in her eyes now that hadn't been there before.

We circled each other, trying to anticipate the other's move. I admired the width of her hips and the way her chest rose and fell rhythmically with each breath as she moved from one foot to the other.

"That's all he taught you?" The smirk on my face matched the insult in my voice as I watched her expression contort with even more anger.

"No. All those moves came from you."

I couldn't stop the chuckle that bubbled out of my throat, and she took advantage of the distraction. She shot forward and slammed her knee into my thigh, and I cursed as a shot of pain lanced through me.

She quickly wrapped her arms around my neck as if she thought she would be able to pull me down, but it did nothing except lift her from the ground.

I tightened my own arms around her middle, holding her tightly against me, and she shoved against my shoulders, trying to get away.

"I see your time with Eiran has taught you a lot." I tugged her harder against me, feeling her body perfectly lined up against mine. "Was he trying to teach you anything other than how to get in his bed?" Nyra's body went rigid against mine.

"What the hell is wrong with you?" Her voice was low and breathy as she struggled against my grasp. Her body writhed against mine, and I felt utterly out of control.

I released my hold on her, dropping her to her feet as she stumbled and took a step back.

"Get out of here." I pointed toward the path that led back to our quarters.

"What?" She crossed her arms over her chest as if that would protect her. "You can't just dismiss me like that."

"I just did." I glared at her as I tried to control my breathing, tried to control any part of me. "You're not learning anything else from Eiran. You're mine to train."

"I'm not yours to do anything with." She took the smallest step back from me.

I was angry and frustrated and had no control over the possessiveness I felt. "You'll train with me and only me. If I catch you with him again…"

"You'll do what?" she snapped with her hands on her hips. "You'll kill me?"

I took a step closer to her, my eyes locked on hers. They were so blue in that moment that I felt like I was lost at sea. "Did you show him your power?"

"I don't have any." The muscles in her neck bulged as she spat out the words.

"Everyone has magic." I said it so flippantly, and she looked away for a moment, unable to hold my stare.

She was hiding something.

"That's what my father said too." Her gaze looked haunted now even as her rage simmered. "Do you know how many hours I spent trying to train myself into finding my magic? How many different people were brought into the palace to make me find it?"

She clamped her mouth shut, and I narrowed my gaze on her. "For a handmaiden's daughter?"

"I'm done with this conversation." She started to turn from me, but I snatched her wrist in my hand before she could.

"I'm not. What the hell did you really do in that palace?" *Just tell me one of your truths.*

"It's none of your business."

"Lies make you a traitor." I tightened my grip on her wrist, but not enough to hurt her.

"You already think I'm a traitor. Me keeping secrets isn't going to change that."

"You keeping secrets is exactly what will get you killed." I tugged on her wrist until she was right in front of me. The toes of her boots knocked against mine, but I paid them no attention when her chest heaved and pressed against my own.

I could feel the heat of her body against mine, and for a moment, I allowed myself to indulge in the desire that had been simmering beneath the surface.

I leaned in closer to her, our faces only inches apart. "You know I won't stop until I find out the truth," I whispered, my lips brushing against her temple.

She said nothing, just stared straight ahead at my chest.

"Don't say I didn't warn you." I released her wrist and took a step back before I did something foolish.

Nyra's breath caught in her throat, and for a moment, I thought I saw the same desire that was somehow drowning my anger staring back at me.

I took another step away from her. "Don't train with Eiran again."

"Of course, sir." She made a show of bowing before me. "I wouldn't dare disobey you."

I bit down on my tongue so I wouldn't say something I was going to regret. Or *did* something I would regret.

I turned my back to her and walked away, making my way toward the edge of the room. I needed to cool off.

"Get some sleep. We'll begin training early tomorrow."

I heard no sounds of her movement, and when I turned back around, Nyra was still standing exactly where I had left her.

"Yes?"

She clenched her fists at her sides and looked toward the mouth of the cave, then back at me. "I don't know how to get back to my room."

I ducked my head as I grinned at her frustration. Figuring out the cave system of our hidden city was tough, but I had lived here so long that I knew it like the back of my hand. I sometimes forget how difficult it could be.

"All you had to say was that you needed my help." I openly smiled at her, and she narrowed her eyes.

"I didn't say I needed your help." She crossed her arms. "Can't you use your magic to call for Wren or Eiran?"

Her words felt like tiny daggers piercing my skin. The anger inside me built up until I was sure it would burst out at any second. "What's your goal here? Are you just trying to piss me off tonight?"

She shrugged her shoulders as she glanced away. "Is it working?"

I rubbed my lips together as I watched her, then headed

for the exit, and she followed me. "Just so you know, the more you piss me off tonight, the harder training will be tomorrow."

She scoffed as she caught up to my side. "I doubt you would take it easy on me even if I was on my best behavior."

She wasn't wrong. "I'm not going to deny that," I replied gruffly. "But if you keep pushing me, I'll be rougher with you."

Nyra's eyes widened, and I could feel the heat grow in my stomach.

I felt the swelling in the front of my trousers as thoughts of being *rough* with her clouded my mind.

She was a traitor.

I adjusted myself covertly as we walked in silence, then I waved her forward as we crouched below the low-hanging rock that kept the training grounds separate from the rest of the city.

We reached a fork in the path, and Nyra's nose scrunched. "Which way?" she asked as she looked around the dimly lit tunnels.

I pointed. "To the right."

She nodded and led us down the path, her light foot-steps echoing off the walls.

"I'm guessing there's no chance of me sleeping in tomorrow since you kept me out while the rest of this damn city is sleeping, huh?"

The city was eerily quiet, and a sliver of guilt crept up on me.

"Not a chance."

"Figures." She lifted her hand and let her fingers trail

over the damp wall of the cave. "I still can't believe this has all been down here this entire time. It's like a whole other world."

She sounded as if she were talking to herself instead of me, but still, I answered her.

"It's our world, and it keeps us safe."

She let out a soft "hmm," and I had a sudden desperation to know what was going through her mind.

But she didn't share another thought.

We walked in silence for a few more minutes before we finally reached the warrior quarters.

She turned to me, and for a second, I thought she was going to say something.

But she simply nodded her head once and shoved her hands into her pockets before she disappeared through the door.

I followed after her, and she looked back over her shoulder as she heard me coming up the steps behind her.

We were housed on the same floor. Wren's safety was my top priority.

"Are you following me?" She turned to face me fully as we reached the top of the stairs.

"No." I scoffed and kept moving until I had to slide my body past hers to get through the narrow stairwell. She sucked in a breath as my chest brushed against hers. "I'm headed to my room."

She huffed as she followed me into the hall and stopped at her door.

"Your room is this close to mine?" She scrunched her nose.

"Trust me, I wished we had an open room elsewhere, but this is where they put you."

She pressed her lips together before her hand moved to the handle of her door.

"I'll see you in the morning, traitor."

"I can't wait," she threw over her shoulder before she let it shut behind her.

CHAPTER 11

NYRA

I winced when Dacre landed another slap against my stomach.

He had taken to barely hitting me after the last three days of training. His eyes had narrowed on the way I stumbled into the training ground this morning, and he'd been gentler today than he had ever been before.

But I didn't trust him.

"Pay attention." He growled. "You're letting me get in hits I shouldn't be able to."

"I'm sore," I protested, gasping for air as I tried to catch my breath.

"Soreness is not an excuse." Dacre's voice was stern as his eyes flicked between mine. "You need to push past the pain."

He lunged forward, and I ducked and spun away at the last second, feeling the rush of air as his hand barely missed me. "You're not even trying."

I gritted my teeth and forced myself to focus. Dacre had

been relentless in his training the last couple days, and his instructions echoed in my ear. But memories of his hands hot on my skin as we moved through the routines made me lose my concentration. All around us, the air swirled thick with the scent of our sweat, and beads of perspiration trickled down his broad shoulders and chest.

I took a deep breath, shaking off the thoughts that were plaguing me, and launched myself forward, my fist flying toward his face. He easily dodged it, but I didn't let that stop me. I followed up with a kick toward his stomach, and it connected with a satisfying thud.

Dacre stumbled back, caught off guard by my sudden attempt to actually train, and he snatched my hand, jerking me with him.

He hit the ground, and a cloud of dust floated around him just before I landed at his side.

Without hesitation, I pushed to my knees and lunged toward him. I grabbed his shoulders, trying to push him to the ground, but he was so damn strong. He quickly over-powered me, pinning me beneath him as he straddled my torso. He held my wrists tightly above my head as we struggled on the ground.

I could feel the heat of his body everywhere.

"Good." He grunted. "You're finally trying."

I lay on the ground, my body frozen under the intensity of the way he watched me. We were both breathless from the exertion, but I was panting for more reasons than that alone.

"Hey, Nyra." I heard the sound of Eiran's voice, and I tore my gaze from Dacre to see Eiran standing at the edge of our sparring circle with his arms crossed.

I attempted to pull my wrists out of Dacre's hold, but his fingers were clamped like a vise, and I could feel slight tremors in my fingers.

"Hi, Eiran." I swallowed hard against the lump forming in my throat. Dacre's grip stiffened against my hands when Eiran's name passed my lips.

Eiran's gaze darted back and forth between us, his eyes lingering on me a little longer each time. I could feel heat rise in my cheeks as I realized the position Dacre currently had me in.

"Is there something we can help you with, Eiran?" Dacre's gaze reluctantly drifted from my face to Eiran, but his strong hands remained firmly pressed against my wrists. My muscles tensed beneath him as I squirmed, and the hardness of his thighs pressed into my sides as he shifted his weight.

"A few of us are going out for drinks tonight, and I was going to see if you'd like to come, Nyra." Eiran looked directly at me, and the way he specifically said my name didn't go unnoticed.

I opened my mouth to answer him, to tell him that I was far too tired to even consider his offer, but Dacre sat up straighter, releasing my hands and answering before I could.

"Nyra and I are actually about to hit the springs. She's not going to make another day of training if she doesn't heal her body a bit."

I whipped my head toward him, startled by what he'd just said, but he was still staring up at Eiran.

"Thank you for the invitation though." Dacre gave Eiran a smile that felt anything but friendly.

Dacre finally pushed off me, and Eiran's mouth opened and closed as Dacre held his hand out to help pull me up. I wanted to refuse him, but I knew there was a chance I wouldn't be able to get off this ground if he didn't help me.

He wrapped his hand around mine and effortlessly lifted me to my feet. As I stumbled forward, my chest bumped against his, and I had to press my hands against his arms to stop myself from falling into him farther. My face flushed as I quickly averted my gaze from his intense dark eyes. "Thank you, Eiran. Maybe tomorrow?"

"Yeah." He pushed his hand through his hair, but his gaze was narrowed on Dacre as he turned away. "I'll get with you tomorrow."

As soon as his footsteps faded, I pivoted on my heel and found myself staring into Dacre's chest. I looked up until I finally met his dark irises that glimmered in the low light of the room.

He leaned closer, and his breath tickled my cheek as he whispered, "What?"

"What if I wanted to go?" I didn't, but that fact didn't matter.

"Too bad." He ran his hands over his chest, checking meticulously over his weapons. "You just told me how sore you were. You need an evening in the springs."

"I don't know. A night full of drinking wine could make me forget my sore body."

His gaze ran over said body from the bottom of my feet until he finally reached my gaze. It felt like a slow caress, like an exploration that neither one of us should have allowed.

"And you would wake up tomorrow with a headache

and your body just as sore as it is now. You want to drink? I'll grab some wine on our way." He moved back from me and grabbed all his things before he started walking off, leaving me behind.

I quickly caught up to him, even though my legs were screaming at me at the effort.

Dacre didn't say anything as we weaved through the tunnels and past several people who were milling about. I noted the way almost everyone nodded in his direction as he passed.

They didn't trust me.

"These people really worship you, don't they?"

Dacre grumbled as he stopped at a small building and quickly knocked on the door. "They don't worship me. They respect me."

The door opened, and a beautiful woman with long red hair answered with a smile on her face. A smile that was directed at Dacre.

"Can I get a bottle?" Dacre asked instead of greeting her, but the woman simply nodded.

She disappeared for only a second before she came back with a large dark olive bottle and placed it in Dacre's hand. "This one is dangerous. But nothing you can't handle."

"Thanks," Dacre answered gruffly before walking away without another word.

The woman watched him leave, and I chuckled even as jealousy twisted in my gut. "You could have fooled me."

"What?" He looked down at me, and his brows were drawn together as if he had no idea what I was talking about.

"You barely said two words to that girl back there, and she was looking at you like you hung the moon. Clearly, these people have never trained with you."

That caused a laugh to escape Dacre's mouth, and I smiled. "A lot of these people have trained with me actually."

"Well, I can guarantee that I'm not going to like you after I finish training with you. I might even be plotting your death as we speak." I was joking, but I still winced at my words. The man didn't trust me already. The last thing I needed was to make him question my motives even more.

"I could train you for a century, and you still wouldn't be able to take me out."

"You're very full of yourself." I huffed as we rounded the corner toward the hot springs, and the cloying heat in the air caused my breath to catch in my chest.

Dacre chuckled. "I have reason to be. I've been fighting for this rebellion for most of my life."

We stepped up to one of the closest springs, and I looked around and realized that there was only one other person here. A woman in the back corner, and from the way her head was laid back against the rocks, she appeared to be asleep.

"Where is everyone?"

Dacre set the wine down near the edge of the spring before toeing off his boots.

"It's late." He groaned softly as he pulled his vest full of weapons away from his chest. "Most of our warriors have already been here if they needed it."

I wished Wren was with us, or Eiran. Or anyone for that matter.

Because this felt too *intimate.*

The air around us felt like it was pressing in, suffocating us both. It was as if the space between us had turned into a mix of heat and tension, completely different from the icy chill of the training grounds that I had started to become accustomed to.

"Strip down, traitor." Dacre paused, his gaze tracing the form of my body before sliding up to meet my eyes. He then grabbed the hem of his shirt at the back of his neck and pulled it off in one swift motion, revealing his toned chest. "You can't get into the springs in full leathers."

"I don't think I need the springs today." I stuttered the words as I averted my gaze from his abdomen, the ripples of muscle visible beneath his tan skin.

His eyes narrowed on me as he crossed his arms. "I could hear your little whimpers with every step we took here. You're getting in this water."

He was right, of course, but that didn't make me any less self-conscious. I winced as I squatted down and untied my boots before pulling them from my feet.

Dacre unfastened his trousers and dropped them to the ground. He stepped over the bottle of wine he had left lying there, and without hesitation, moved toward the steaming pool. His back was broad and toned as he descended into the steam-laced water.

My eyes traced his defined muscles, appreciating the way they flexed with each movement. But my gaze then fell upon a dark, mottled bruise that marred the smoothness of his skin. It started at his shoulder blade and extended down his side, its angry hues standing out against the tan of his body.

"What happened?" I shrugged out of my vest, letting it fall to the ground next to me.

"What do you mean?" The steam crept up his body as he inhaled sharply against the water that lapped around his neck and shoulders. His skin glistened with water in the dim light, and his fingers dug deep into the coarse stones on the edge of the pool as he settled back against it.

"Your side." I nodded toward his body as I undid my trousers with trembling fingers and pulled them down my legs.

Dacre's eyes roamed over my body, lingering on each curve with a hunger that sent shivers down my spine. His gaze was intense, like a predator sizing up its prey, and I couldn't help but feel exposed under his scrutiny.

"What happened to your side?" I crossed my arms as I inched closer to the water even as my heart rate rose.

"Shirt too."

"What?" I scrutinized his face, noting the dark shadows under his eyes.

"Lose the shirt too. The water needs to touch your skin if it's going to speed up your healing."

"You're avoiding my question."

"And you're avoiding taking off that damned shirt." The way Dacre cocked his head made me feel uneasy. He had barely moved, yet every part of him felt like a threat.

I groaned as I stepped into the steaming pool of water, the heat radiating around my aching ankles. His gaze was heavy on me as I inched farther in, and soon, the fabric of my shirt clung to my skin, weighed down by the water.

Dacre's gaze lingered on the damp patches of my shirt sticking to my skin in the sweltering heat. Goose bumps rose on my arms as a chill ran down my spine. I pushed through the water, feeling its soothing warmth seep into my muscles until it reached my chest.

"It's nothing," Dacre finally mumbled, his voice low and throaty. "Just a little run-in with a group of your people."

I winced at his words. *My people.*

"Does it hurt?" I asked, gesturing toward his bruised side.

Dacre's lips were pressed together in a thin line as he shook his head, and a thin sheen of sweat was forming along his forehead. "It's fine. Just a little sore. What about you?"

"Everything hurts," I said through gritted teeth. A faint chuckle escaped my lips as I tried not to think about how sore I was.

Dacre's lips curved ever so slightly, and his eyes crinkled as he smiled. "You'll start to get used to it."

"I can't wait," I said dramatically, and he laughed.

We soaked in silence for a few moments, the only sounds came from the gentle lapping of the water and the occasional sigh from one of us.

Dacre grabbed the bottle of wine and expertly removed the cork with a satisfying pop. He tilted his head back, letting the deep red liquid pour like a waterfall into his mouth. When he finished, he ran the back of his hand against his lips before he passed the bottle to me, and I eagerly accepted it.

It had been so long since I had tasted wine, and even in the palace, I was only allowed a respectable amount at formal dinners.

If I was allowed to attend the dinners at all.

My hands trembled as I slowly raised the bottle to my lips. I closed my eyes and relished the rich, bitter taste that filled my mouth, followed by a deep, satisfying groan.

It was sweet and earthy and far better than any I had ever had before.

"This is good," I said before pressing the bottle back to my lips and taking another drink.

"It is." Dacre reached forward and took the bottle from my hands before taking another drink himself. "It's also dangerous. Especially in this heat."

He held the bottle aloft, and the glint of firelight caught the outline of his profile, the curve of his chin and the sharpness of his jawline. He tilted his head back and took a long pull, his throat muscles working as he swallowed down the wine.

"It would seem everything around here is dangerous." I pressed my hands to the spring floor, curled my fingers into the layer of pebbles that felt like a mosaic beneath me, and pushed the heels of my hands against the firm surface. The tiny stones shifted around my fingers as I dug into them.

"For you, absolutely." He leaned forward until his frame drowned out the firelight and pressed the bottle back into my hand.

I hesitated, knowing I shouldn't drink any more, but I didn't want to say no, so I took the bottle from him and held it tightly against my chest.

"But not for you?" I tilted my head and scrutinized him. He appeared to be so confident and sure of himself, but now, a small part of me questioned how much of it was merely for show. His eyes shifted, avoiding mine, and his lips pressed into a thin line.

"There are dangers for me here, sure." He locked his gaze back on me, and my heart thundered in my chest. I looked away from him as I brought the wine bottle to my lips.

"You could have gone drinking with everyone else tonight. I could have done this spring thing on my own." I swiped my wet sleeve across my lips, feeling the warmth of the wine and the intensity of the spring surge through my veins and heat up my cheeks.

"And let you get lost?" A mischievous glimmer danced in his eye and the right corner of his mouth twitched up in a smirk as he said, "We would have probably never found you again."

"Would that have been so bad?" I felt my shoulders rise close to my ears and fall again before I could stop myself, wishing I could retract the words from the air.

"I don't know." His eyes were glassy and searching. "Is there something worth you running back to?"

My voice came out as a whisper as I said, "I wouldn't go back." The hot, humid air was oppressive as I looked up and saw a single drop of water hanging suspended from the edge of the low ceiling. It slowly cascaded down until it hit my cheek, cool against my overheated skin. I closed my eyes and let myself feel the longing for home, for my mother. But she was gone, and with her, so was every trace of the home I had once known. "There's nothing left for me there."

I waited, expecting some kind of response from Dacre,

but none came. The stagnant air seemed to vibrate around me as I breathed in the heavy silence.

"What hurts the most?" I jumped at the sound of Dacre's voice, and when I turned my head toward him, his gaze caught mine.

I clenched my fist as I looked into his eyes, searching for the right words. Memories of all the times my father had hurt me flooded my thoughts, but I knew that wasn't what he was asking. The silence between us hung heavy like a humid summer afternoon, and I felt sweat roll down the side of my neck.

"My left ankle."

Dacre slowly nodded, his eyes locked on mine as he motioned to the edge of the spring. He stood until the water lapped against his stomach. His gaze never wavered as he reached out and extended his arm toward me, his open palm facing up. "Let me see."

My throat tightened as he stepped closer, and his dark eyes bore into me. "What?" The word trembled in the air.

"Up." He stopped in front of me, and I paused before slowly rising to my feet.

My shirt clung to my skin, exposing the outline of my body as I perched on the edge of the spring. His eyes ran over every dip and curve and lingered for what felt like an eternity, sending shivers through my skin.

The wine swirled through my veins like wildfire, clouding my judgment, but I didn't want him to stop.

He had been cruel to me, but I still didn't want him to stop.

He slowly reached out toward me, and before I had a chance to react, he was already grasping my ankle. His thumb traced small circles along its bone, and I couldn't stop my body's reaction to the sudden contact. Despite every instinct telling me to move away, I stayed rooted in place.

Gently, he lifted my ankle above the water and tenderly inspected it. His fingertips lightly grazed over the swollen joint, his shoulders lifting as he examined it with careful scrutiny.

"It's just a sprain," he said finally, his fingers still resting on my skin. "The springs will help it, but it will still need a few days to heal."

I nodded, not trusting myself to speak. Every inch of my skin seemed to come alive beneath his gentle caress, each tiny spark of electricity sending goose bumps rippling through my body. I suddenly never wanted him to stop touching me, but I didn't know how much longer I could handle being this close to him.

"Or I could heal it?" His gaze flicked up to mine and smoldered with an intensity that seemed to reach out and caress my skin as intensely as his fingers.

I nodded, my eyes closing as his fingers began kneading the sore muscles of my lower calf. His touch grew firmer with each slow circle he drew along my skin, the warmth of it sending a trail of pins and needles up my leg. I bit down hard on my lip to keep in the soft moan that threatened to escape.

I shifted my weight, and Dacre's eyes followed the movement of my legs as I pressed my thighs together. His gaze was searing.

"This may hurt a little bit."

I had been healed dozens of times before by the healers

at the palace because my father wanted no proof of his merciless methods. The palace healers were no ordinary fae; they were a league above the rest, trained to heal the king himself. My father had made sure that not a single blemish was left behind after their work was finished.

I was the powerless heir, but he made sure I was unmarred by his cruelty.

The scars that were left behind after Micah healed me were the only ones that remained. The first time had been just after the raid. My father's healers had no time to correct his brutality before the rebels stormed our palace.

And still I had lied to Micah about where the lashings that wrapped around my back to the edges of my stomach had come from. I lied to him even as he healed a complete stranger who he found hiding in the slums.

"It's okay." My voice was barely audible as his calloused fingertips skirted the edge of my ankle bone.

Without warning, his other hand came up and his damp fingers slid around the back of my calf, holding it higher out of the water. The move made my legs spread ever so slightly, and I breathed in harshly as I felt his power spread from his fingers and bleed into my skin.

The pull of pain was faint but kept me grounded as I panted and my lungs burned for air. A swirling warmth seemed to course through my veins, and I felt like I was in a trance as his fingertips grazed my skin and a soft golden light encircled my ankle.

He held me tightly for a long moment as his magic burned against my skin before he finally looked back up at me. "How does that feel?"

"Good," I answered, but I wasn't thinking about my

damn ankle. I could hardly think of anything other than the way his fingers were still gripping me and the rivulets of water that were running down his bare chest before me.

"Good." He cleared his throat softly and lowered my ankle until it was surrounded again by the hot water. His gaze fell to my mouth, and I rolled my tongue against my lips to taste the wine that still lingered there.

"We should head back." He spoke the words, but he didn't move away from me. I could feel the heat from his skin as he watched me intently, and I felt so exposed.

"We should." I nodded, and the spring water lapped at my thighs.

He still didn't move, and neither did I.

The air around us felt heavy and still, punctuated only by the sound of our shallow breathing.

"I should get you back to your room." He turned away from me, focusing on the pile of our belongings that lay on the ground near us.

"Okay." I nodded again and ran a trembling hand against my throat.

Dacre glanced back at me, but I was already climbing to my feet, my legs shaking beneath me as I passed by him and stepped out of the spring, my shirt clinging to my body like a second skin.

He sucked in a sharp breath, and the sound echoed through the caves. My heart raced as I forced my gaze away from him. Fingers trembling, I grabbed a towel that hung near the pool's edge and hastily dried my legs.

I held the towel in my hands and brought it up to my chest, feeling the rough, damp fabric of my shirt sticking to me as if it were glued on. I ran the towel over it to try to collect at least a bit of the moisture, but it was no use.

Dacre's heavy presence was overwhelming behind me, and I heard the soft thudding of his feet as he walked. I didn't dare turn around, my head still foggy from the wine and far too aware of how attractive he was when he wasn't being an ass.

I didn't trust myself.

So I quickly grabbed my trousers and struggled to pull them on over my damp skin before I shoved my feet into my boots. I snatched my vest from the ground and held it against my chest.

Feeling a bit more secure, I turned and cautiously met his gaze. He was almost fully dressed himself, and I let myself watch as he slowly pulled the black fabric of his shirt over his head, hiding his toned arms and a broad chest, sending a wave of heat through my body.

He watched me carefully, too carefully, as he leaned forward and grabbed his own vest and weapons from the ground. He pulled it over his head, attaching everything, before he waved me forward.

And I followed.

CHAPTER 12
NYRA

We trudged through the darkness, arms brushing against each other's. The silent air was heavy with unspoken words. Heat filled my cheeks from the wine, and every once in a while, a sentence would form in my mind, only to be quickly swallowed back down by dread at the thought of voicing it.

"Thank you for healing my ankle." I studied the worn boards of the bridge we were walking over. "It really does feel better."

"You're welcome." He nodded, his gaze lingering on me. "You're not worth anything if you aren't able to fight, let alone walk."

I jolted as his words pierced through the haze of wine that clouded my mind. The icy clarity stung like a thousand needles, bringing me back to reality.

"Of course." I saluted him as we approached the main door, and I hated how my stomach ached as he watched me.

"I assume you do that kind of healing for all of your warriors."

As soon as the words left my mouth, I was bombarded with thoughts of him touching other women in the same way, of him touching Mal.

Someone he respected.

An irrational anger boiled inside me and made me think clearly for the first time all night.

Before he had the chance to respond, I raced up the dark stairwell and pushed into the shadowy hallway. My heart thudded in my chest as I frantically strode away from him.

I would have to face him in only a few hours when training would begin again, but I needed to breathe for a moment where the scent of him wasn't clouding the air.

"What the...?" I stopped short at my door and stared down at the pair of boots that were hanging from their laces on my handle.

The deep rumble of Dacre's throaty laugh filled the hallway as he ambled past me on his way to his own door.

"Good luck with that one." He ran a hand through his dark hair.

"I don't understand."

His response was another deep laugh that shook his body in waves of mirth. He lifted one arm and waved it toward the door. "Boots on the door. It only has one meaning."

"Which is?"

"Don't disturb." As soon as he said the words, a soft moan came from my room, and I jolted back a step.

"You mean Wren is in there with...?"

"That's information I don't want to know." He shook his head and reached for his doorknob. "My sister is a woman and can do whatever she wants, but I have zero interest in knowing who it is she's doing it with."

I took another small step back and sent up a silent prayer to the gods that whatever they were doing, they weren't doing it in my bed.

It was the one thing I had come to look forward to every evening.

I moved across the hall and slumped against the wall. I was so tired, exhausted in a way that I had never experienced before, not even when I was on the streets.

"There's a couch downstairs, right?" I turned my head to look at Dacre and was surprised by the way he was watching me.

"There is, but you're not sleeping down there." His voice was calm, but his jaw twitched.

"Why not?" I hugged myself, trying to contain the wave of shivers that swept over me as the damp fabric of my shirt chilled my skin.

"Because no one here trusts you, and I don't trust them with you." His words made no sense to me, yet they still managed to fill me with anger.

"Do you have any idea what room is Eiran's then? I'm sure he'll take me in for the night."

Dacre's low, menacing growl rippled through the hall, sending an icy chill down my spine. His eyes were fixed on mine, and I could see his clenched jaw bulging out in anger. Despite how badly I wanted to, I didn't look away.

"That's not going to fucking happen." He tossed something through the open doorway to his room before he turned back to face me.

"I'm also an adult," I said, pointing emphatically at my chest. "Just like your sister. I can sleep anywhere I want to."

"Get in," he growled as he pointed inside his room, and my stomach bottomed out.

"I'm not sleeping in there. I trust you least of everyone in this damned place."

His nostrils flared at my words, and I was mesmerized by the way his throat moved as he swallowed.

"My room or the hall until she's done. It's your choice." His voice was low and dangerous, and his dark gaze was narrowed on me.

I knew the answer without hesitating. "The hall," I said, my voice cracking as I slid down the wall, barely catching myself before my bottom hit the floor.

Dacre gave a heavy sigh. My stomach twisted into knots, and I fought the urge to climb to my feet and barge into my room. Even though I had no idea what Wren was doing, it couldn't be worse than spending the night with her brother.

"Get in my room, Nyra. I'm tired, and I'm not going to worry about you being out in this hall all night." The casualness of his words betrayed the intensity in his gaze.

I slowly tilted my head back until it rested against the wall. "Are you worried about me?"

He let out a deep, guttural growl that reverberated between us before he let his door slam shut and marched toward me. My heart pounded as I clutched my vest tighter against my chest, feeling the cool metal of my dagger handle press into my skin. His footsteps thundered against the floor, echoing throughout the hall.

I scrambled to recall any training he had imparted over the past few days, but my mind was blank as he loomed closer.

Without hesitation, he bent down and cupped his rough hands around the backs of my thighs, lifting me up. I let out an involuntary yelp as my stomach hit his hard shoulder.

I pounded my fist against his broad, muscular back, but he remained unfazed. "Put me down," I cried, my voice shaking with rage. "I'm not kidding, Dacre. Put me down or..."

He kicked his door shut behind us as he entered before he tossed me down on the bed.

"Or what?" He leaned forward, his jaw clenched and a challenge in his eyes. His lips parted slightly, and he leaned in so close that I could feel the warmth of his breath on my face.

"I'm not sleeping in here." I could barely see past his broad shoulders and outstretched arms where they were pressed into the mattress at my sides.

"You don't have any other options." He hesitated for a moment, his breath heavy and his eyes on my lips. Then he suddenly pushed away and strode over to the tall dresser in one corner of the room and yanked open the top drawer, extracting a wrinkled white shirt and a pair of soft gray pants before throwing them on the bed without looking back. "The bathroom is right over there." He pointed to the door on the right. "At least change out of that shirt so you don't get my bed wet."

I stared back at him defiantly, unmoving, unwilling to

yield to the irritation radiating from him. At that moment, I knew I wouldn't be obeying him anytime soon. Not tonight. Not in this room.

I tossed my vest carelessly onto a chair before kicking off my boots. They skidded across the hard floor and landed near the end of the bed. Dacre still had his back to me as he moved to the other side of the bed, and I glared at the ceiling.

I bit my lip and inhaled sharply as I yanked my shirt over my head. My trembling fingers fought with the wet fabric before I dropped it to the floor near my boots, exposing the goose bumps on my skin.

I hadn't wanted to be bare in front of him in the springs, but now, I wanted to push him. I wanted to prove to him that he wasn't the only one who could wield control even though it felt that way.

I hooked my fingers into the waistband of my pants, slowly tugging them down over my hips, revealing inch by inch of bare skin. I glanced over my shoulder as I sat on his bed and saw Dacre's muscles tense beneath his shirt, even though he still refused to look at me. The air prickled with a charged tension that seemed to hum between us.

"Are you done yet?" His voice was harsh and clipped as if he were speaking through gritted teeth.

"You just saw me practically naked in the springs." I tried to keep my voice level. "What's the difference?"

"You're in my room," he snarled, emphasizing each word.

"I can leave," I shot back without hesitation.

He slowly turned to face me, his jaw clenched and his

eyes narrowed. He scrutinized my face for a few seconds before speaking. "Do you always have to be so difficult?"

"Do you always have to be such an ass?"

Dacre's gaze grew colder, as if a dark storm cloud had passed over him, and I knew that I was playing with fire, but I couldn't help myself.

He opened his mouth, and I prepared myself for his arrogant response. But it didn't come.

Instead, his gaze lingered over my back, and he stilled. He looked like he had seen a ghost or...

My scars.

"Who did that to you?" His voice lacked every bit of his control.

I quickly grabbed the T-shirt he had thrown me and pulled it over my head.

"It's nothing."

"It's not nothing." He was staring at the shirt as if he could still see the scars beneath.

"Who the fuck did that to you?" He enunciated every word, and fear coated every bit of me. I had never seen him this angry before.

"It doesn't matter."

"It doesn't matter," he repeated my words on a laugh that had no trace of humor. "Who would do that?"

"I'm a traitor, remember?" I threw the name he had given me back in his face. "Traitors don't go without scars.

"Finish getting dressed," he growled, his voice so low that my stomach ached at the tone.

I met his gaze and said firmly, "You can't tell me what to do."

His eyes roamed down my body, scanning every curve

and plane with a hunger and irritation I'd never seen before. When his gaze finally met mine again, it was like being plunged into the depths of the darkness that seemed to consume this city. The gravity of it threatened to swallow me whole.

He ran his hand over his jaw, his fingers trailing over his full lips. His silence was heavy and filled the room like a bank of fog, leaving me exposed to its cold and weighty presence.

I carefully unfolded the trousers he had given me from my bed. His eyes followed my every movement as I stood and slipped my legs inside. They were several sizes too big, so I bunched and rolled them up around my waist.

I opened my mouth to speak, but he cut me off. His gaze still lingered on my body as he spoke. "Get in bed. Tomorrow morning is going to come early."

I clenched my fists, anger clouding every other emotion at his orders. But there was something in the way he spoke that weakened my resolve, and I found myself climbing onto the bed, my movements hesitant.

Dacre moved to the other side of the bed, and I could hear the rustle of his clothing as I turned my back to him and tugged the blanket high above my shoulders.

I was as far on the edge of the bed as I could possibly get, but I could still feel the heat radiating from him as the mattress shifted under his weight.

The wooden bed frame creaked as he settled onto the mattress. His chest heaved with each breath, and I shivered as I sensed a subtle hum of energy in the air, the same feeling as when he used his power on my ankle. Before I could utter a word, the lantern lights in the room quietly extinguished.

The silence was punctuated by our shallow breathing. My eyelids felt heavy, yet sleep was elusive as I lay there, listening to the slight creaking of the bed behind me that signaled every movement Dacre made.

I twisted and squirmed in bed, struggling to find a comfortable position, until I gave up and ended up flat on my back. My eyes locked on to the ceiling, and I tried to relax, but my gaze drifted to Dacre, and I noticed that he was lying in the exact same position. His arm rested on his stomach, his elbow an inch away from brushing mine, and the heat emanating from him seemed to fill the room.

The way his chest rose and fell with each of his inhales and exhales, the way his arm brushed against mine as he shifted. I was acutely aware of his every movement.

My body was betraying me.

"Go to sleep, Nyra." His low voice pierced through the silent night air, and I jumped, startled by the noise.

"I'm trying to go to sleep," I breathed out and shifted under the blanket. "I can't seem to shut my mind off."

Silence blanketed the room for a few moments, and I glanced over at him. His eyes were closed as he breathed slowly and steadily. Then, all of a sudden, he spoke in a low murmur that filled the space like a balm.

"Close your eyes and focus on your breathing."

I took a deep breath, my eyes fluttering shut as I did what he instructed. My chest rose with each inhale, then sank back into the mattress as I exhaled slowly. A wave of calmness washed over me, and my muscles began to unwind.

Dacre's arm brushed mine as he reached up to adjust his arm above his head, and before I realized what I was doing, I found myself leaning into him.

Even with the warmth of his body enveloping me, my skin still broke out in a thousand chill bumps as I felt his body against mine. He didn't make a single move to pull away from the spot where we touched, and neither did I.

The thick darkness of the room embraced me as I lay there and allowed myself to think about what it would be like if this wasn't my life. If this wasn't our world.

I let that tiny spot where we were touching fuel me, and I imagined what it would be like to let his hands roam over my body. My thighs clamped together as tightly as my eyes, and I took a deep breath.

Dacre's arm shifted again, and I could feel his body moving closer to mine. I let myself sink into his touch, the warmth of his body seeping into mine. And before I knew it, I was drifting off to sleep.

CHAPTER 13
DACRE

The thunderous pounding of a fist against my door woke me abruptly, and I groaned in frustration. My eyes felt heavy as I blinked them open and saw the dull lantern light from outside streaming in through my window.

My muscles were stiff, and my shoulder throbbed slightly from how I had slept on it. I attempted to shift position, but a soft warmth pressed into my skin.

I squinted against the light as I took in Nyra's sleeping form next to me. Her pale skin was illuminated with a golden hue as her chest rose and fell with each breath, and I could feel the plushness of her curves through our clothing. My chest was flush against her, and the rest of us were intertwined, her thigh grazing mine as she snuggled closer.

She had made sure to keep her distance from me last night before we fell asleep, and I had been thankful.

That was, until she didn't.

Having her in my space had been a bad idea.

I didn't trust her. Hell, I didn't even like her, but there was something about being surrounded by the scent of her in my room, about not being able to look anywhere without seeing her curves, that drove me crazy. Even now, I found myself glancing at her full lips before tracing down her body to the deep curve at her hip.

The knocking at the door came again, and I cursed under my breath before carefully untangling myself from beneath Nyra and sitting up in my bed.

I pulled the blanket up to cover her body, her body that was covered in my clothing, before I quickly moved to the door.

I grasped the cold brass handle and heaved open the door. The warm glow of the lanterns spilled into the dark room like liquid sunlight, casting shadows on the wall. Taking care to be as quiet as possible, I stepped out into the hallway and gently pulled the door closed behind me.

My father stood before me, fully dressed in his leathers with all his weapons strapped to him, and his face was unreadable as always.

"What time is it?" I asked, my voice rough with sleep.

"Early." He crossed his arms, and I could feel him assessing as his gaze ran over me. "One of the new recruits gave information about how to access the palace from beneath."

My gaze shot up at that. "Beneath?" We had been searching for different ways to get into the palace for my entire life, but with the way it was surrounded by water and the massive falls, there had never been any way other than going through the front gate and being met with the king's army.

"The tunnels." My father's answer was clipped as he shifted on his feet.

Legends told of a secret tunnel that led directly beneath the waterfalls, but we had searched high and low without finding any trace.

My mind automatically went to Nyra who was still lying in my bed. If she had worked in the castle all that time, there was a good chance that she knew.

She was one of the first recruits we had gotten that had spent her entire life in that place, but even though I knew she could be the key to the answers we sought, I didn't want to bring her up to my father.

Not when she was currently sleeping in my bed.

"Okay. Let me get dressed. I'll meet you at the training grounds."

My father nodded without saying another word, and I quietly slipped back into my room. Nyra was still sprawled out where I left her, except her left arm was now wrapped around my pillow and she had it tugged tightly against her chest.

I let myself stare at her as I undressed and pulled on clean leathers. I should have probably woken her to let her know I was leaving, but it was still early, and I was almost certain that she would demand to go back to her room.

Knowing Wren, she had probably already kicked out whatever man she had in there last night. Nyra could have easily gone back there and slept the rest of the morning in her own bed, but I didn't wake her.

And that frustrated the hell out of me.

I strapped my daggers into the sheaths on my chest as I looked over the smooth curve of her neck.

As she lay in my bed, her small frame seemed to sink into the soft sheets. My gaze traveled over every inch of her body, lingering on the way the sheets draped over her breasts and the way her hair fanned out on my pillow. Desire flooded through me, and I felt desperate to learn if she would have the same boldness when I spread her open and tasted her with my tongue.

I snapped my gaze away from her body and started lacing up my boots.

I had no business thinking about her like that. I had no business bringing her back to my room at all, but when she had mentioned Eiran and going to find him, I was consumed with the sudden desire to drag her back here.

Eiran was a jackass. He had been placed into the warrior unit simply because his father was close with mine. I didn't trust him or his slimy hands anywhere near her.

But he had clung to her the moment he saw her with me.

I wasn't surprised. He had never been able to stand for me having anything that he didn't.

It was why he had become so close to my father the moment he saw us drifting apart.

I allowed myself another moment, memorizing the details of her face, the way her dark lashes pressed against her soft cheeks, before dragging my eyes away. A heaviness pressed against my chest as I pushed out of my room and into the hallway. The air felt thick and damp, making it difficult to breathe as I thought of her and the way she had looked in the springs the night before.

Fuck, those damn springs.

That had really been a bad idea.

I stepped out of the building and breathed deeply in an attempt to clear my mind. I had a job to do, and I couldn't do it while thinking about the way she would have looked in my bed if I had stripped her of my clothes and touched her in the ways that flooded my mind when we were training.

The city still slept around me, and I should have been eager to find out the information my father had been fed.

But all I could think about was her.

I crossed the path and headed toward the training grounds where my father was waiting for me.

The buildings I passed were ancient and worn, and the pathways were crumbling from years of being hidden with no one to care for them.

I slowed my steps as my eyes fell on a lowly lit lantern in the shop across from me.

My eyes fell on the etching on the glass window, and my heart lodged in my throat. My chest ached, and I swallowed a hard lump as I let my eyes fall over the stained glass.

Light pink camellia flowers covered the window and thoughts of my mother flooded me.

My mother had been a warrior in every sense of the word, but she had always been mine and Wren's mother first. It was a job she took seriously, and I hated that everyone in this city celebrated her for the way she fought, for the way she died, rather than the way she loved us.

Even my father.

Part of me wondered if he could even recall the way she had loved all three of us before the raid.

I could.

She wasn't a warrior to me.

She was my mother, and as I passed by the glass and left it behind me, grief threatened to cave in my chest.

I reached the training grounds and ducked beneath the low-hanging rock as I tried to tuck the memories of her away. I shoved down thoughts of everything except what would be expected of me when I stepped foot onto the training grounds.

My father was there on the other side waiting for me, and he stood with Eiran's father, Reed, and three others that were always at his side.

"Let's head out," my father commanded as soon as I made my way to them.

CHAPTER 14
NYRA

When I had awakened this morning, Dacre had been missing from his room. I laid there in his bed with his sheets tangled around my legs. I was still wearing his clothes, covered in his scent, and he was nowhere to be seen.

I was half angry and half mortified when I woke up, clinging to a pillow that smelled exactly like him.

I quickly gathered my scattered clothes from the floor, tiptoeing out of his room like a thief in the night, sneaking back to my room as if I had done something wrong.

And the way Wren hadn't been able to stop smiling at me, even throughout our training today, made me feel like I had.

"You're getting a lot better." Eiran ran a hand over his face and wiped the sweat from his brow. He had just handed me my ass in the training circle, but I would take his compliment over Dacre yelling at me about what I had done wrong.

Which was why I hated myself for searching the grounds for him now.

Not only had he not been in his room when I woke, he also hadn't been at the training grounds when I showed up this morning.

I had been fully prepared to ignore him and try as hard as I could while barely speaking a word in his direction, but I didn't get the chance.

And that just made me angrier than I had been this morning.

"We're all hanging out tonight." Wren wrapped her arm around my shoulders, and I had been so distracted by looking for her brother that I hadn't seen her approach.

"What?" I was still trying to catch my breath from where Eiran had knocked me on my ass.

"We've been training hard and deserve a break." She grinned like it was the best news she could deliver, and honestly, it was. My body needed a break, and apparently, I needed an even bigger one from Dacre. "So, you, my dear, are stuck with me tonight." She wagged her eyebrows, and I nudged her side with my elbow.

I didn't want anyone to know I spent the night in her brother's room, let alone Eiran.

"You're stuck with me as well." Eiran smiled, and it was a smile that should have made my stomach flip. But it didn't. "I'm going to head back to clean up, then I'll meet you all before we head out?"

"Sounds good." Wren tucked her arm around mine and didn't give me a choice as she led me away from the training grounds and back to our room.

She also hadn't given me a choice when she tossed clothes at me as soon as I had finished bathing.

"Everyone is used to seeing you in your leathers. If we're going to find you a man in this rebellion, we need to change it up."

"I'm not interested in finding anything," I huffed as I flopped onto the bed and tossed the clothes to the side.

"Uh-huh." Her eyes narrowed, and she studied me. Her lips thinned before a sneaky smile slipped through before she could stop it. "That's why you came back this morning wearing my brother's clothes."

"That's because of you!" I pointed at her, and her smile finally slipped.

"Do you know how many of my roommates have hung out in the hall while I had a visitor?" She arched an eyebrow.

"Gods, I don't want to know."

"Far too many." She chuckled and pressed her hand against her hip. "Do you know how many of them Dacre has let sleep in his bed because he didn't want them out there in the cold?"

"No, but I'm sure you're going to tell me."

"None." She said it so quickly I was barely able to finish my sentence. "And he certainly doesn't have girls in his bed that don't look thoroughly ruined the next morning."

I winced as jealousy raged through me. I couldn't help but think of the woman from the night before who gave him the wine and looked at him as if she *knew* him. "That's your brother."

"Trust me. I'm aware." She made a gagging noise, and I

rolled my eyes. "The fact that he insisted that our rooms be side by side so he could watch over me has completely backfired on both of us."

I held up the shirt she had handed me, and my eyes widened. It contained less fabric than any shirt I had ever seen before, and I quickly dropped it back to my side. "I think you might be as insane as your brother."

"Maybe." She shrugged before pointing at me. "Now get dressed. It's already late."

I scowled and grumbled as I reluctantly pulled on the too tight shirt, desperately trying to make it reach the waistband of my trousers. No matter how hard I tugged, the fabric strained against my chest and refused to stretch.

"Stop fidgeting. You look gorgeous," Wren whispered as we made our way down the stairs.

Eiran turned in our direction and his eyes ran over me appreciatively.

"Let's get out of here." He grinned and motioned us forward.

Wren led us through the city, and Eiran pulled me alongside him. He kept looking over at me with a soft smile on his face, and I returned it.

It wasn't until we had gone over around half a dozen bridges and the floating lanterns started becoming more scarce that I started wondering where we were going.

"Where are you two taking me?" My voice echoed off the cave walls, and Wren laughed.

"Can't tell you." She leaned in and inclined her head toward me. "We're not supposed to be there."

"That sounds promising." I sighed heavily and glanced at Eiran.

Even though I desperately wanted to trust Wren, she was a part of the rebellion, and I couldn't trust any of them completely.

Wren was my friend now, but if she knew the truth...

As we walked farther into the cave, the air grew colder and the light grew dimmer. I could hardly see as Eiran led me forward, but he reached out and took my hand in his to help me.

I tried not to let myself think about how it felt so different from Dacre's. How the simple slip of his skin against mine had me burning like an inferno while Eiran's fingers wrapped around mine felt nice.

Dacre had felt anything but nice.

We edged around the bend, and a faint orange glow appeared in the distance. The farther we walked, the brighter it grew until the leaping tongues of fire illuminated our way forward. When we emerged from the shadows, I saw several people gathered around the fire, their faces lit up by the dancing flames. Bottles of wine were scattered on the ground next to them, and laughter echoed off the walls.

The darkness in this part of the cave was almost absolute, with the only source of light coming from the flickering flames of the fire. Stalactites jutted from the rocky walls like sharpened teeth.

"This is our secret spot." Wren turned toward me and walked backward as a smile lit up her face. "Us bringing you here means you can't tell anyone else."

"Who am I going to tell?" I chuckled as I glanced around.

"Me." Dacre's voice raked down my spine, and I turned to see him lounging against a large boulder. He had one knee bent with an arm draped over it and the other hanging down loosely with an almost empty bottle of wine gripped between his fingers. His dark eyes were piercing as he spoke. "I am in charge of your training. You shouldn't even be here."

My body went rigid beside Eiran, and a deep flush crept up my neck as Dacre spoke. His tone was condescending, and a part of me wanted to just ignore him and walk away, but my pride kept me rooted in place.

"Well, seeing as you didn't show up to training today, Eiran took over for you, and he invited me." As the words tumbled out of my mouth, I could feel my cheeks redden further and wished fervently that Dacre couldn't see it. The truth was, I wouldn't have come at all if it hadn't been for Wren.

Dacre cocked his head and studied me. Gods, he looked over every inch of me with his slow perusal as if he didn't care that everyone around us could see exactly what he was doing. Eiran's hand tightened around mine as if he could protect me against Dacre's scrutiny.

Dacre was wearing his leathers, but his vest was missing, and I only noted one dagger at his side. His body was relaxed, his gaze glazed over from the wine, and he was devastatingly handsome.

"Eiran took over, did he?" He lifted the bottle to his mouth and took a long drink. His Adam's apple bobbed as he swallowed, and the bottle clinked against his teeth before he lowered it again.

I could see Wren looking back and forth between us out of my peripheral, but I didn't dare take my eyes off him.

"Does that mean you're going to strip down in his room tonight and sleep in *his* bed?"

Eiran went rigid beside me, and Wren sucked in a sharp breath that echoed in the silence as everyone watched the exchange. But Dacre was only looking at me.

Heat crept up my neck, and I became acutely aware of how small my shirt was, how tight it felt pressed against my skin. Eiran's fingers twitched against mine as he held on tighter, but I was too focused on the way Dacre's gaze smoldered as if a fire would erupt at any moment.

"What the hell is wrong with you?" I bared my teeth as I spat out the words.

Dacre leaned forward, his eyes glittering with an unsettling amusement. His chuckle was low and twisted, sending shivers up my spine.

"What's wrong with me? Nothing at all. I was just telling the man the truth." He lifted the wine bottle and pointed the neck toward Eiran. "Don't you think he deserves to know you were in my bed last night since he's clinging to you as if tonight you'll be in his?"

My whole body tensed as a wave of humiliation crashed over me. I wanted to snatch my hand away from Eiran, but I refused to give Dacre the satisfaction.

I didn't trust myself to speak, so I pivoted on my heel and let my silence settle in. I felt his eyes on me, burning holes into my back like a thousand suns. I shifted my weight and looked instead at Eiran. His eyes were narrowed so tightly on Dacre that he hadn't even noticed me looking at him.

I opened my mouth to speak, but Dacre wasn't finished.

"Come here, little traitor," he whispered, and I shivered, hating that he drew a reaction from me so easily. "Come show me what Eiran taught you today."

I could hear the others snickering around us. Every part of my body screamed at me to leave, but I couldn't control the rage that made me clench my fist at my side.

I felt my palm slide from Eiran's as I spun back around, my face hot. When Dacre noticed my expression, his lips stretched into a cocky smirk, a dimple making its appearance on his right cheek. He climbed to his feet and the glass neck of his wine bottle dangled between two fingers.

I stormed toward him, leaving Eiran and Wren behind, blocking out everyone else.

"Have a drink." He held the bottle out in my direction. "It helped you relax last night."

The sound of his voice was teasing, but the way he looked over my shoulder at Eiran with dark, narrowed eyes was anything but.

"I'll be right back," Eiran said from behind me, but I didn't turn.

I crossed my arms, drawing Dacre's gaze to the swell of my breasts. My throat felt tight as I asked him, "Why are you so mean?"

He reached out and delicately brushed a strand of hair off my chest, his hand grazing my skin as he leaned in close. His breath was warm on my cheek as he whispered, "You haven't seen me be mean. If I were mean, I'd slide my cock between your lips to keep you from talking when I tire of hearing you speak."

His words hit me like a physical blow, causing my breath to catch in my throat and my muscles to contract involuntarily. He remained close, evaporating the tiny space between us, as his gentle breath tickled my neck. His warmth was palpable despite the fact that we weren't touching.

"You can't say things like that to me." My voice shook, and I wasn't sure if it was anger or lust that coated my words.

"Why not?" His voice was like liquid pouring over me. "Because it pisses you off or because you're getting wet between those perfect thighs you're clamping together as you imagine it yourself?"

I sucked in a breath and stumbled back from him, my heart racing as his dark eyes lingered on my lips. The way he licked his own made me suspect he was far more intoxicated off the wine than I realized.

"That's not true."

His gaze fell to my thighs, and he showed no restraint in the way he was looking at me. "Are you going to show me what he taught you?"

I shifted my weight to the balls of my feet, ready to move. "I think you need some water," I said and started to reach for his bottle of wine. But before I could touch it, his other hand shot forward with lightning speed, and he grabbed my wrist. His grip was strong, but not too tight; even drunk, he was still faster than me.

"Come on." He nodded behind him. "I want to show you something."

I looked over his shoulder, and all I could see was darkness. The fire didn't touch the walls there, but the look in Dacre's eyes dared me to say yes.

My stomach lurched as the word *yes* formed on my

tongue, even though the rational part of my brain was screaming for me to say no. I hesitated, my mouth slightly agape.

"Here." Eiran appeared back by my side, causing me to jump, a small cup of dark red liquid cradled in his hands. "I got you a drink." He offered it to me with a tight smile, but his eyes flicked back and forth between me and Dacre.

"We've got it covered, thanks." Dacre saluted him with the wine bottle, and Eiran's lip curled in disgust as he glared at Dacre.

But I lifted the cup Eiran gave me to my lips and took a large swallow to help calm my nerves. My fingers were trembling around the edge of the cup, and I realized with a start that it wasn't in fear. There was nothing but desire coursing through me.

And that want had nothing to do with Eiran.

"Thank you, Eiran." I pressed my fingers against my lips, wiping at the wine that had clung to them. Dacre watched me intently, his gaze unblinking. "Dacre, I'll show you what I've learned tomorrow on the training grounds."

I whirled around, desperately hoping to escape Dacre's presence, but his smug laughter echoed behind me. Eiran had the same idea as me, though, and he pulled me away from Dacre as quickly as he could.

I took a seat around the fire next to Wren, and Eiran moved to the other side of me.

Wren's brow furrowed as her gaze drifted toward her brother, who was still watching me intently. "What was that about?" she asked, her voice soft yet demanding.

"I don't know." I placed my hands in front of the crackling fire and held them steady until I felt the warmth start to thaw my cool fingertips, even though the rest of me felt as if I were burning from the inside. "He's clearly had too much to drink."

Wren scrunched her nose, but she didn't comment as she watched him.

People were talking around us, about life, about the rebellion, and I tried to listen to them and ignore Dacre. I tried not to be hyperaware of the way he watched me or shift when I noticed him move closer and sit on the ground directly across the fire from me.

"Are you sore?" Eiran's hand touched my outer thigh, and I tensed, jerking away from his touch.

"No." I shook my head and tried to play it off. "I'm okay. I spent a lot of time in the springs last night."

His gaze flickered to where Dacre sat, but I pretended not to notice. "What about you? I didn't go too hard on you out there today, did I?"

Eiran chuckled and brushed his hair back out of his face. "I've had worse, but you were definitely holding your own out there."

He was lying, and we both knew it. But Eiran was kind, and he didn't want to shove it in my face how miserable I was like Dacre would.

"That's sweet of you, but I'm terrible." I patted Eiran's hand, and he chuckled.

"Yeah. You kind of are." He was watching me, and not in the same way Dacre did. Eiran watched me like there was something special about me. Not like I was some secret he had to crack, but like I was a story he couldn't wait to hear. A man like Eiran would take his time with me.

He would worship me in a way that I could never dream of.

But as I tried to imagine it, all I could think of was the man across the fire from me and the way he would destroy me instead.

"Eiran, I was with your father today." Dacre spoke over everyone else, and I closed my eyes as Eiran looked away from me and turned in his direction.

"Oh yeah?"

"Yeah." Dacre slowly raised his bottle, took a long, deep swallow of the dark red wine, and then ran one hand through his thick, dark hair. "It's too bad that you couldn't have come with us."

"Dacre." Wren said his name sternly, but he paid her no attention.

"We really could have used you out there." Dacre's face darkened as he chuckled. "I wouldn't be so sore right now if I had a partner."

I glanced back and forth between him and Eiran, the tension between them so thick I could almost choke on it.

"Maybe you should visit the springs if you're so sore. Lay off the wine." Eiran's voice was harder than it had been only a moment before.

"I could." Dacre nodded as he slowly rotated the bottle between his hands. "But every time I'm in the springs and I close my eyes, all I can think about is her body and the way her legs felt beneath my palms."

"Okay. That's it." Wren stood before Dacre could say anything else, and I could feel my cheeks burning as I shifted my weight. "I think you've had enough."

"That's not going to happen." Dacre moved the bottle out of Wren's reach as she approached him.

"I'm not kidding with you, Dacre. I don't know what's gotten into you tonight, but you've had enough." Wren crossed her arms and quirked a brow, but he avoided her gaze and kept his eyes trained on me.

"I don't think I have." He took another drink, completely ignoring her.

"Dacre, seriously. Give me the bottle."

"Okay." Dacre nodded and leaned his head back to look up at his sister. "I'll give it to you under one condition."

"Which is?"

"Nyra."

I cursed under my breath, and I could feel everyone looking back and forth between us.

"Nyra's a person. Not a condition, you ass."

Dacre rolled his head around before meeting my eyes again. "I want to show her something."

He had to be joking.

"That's not fucking happening," Eiran answered, his voice stern and protective, and while I could appreciate the sentiment, it pissed me off that he felt like he could speak for me.

"She's not a dog, Eiran. You can let her off her leash."

Eiran opened his mouth to answer, but I was already climbing to my feet. "Well, if the two of you are done pissing on me, let's go."

Dacre glanced up at me with a sloppy smile on his face like I hadn't just insulted him. "Let's go then."

He stood, and when Wren went to reach for the bottle,

he tsked at her. "I'll give it up as soon as Nyra holds up her end of the bargain."

Eiran was staring at Dacre, but he didn't say a word as he leaned forward, hiding his face for a moment as he clasped his hands together.

I reluctantly stepped around the roaring fire, keeping my eyes fixed on the shadows as I walked closer to him. He didn't wait for me; he was already striding to the back of the cave, assuming I'd follow without question. And I did.

My body tensed as the light from the fire grew more distant. Pebbles crunched under my boots with each step, echoing off the damp walls of the cave.

"Where are we going?" I hurried to keep pace with him, the darkness looming all around me. I could barely make out his silhouette in the shadows, and my heart pounded with fear at the thought of getting lost back here.

He tilted his head in the direction of the unseen and spoke softly. "You'll see." A chill ran up my spine as I realized there was nothing but a blanket of darkness ahead.

"If you were planning to kill me, you really should have done it the first day." I looked back over my shoulder, but I could hardly make out the others now. "I've become really fond of Wren."

"Just Wren?" He cocked an eyebrow at me. "You looked like you were growing awfully fond of Eiran too."

"Jealousy isn't a good look for such a handsome guy."

He stopped in his tracks, and I slammed into him from behind. His free arm shot out to catch me as I stumbled backward. When he locked eyes with me, his touch was so gentle it sent a shiver down my spine. "Did you just call me handsome?"

"I'm pretty sure I was talking about Eiran."

"I don't think you were." He licked his lips again, and although he seemed to be absently doing the move, it was utterly infuriating. "It's okay if you think I'm handsome."

"I also think you're an ass, but you're really clinging to the handsome thing, aren't you?"

"I am." The smile in his voice made me step forward mindlessly.

"Is this where you were taking me?" I tried to steady my breathing, but it was no use; he could hear every hitch in my breath.

"No." He grabbed my wrist in his hand and pulled me forward. "We're almost there. Watch your head."

He lifted my hand until it touched the cool, damp ceiling that was looming just over my head, then I watched him duck down in front of me and disappear under the low-hanging ceiling. The opening was small, smaller than any other I had seen in the cave, but I shut down the anxiety that was beating in my chest and followed after him.

I could see a hint of blue light as I crawled through, and when I stood back to my full height on the other side, I took in a sharp breath. A pool of water glowed a cool blue, casting an eerie light across the damp walls of the cave. Stalagmites surrounded us as Dacre moved around behind me, his footsteps echoing off the walls as I took it all in.

"What is this place?"

"Most of the water from the waterfall goes there." He pointed to the far left where a small opening seemed to go on forever.

The silence between us was broken by the gentle

gurgling of the river outside, carrying its load of water downstream.

"But for some reason, this pool of water doesn't get pulled in that same direction, and it's always this clear."

Dacre crouched beside the pool, his outstretched fingers disturbing the glassy surface. I stepped closer and marveled at the blue light that seemed to be coming from the bottom of the pool itself.

"Please don't fall in. You'll drown before I'll be able to get you up."

Dacre smirked. "Are you worried about me?"

"I'm worried about finding my way back out of here." I looked back over my shoulder to the small opening we had entered through as he chuckled.

"Don't worry. I'm sure Eiran wouldn't rest until he found you."

"You really don't like him." I turned back and studied him.

His hand was still trailing over the water absently. "That's putting it lightly." He glanced up at me, and I found myself moving closer to him and the edge of the pool.

"Why?"

"That's not something I want to talk about tonight." He reached forward, and I hesitated as his fingers laced through mine, and he pulled me closer.

He tugged me down until I had no choice but to sit next to him at the edge of the water. He settled next to me and held out the bottle of wine in my direction. I took it from him, but I didn't drink. I simply set it on the other side of me, out of his reach.

"Don't ruin the mood." He narrowed his eyes, but I simply rolled mine.

"Why are you drinking so much tonight anyway?" I pushed my hair out of my face before I leaned forward and ran my fingers through the water. It was much cooler than I had anticipated, and chills broke out across my skin.

"I just needed to take the edge off."

"Off of what, exactly?"

Dacre's eyes moved slowly over my face as he pressed his lips together in thought. His gaze was intense and calculating, as if he wanted to know whether I could be trusted with whatever he was about to reveal.

"How much do you know about the rebellion? Like, really know?" If his words hadn't already filled me with hesitation, the way he was looking at me would've.

"All I know is from what I learned at the palace." I shrugged because it was the truth. "You probably don't want to know what they say about the rebellion."

He nodded, and I wondered if he already knew. Was he aware of what my father did whenever they caught someone who was actively conspiring as a rebel? I knew all too well what my father was capable of when it came to those who sought to overthrow the kingdom—memories surged to the surface of *traitors* dangling from the castle walls at dawn, their lifeless bodies swaying in the breeze. A chill ran through me as I recalled all those nights spent struggling to put the images out of my mind.

"Well, our rebellion isn't what the people in that palace would make it seem. I know you hate us for bringing you here and making you join our cause, but do you know how many people we have saved from King Roan's wrath? How many people were fearful for their lives until we brought them here?"

I shook my head because I wasn't sure I wanted to know. I knew of my father's cruelty firsthand, but I couldn't imagine what he would do to strangers after what I had witnessed him do to people he was meant to love.

"Today, when we were on patrol, my father took us to the base of the waterfall." Dacre swallowed so hard I could see his throat work with the tension. "There has been word lately of movement near there, and my father had gotten intel on a possible way into the castle."

I tensed because I half expected Dacre to question me about this, about what I knew, but he simply kept going.

"But when we got there." He shook his head and his gaze darkened as if he were being haunted by his memories. "There were two boys lying at the base of the falls. Both of them were dead. It was their father who had been providing us with the intel." He looked away from me, and a flicker of remorse crossed his eyes. "He had been feeding my father information from inside the castle for years. We have no idea how they found out."

My gut sank at his words. "Who was it?"

"What?" He ran his hand over his hair and looked back at me.

"The man who was giving information. Who was it?" I knew almost every man and woman in that castle. I had spent the entirety of my life with them, and I held my breath as I waited for Dacre to answer.

"Griffin. He was an adviser to the king." He carefully watched me for my reaction.

I gave him none. Even as my heart felt like it was

beating out of my chest. I hadn't liked Griffin during his time as one of my father's advisers, but I had cared for his boys. And if what Dacre was saying was true...

No. I couldn't think about it.

I swallowed down the emotion threatening to drown me and tried not to let Dacre see a trace of it on my face.

Was my father responsible?

"Did you know him?" Dacre asked, but his voice was soft as if he actually cared if I had lost someone I cared for.

My throat tightened and my voice cracked as I replied, "Only in passing." My eyes darted around us, avoiding eye contact. I tried not to think about the time I'd spent with his sons. "I did know his boys, though."

"I'm sorry." Dacre's apology was like an arrow through my chest, and I struggled to keep myself composed. His words made me painfully aware that the only thing keeping me safe from becoming a traitor in my father's eyes was the fact that he had no knowledge of my whereabouts.

But I was a traitor, just as Dacre had named me the moment we met.

I was the princess of Marmoris, and here I sat with our enemy, talking about the cruelties of my king.

A king who should have had no more loyal a subject than his heir.

My heart raced as I imagined the worst. If Dacre discovered my true identity, he would kill me without mercy or perhaps use me in ways that would make me wish for death.

I had heard of the rebellion's cruelties just as much as I had experienced my father's.

I didn't want to think about which of them was worse.

"I like to come here." The sound of Dacre's voice pulled me away from my thoughts, and I watched him as he looked out over the water. "I come here whenever the day has been too rough or when thoughts of my mother won't quit plaguing my mind."

"I'm sorry about your mother." I couldn't remember if I had already told him that, but it felt imperative for me to say it now. I wanted to tell him that I was sorry that my own family had a hand in taking his mother away from him. That I was sorry that his mother had spent her life fighting a king who hadn't cared if she lived or died.

My father thought of the rebellion as a nuisance, and I didn't think he truly took them seriously until they raided the castle. But I had seen the fear in his eyes then. My father was hoarding magic from the tithe, keeping it as a way to fuel his greed for power, but I had seen the trace of doubt on his face that day. Everything he had taken from them may not have been enough.

The man had everything, and still, it wasn't enough to protect him when his people finally decided to fight back.

I didn't think anything ever would be.

Dacre nodded his head before he leaned back and pressed his eyes closed. "I'm too drunk for this conversation."

I chuckled softly even though it lacked humor. "What would you like to talk about then?"

"You wearing nothing but my shirt." He didn't hesitate, his words coming out slow as if he could taste them, and they hung in the air like an unspoken promise, making my skin tingle with anticipation. "It's really the only thing I can seem to think about since last night."

I swallowed hard as I stared at him. His lashes were fanned out over his cheeks, and he looked so peaceful like this. "I was wearing more than just your shirt."

"I know," he groaned softly. "But all I could think about while lying there in the dark is what if you weren't."

He slowly turned his head toward me and looked into my eyes with an intensity that made my breath catch. His voice surprised me, soft and deep. "I kept dreaming of stripping you bare of everything else until you had nothing left to hide behind."

I could feel the heat rising to my face as I looked away, unable to meet his gaze. "I think it's time for us to go," I said, my voice tight as I bit back the words I wanted to say.

"That would be smart." He reached forward and ran his fingers over the edge of my shirt. He played with the material mindlessly, but it was a stark contrast to the fire he was stoking inside me with each assured touch. "Did you wear this tonight to punish me?"

"How in the world would this be punishing you?"

"Because you're not mine."

His words intoxicated me far more than any wine ever could. "I'm not anyone's."

His gaze darkened as it followed the trail of his hands, his touch becoming firmer. "Has Eiran touched you?"

I stumbled over my words, barely managing to squeeze out a "What?" before an incredulous scoff escaped my lips. I shook my head in disbelief. "You can't be serious."

"I'm completely serious." He lifted his gaze from my abdomen to my face, and I felt a wave of rage surge through me. His eyes were taunting me with the same disdain that had been laced through every training session he'd put me through.

I quickly stood and moved away from him before I did something I would regret.

He called out my name, but I didn't stop as I moved back toward the entrance of the small cave. Dacre was drunk, and I wasn't in the mood to deal with him tonight. Not when he was touching me like that.

Not when I would beg him even when he was cruel.

I squatted carefully, craning my neck downward, and felt the cold, jagged edge of rock scrape against my back. I exhaled with relief when I finally emerged on the other side of the narrow passageway, only to be met by a terrifying darkness. The faint glimmer of light, which had guided me through the tight tunnel, was now completely obscured, and I fought back my rising panic as I contemplated returning to it.

"Nyra, wait."

I was about to walk away when Dacre stumbled out of the shadowy opening, slamming into my back. His hands shot out and caught my arms before I could fall.

"What are you doing?"

"I can't fucking see!" I said a bit hysterically.

"If you used your magic, you could produce light."

"Oh, thank the gods. You didn't lose your ability to be an ass in there." I should have moved away from him.

"We wouldn't be able to go on without that." He chuckled behind me, and I could feel the warmth of his breath against the back of my neck.

I shivered, and I knew that he could feel it.

"*You* wouldn't be able to go on without that because it's your entire personality. I would be just fine."

I jumped as Dacre touched the nape of my neck, and I could practically feel him smiling as he ran his nose along my skin.

"What are you doing?"

"Enjoying you for a moment." He breathed me in, and I pressed my thighs together as the deep rumble of his voice washed over me. "There's nowhere for you to run away to now."

"I could yell for Eiran." I didn't mean it, but I knew the words would piss him off. And I wanted to be able to get under his skin as easily as he was getting under mine.

"Do it." He pulled me closer, his muscled arm wrapping around my waist. His fingertips grazed my bare stomach as he murmured in my ear, "I would love for Eiran to come back here and see us exactly like this."

"It wouldn't matter." My body trembled beneath his strong grip as he stepped closer, pressing himself against my back. His warm breath hitched in my ear as I said, "We're not doing anything."

"Aren't we, though?" He pushed in closer to me, pressing his hips against mine, and I could feel the hard bulge of his arousal pressing against my ass, sending a thrill through me at the realization of my power over him.

I closed my eyes and felt his warmth through my clothes as strong arms wrapped around me. I wanted to stay in this moment, but we shouldn't. "We should go back," I said quietly.

"We shouldn't," Dacre groaned against my neck, and

the sound made my stomach ache as it tightened. "I'm not ready to go back yet."

It was on the tip of my tongue to beg him to touch me, but I didn't want to give him anything to use against me later.

"You're drunk, Dacre." My words were low as if I didn't want them to be true.

"I'm thinking more clearly than I have in a very long time."

The words washed over me like a wave of warmth as his lips ran over the edge of my earlobe.

"I swear they went this way." Eiran's voice carried to the back of the cave where we stood, even though we couldn't see him, and Dacre stiffened behind me. "Do you see them?"

"No. Come on, Eiran." That was Wren. "Dacre is more than capable of taking care of Nyra."

Dacre's hand traveled slowly across my body, sending a shiver through me as his fingers lingered along the soft skin of my neck. He moved upward and cupped my mouth with long, gentle fingers, pressing just hard enough to keep me quiet.

His hot breath breezed over my ear as he uttered an emphatic "Shhh," and his other hand slid under the hem of my shirt, pressing lightly against my belly.

"Dacre." The sound of his name was muffled against his palm, and he groaned against the back of my neck.

"Gods, I love when you say my name." His hand flattened on my stomach and tugged me harder against him, harder against the evidence of how badly he wanted me. "I love it even more knowing that Eiran is looking for you."

My mouth opened, poised to return a witty retort, but before I could utter a word, his finger grazed just between my lips until he ran it along the tip of my tongue.

"Nyra!" Eiran called out, and Dacre chuckled softly.

"I'll let you go back to him on one condition," Dacre breathed against my ear. "Tell me you don't want me, and I'll let you run off with him."

I opened my mouth, ready to do exactly as he instructed. But before I could speak, one of his hands slipped from my mouth, trailing down my neck, and the other moved slowly against the edge of my trousers, his fingers tracing gentle circles that left me breathless.

All I could think about was that damned hand of his and how the tip of one of his fingers slipped just below the edge of my pants.

"Are you wet, little traitor?" he whispered in my ear, and a moan passed through my lips that I couldn't stop.

I wished I could stop my reaction to him, but I had told so many lies that I couldn't resist telling him the truth.

I nodded my head, but that wasn't enough for him.

"Use your words, Nyra. I need to hear you say how badly you want me."

Embarrassment flooded me, but I couldn't bring myself to care. Not in the dark where no one else could see me or hear me. "I am."

"You are what?" His words were a growl.

"I'm wet for you." I could feel the moisture pooling between my thighs, and I felt like I was going to die if he didn't touch me.

A low, guttural moan left my throat as his hands explored my body. His fingers were sure against my skin, and I felt a warmth radiating from him as he slowly slipped them beneath my clothes. My breath quivered as his fingers curved around my flesh, drawing circles that made my legs tremble with anticipation.

He took my chin in his hand, his calloused thumb gentle against my skin until my lips collided with his.

The kiss wasn't gentle or teasing, it was punishing and brutal, and he grazed his teeth over my lips before he forced himself inside and tasted my tongue with his. His fingers explored and pushed more firmly against me, and I jerked forward in his arms.

It was the first time I had been kissed, and it was nothing like I expected. I had dreamed of this moment for years, but somehow, this was more.

His fingers slipped lower, toying with me as he traced over every part of me, and he groaned when he was met with the moisture that waited there for him. "Gods, you *are* so wet for me."

I kissed him hard, trying to keep my whimpers of pleasure contained, but he lifted his thumb and pulled my lip from my teeth. He rubbed the tip of his thumb roughly over my lip before he moved his mouth back to mine and teased it open with his tongue just as a finger slid inside me. I froze for a second before his palm began to rub soft circles on my sensitive clit.

I had never been touched like this before, never felt so utterly out of control.

I leaned back into him, feeling his muscles flex under my touch. His breath hitched against my mouth as I ran my hand up his thigh and dug my fingernails into his leathers.

"Nyra!" Eiran called again, and I quickly turned my

head in the direction of his voice. I still couldn't see him, but I could see the edge of a light coming our way.

"Dacre."

"Don't you dare." His fingers started pumping in and out of me gently, and my thighs tightened around his hand. "I'm not letting you go anywhere until I can taste your cum on my fingers."

I sucked in a sharp breath because I had never been spoken to like this before. I was the princess, and everyone treated me as if I were going to break at any moment.

But Dacre didn't.

And his words did nothing but make more wetness coat his fingers as he continued to work me.

"Do you want to come?" he asked so quietly I thought I imagined it.

"Yes," I breathed, and he entered a second finger inside me.

I felt so full. Too full, and I whimpered as he moved his hand harder and faster.

"You're taking me so good, little traitor." He nipped at my ear, and I felt the move all the way to my core. "Gods, I can imagine how well you'll take my cock. I could die thinking about this tight little pussy wrapped around me like it was made for me."

My stomach tightened to the point of pain, and I pressed back against Dacre, letting him support my weight as I focused on nothing but chasing the high he was giving me.

"You like that idea, don't you? Me buried inside you while you cry out my name."

I nodded, but his command was immediate. "Words."

"Yes."

"Good girl." He pressed his length against my ass, and I whimpered. "I would reward you so well." His palm pressed harder against my clit, and I didn't think I could handle another second of it. "I would feast upon this pussy like I had been starved for years."

I cried out, but he wasn't done.

"I have been starved, Nyra. Until you."

The dam broke inside me, and I cried out his name as pleasure coursed through every inch of me. His hand didn't stop its assault on me, and the high I was feeling was enough to make me want to cry. It was too much, the pleasure too extreme, and I pressed my lips together so everyone in this entire damn city wouldn't hear me screaming his name.

"Nyra." It was Eiran's voice again, this time closer, and Dacre slipped his hand out of my trousers easily.

I whimpered at the loss of him, and he chuckled softly behind me.

"Clean them." He brought his fingers to my lips. "Unless you want Eiran to see you still dripping off my fingers when he gets over here."

I opened my mouth immediately, greedily, and I didn't want to admit to myself that it had absolutely nothing to do with Eiran or what he would see.

I tasted myself on Dacre's fingers, and he pressed them into my mouth until they hit the back of my throat. Right before I thought I would gag, he stopped.

"Suck," he demanded softly, and I obeyed.

I hollowed out my cheeks and sucked his fingers farther into my mouth. I ran my tongue over his fingers, tasting every inch of him that he gave me, until he finally pulled out of my mouth. He kissed me then, tasting me off my lips, and he groaned into my mouth just as light flooded my vision.

"Nyra, are you okay?"

Dacre let me go, and I blinked up at him before I glanced over at Eiran. He was standing about fifteen feet away from us, and he truly looked concerned. I couldn't possibly imagine what I looked like right now to him, but shame flooded me as the shocks of pleasure still clung to every part of me.

"Yes. I'm fine." My voice trembled, and I hoped that Eiran couldn't hear it. "We were just heading back."

His gaze jumped from me to Dacre before coming back to me again. "We were getting worried about you. We know how much Dacre has had to drink tonight."

His words slammed into me, and the shame I felt a second ago didn't hold a candle to what I felt now. It was as if Eiran was reminding me that whatever happened between Dacre and me tonight was a result of the wine and nothing else, and maybe he was right.

Dacre hated me, but tonight, he was...well, I did't know what he was, but I could still feel his touch between my thighs.

I could feel his touch *everywhere.*

"I'm perfectly fine, Eiran," Dacre said from behind me, and I startled at the sound of his voice. "Thank you for your concern though."

"I wasn't concerned about you. Only her."

"I'd say she's more than alright. Aren't you, little trai-tor?" Dacre moved around the front of me, and my mouth gaped open as I watched him slip two of his fingers between his lips. He winked at me as he slipped his tongue between them. He didn't shield what he was doing in front of Eiran, and I wanted to kill him when he finally pulled those fingers from his mouth. "Perfect even."

"Okay." Eiran's narrowed gaze looked back to me, and I hated how cautious it was. Did he know exactly what Dacre had just done? What I had allowed him to do? "Do you want me to leave you?"

"No." I stepped forward quickly and passed by Dacre before I could think better of it. "Please take me back."

Dacre chuckled behind me, but Eiran simply nodded.

I moved to his side, but this time, he didn't reach out to take my hand as he did earlier.

He was still watching Dacre, and the look of disgust on his face was anything but hidden.

"Come on." Eiran waved me forward, and I walked in front of him, not waiting for him to follow.

"I'll see you at training." Dacre's voice echoed off the walls, but I didn't stop.

I needed to get out of here.

CHAPTER 15

NYRA

My palms were slick with sweat as I glanced around the training grounds, taking in every detail. Wren was to my right, her long legs stretching out before her, and I nodded at something she was saying.

"Did you hear me?"

"What?" I blinked and looked down at her.

"You should stretch more. I promise it will help with the soreness later." She leaned forward and touched her toes, and I followed suit.

The soreness. The only soreness I could think of was the way I ached between my thighs with the memory of Dacre's touch. Dacre, who had all but disappeared after I walked off with Eiran last night.

"Have you seen your brother this morning?" I stretched my arms over my head while I looked around.

"No." She chuckled. "I'd say he's probably sleeping off that wine if I had to guess. I don't know what got into him last night."

I bit down on my tongue because I didn't know what had gotten into him either, but it wasn't something I was ready to discuss with her.

He was her brother.

"Does that mean I can go back to our room and get some more sleep?" I chuckled because I knew that was never going to happen.

"Not today," a deep male voice I didn't recognize said from behind me.

"Dad." Wren climbed to her feet and stood up straight in front of her father. She didn't approach him or embrace him like I expected her to. Instead, she stood like a warrior before a commanding officer.

So I did the same.

"You must be Nyra." Her father looked at me, and he looked so much like his son it was unsettling. He had graying hair at his temples, and his face was worn with his years, but his features were the same.

All except for his eyes.

I had seen him only once before when he pulled Dacre from training, but this was the first time he had spoken to me.

"I am." I nodded and shifted on my feet, uncomfortable under his attention.

"I hear my son has been training you." He looked around the grounds. "Any idea where he is now?"

"He wasn't feeling well last night," Wren answered before I could say anything. "I could hear him getting sick through the walls."

I kept my mouth shut because her lies to her father were none of my business.

I had my own lies to worry about.

"Then you're with me today, Wren." His words were a command, and she simply nodded.

"What about you?" He cocked his head and studied me. His expression so similar to Dacre's, but he unnerved me in a way that Dacre never had.

My spine straightened under his scrutiny. "What about me?"

"Have you been out on the field yet?"

"She's only had a few days of training," Wren answered for me, but her father paid her no attention.

"You'll come with us then." He turned away from both of us. "We're leaving now."

"Shit," Wren cursed under her breath, and I widened my eyes.

Her father was already walking away from us, but she pulled two different daggers from their sheaths on her vest before tucking them into mine.

"I'm going to kill Dacre." She looked over my shoulder as if he would suddenly appear.

"Should I be worried?" My hands were trembling at my sides, but I had no idea what going out on the field meant. But I couldn't get the image of what Dacre had told me in that cave yesterday out of my mind. Those boys. I didn't know how I would handle that. I didn't know if I could.

I didn't know what I'd do if he forced me to go anywhere near the palace.

"Just stick to my side." She tugged on the straps of my vest before her worried gaze met mine. "You'll be fine."

She followed after her father, and I did exactly as she

said and stuck to her side as we walked up to him, two other men, and Mal.

She opened her mouth as if she was about to speak before closing it again. I hadn't seen her since the day I had arrived, and honestly, I had been thankful for that.

"Good. Let's go." Wren's father barely spared us a glance before he was leading us down a winding path that led us away from the training grounds and deeper into the narrowing caves.

He was walking so quickly that I could barely keep up, but I stayed at Wren's side as we reached the end of a massive cave and started ascending a winding staircase that was so covered in vines that I wouldn't have known it was there without being shown.

When Wren's father reached the top, he lifted open the circular rock that gave way and allowed the blinding sunlight to come in. I had spent so many days already in the hidden city that I had to shield my eyes as I let them adjust to the daylight.

Wren's father and the others disappeared through the hole in the ceiling, and Wren and I followed after them. Wren reached her hand forward to grab mine and helped pull me up before the two of us shifted the rock back over the opening.

We were in the middle of woods, surrounded by trees and a thick mossy forest floor. I had no idea where we were, or how far from the palace, but I could hear the loud crashing water where the waterfall hit the surface. It was a sound I used to crave at night. I would open my window and let the familiar sound lull me to sleep after my mother was no longer there to do it.

But now the sound made me shudder, and anxiety coated my veins. We were close enough to hear it, which meant we were also close to my father.

"Davian, we need to head east," Mal said as she looked around. "We're supposed to meet him shortly."

Wren's father looked over at us once before nodding his head. "Let's get this over with."

We followed behind them as they moved through the forest as if they were a part of it. Their steps were soundless, and they moved so quickly that my breaths were rushing in and out of my chest, trying to keep up with them. Wren was almost as stealthy as they were, but I could easily spot the years of training they had over her. Even Mal.

Sweat was dripping down the back of my neck by the time they finally stopped behind a cluster of large trees, and I tried to quiet my panting as they watched the small clearing before us.

I didn't know what they were waiting for, but the tension in the air was thick and suffocating. I could hear my own heartbeat in my ears as I watched the men in front of us, their eyes focused on something in the clearing.

"Why would you bring her here?" Mal spoke quietly as she moved to Wren's side.

"Davian demanded it." Wren narrowed her eyes at Mal. "Would you like to be the one to tell him no?"

Mal didn't answer her; instead, she crouched and looked out toward the clearing.

I gasped as movement in the nearby bushes revealed a tall, broad-shouldered figure with a strong jaw and short black hair. Faris.

We had known each other for years—ever since I was a tiny girl playing in the castle courtyards. He was one of the top commanders in my father's army, and there was no chance of him not recognizing me. I felt lightheaded as fear surged through me, and I forced myself to take a deep breath.

Davian motioned for us to stay put as he and the other men disappeared around the trees. Wren grabbed my hand and pulled me closer to her, her grip tight and reassuring. We both crouched down near the base of a massive tree, near Mal, and I could feel the tension in Wren's body.

There was no doubt that they could feel it in mine as well.

"Do you know who that is?" I asked Wren so quietly that I barely heard my own question.

She shook her head without taking her eyes off of Faris. "I've never seen him before."

"He's a commander in King Roan's army," Mal hissed without turning to face us.

I watched as Faris paced back and forth in the clearing, his eyes darting rapidly. He looked like he hadn't slept in days, his face drawn and gaunt.

I felt a chill run down my spine as I watched him. Faris was known for how ruthless he could be in battle. The stories my father used to tell about his great war efforts had been enough to turn my stomach, and I didn't feel safe that he stood before us now.

"He knows me." I spoke the words into Wren's ear before I could think better of them, but if I was going to have to face this, I wanted to do it with someone I trusted at least knowing part of the truth.

The only truth I could give her.

Wren looked at me, and her eyes were assessing, but there was no judgment there. No hatred.

"We wait and we watch." Her voice was steady and calm. "We stay hidden unless my father tells us otherwise."

I nodded, my heart pounding in my chest.

"You're the one who asked for this meeting." Davian stood before the others. "What do you want?"

Faris's eyes flicked toward Wren's father, and he took a step forward. "I have information that could be of great use to you."

Davian's expression was unreadable as he stood there waiting for Faris to continue.

"I have information on the whereabouts of the princess." Faris's voice was low, and I felt Wren's grip on my hand tighten.

"What makes you think we would be interested in that?" Davian's tone was hard, but I saw the way he leaned toward Faris just a fraction.

"Princess Verena is a valuable bargaining chip," Faris replied, his eyes darting around the clearing. "The king has had men searching for her for months."

It was the first time I had heard my name in months, and I felt unsteady.

Davian rolled his shoulders back and shifted on his feet.

"Because she's his daughter." He almost sounded bored by the conversation, but he was watching Faris carefully for his answer. "That doesn't make her valuable to me."

"He doesn't care about her because she's his daughter," Faris spat, and shame flooded me. "If she had been enough for him, he wouldn't have spent years killing his queen by forcing her to try to bear him another heir."

Guilt and grief were worse than any blade someone could throw at me, and my hands trembled as his words assaulted me.

"Then what does he want with her? He has a new queen now." Davian's hand moved almost unnoticeably, but I saw the way it inched closer to the blades at his side.

Faris shook his head and his gaze fell to Davian's hand then back to his face. "He is desperate to find her."

My father hadn't even looked in my direction when the rebels raided the palace. His new queen was protected, but me? I wasn't a thought on his mind, and it was the only reason I was able to escape without any of them finding me.

Faris leaned in, his voice lowered to a whisper, his gaze still erratic as it searched around him. "She is his only heir. It is rumored that his new queen is failing him just as the first one had."

My breath caught in my throat and the pressure in my chest threatened to cave in on me. He had always been cruel, but he was still my father.

I was still the only child born from the queen he once loved.

My hand shot out before me, pressing into the tree and catching myself before I fell. Wren's hand squeezed mine, trying to get me to look at her, but I couldn't think past what Faris had just said. If my father wanted me dead, there would be no stopping him.

"What was that?" Faris's hand went to his own dagger

as he shuffled backward and his gaze darted in our direction. "Is someone else here?"

Davian's eyes shifted in our direction, and I felt Wren pull me closer to her. The tension in the air was suffocating, and I had already barely been able to breathe.

"Who's there?" Faris called out, his dagger now fully drawn as he scanned the area.

Davian stepped forward, his hand resting on the hilt of his own blade as he blocked us from view. "Stand down, Faris. It's just two of my trainees."

"What are they doing here?" Faris sidestepped Davian and tried to get a better look at us. "Show yourself."

Davian nodded once in our direction, and Wren stood. She pulled me with her, but I hesitated.

Fear, pure and relentless, raced through me, paralyzing me. I couldn't move. I couldn't breathe. I felt Wren pulling on my arm, but I couldn't bring myself to face Faris.

"It's alright, Nyra." Wren's voice was calm and reassuring, but she didn't understand.

I watched as Faris turned his dagger over in his hand, and I was eager to reach for my own. But even with how much Dacre had been pushing me in training, I wouldn't stand a chance in fighting him off, let alone the others.

"Faris," Davian warned, his hand still resting on his own blade as Wren stepped out from behind the shelter of the tree.

Her hand still tightly gripping mine, she stood tall and proud, her chin held high. Her eyes never once left Faris as I took in a harsh breath and stepped out behind her.

Faris's eyes flickered between the two of us, his dagger

still held tightly in his hand, before his eyes widened as he stared at me.

"What are you doing here?" he demanded, his voice low and dangerous.

I could feel Davian and the others turning to look at me, but I didn't dare take my gaze off of Faris.

"Faris, please." I lifted my hand toward him, hoping to calm him down.

But his eyes narrowed only a second before I saw the blade leave his hand.

My heart raced as I watched the glint of the blade fly toward us, aimed straight at Wren who was still blocking me from Faris's full view. Time slowed to a crawl, and everything around me seemed to blur together.

My grip tightened on Wren's hand, and I jerked her behind me forcefully. The blade was moving so quickly that I hardly noticed it as the sharp tip lanced through my shirt, grazing my arm, and a fiery pain bled into my arm before the dagger buried itself deep into the tree behind us.

Wren's father had his sword drawn, but not before Faris had yet another dagger in his hand.

But Wren didn't flinch, didn't waver.

She already had her own blade drawn in her hand that didn't tremble as mine did.

"How do you know her?" her father asked Faris, pointing the tip of his sword in my direction, but as Faris growled, Wren was already moving.

I couldn't believe the speed with which she had reacted. Her movements were graceful and fluid as she threw her blade with practiced ease.

Her blade was lethal as it caught Faris in the side of his

neck. Blood spurted from the wound, and Faris stumbled back, his eyes wide in shock.

"The princess." Faris's words were muffled as he struggled to breathe, but there was no mistaking what he had said.

"What about the princess?" Davian demanded, his voice booming and chaotic.

"He will kill you all for her." He didn't take his gaze off me. "He will kill you."

Faris fell forward, his knees slamming into the hard earth with a loud thud as his dagger dropped to his side from his lifeless fingers.

As he stared at me, his body seemed to weaken, and he collapsed to the ground, his face landing on the damp earth overrun with patches of moss. I stood frozen, my heart pounding against my chest as I watched him struggle for breath in the grass.

"What the fuck was that?" one of the men with Wren's father cursed just as Davian turned in my direction.

His brow furrowed and his jaw clenched, anger and confusion etched on his face. My hands trembled uncontrollably at my sides, and the pain shooting through my arm intensified with every passing second.

Blood trailed down my arm until it dripped from my fingers and hit the ground, but I didn't dare take my eyes off the men in front of me long enough to check the damage. Davian's expression twisted into one of pure rage, his muscles tensing as he charged toward me. I braced myself for the impact, knowing that my own injuries were nothing compared to what he would do.

I stumbled backward, tripping over the thick moss and

roots that were breaching the surface as if trying to grab my ankles. I barely managed to catch myself against the trunk of the large tree behind me, and I winced as I put weight on my injured arm.

Davian was on me before I could think or even breathe, and even though I could hear Wren as she told her father to stop, he was all I could see.

His hand wrapped around my neck as his other pressed into the wound on my arm carelessly, and I cried out in pain, even though I was struggling to draw in air.

"Who the hell are you?" he demanded, and his spittle landed on my chin.

I raised my other hand, clawing at his hand that was cutting off my air. I couldn't speak, but even if I could, I could never tell him the truth.

My mind raced, panic setting in as he pressed harder into my wound.

"How the hell is she supposed to answer you?" Wren yelled from behind me, but I could only see Davian's face that resembled his son's so much that it was startling.

Davian's gaze dropped to his hand on my neck for a moment before he finally loosened his grip, but only enough to allow me to sneak in enough breath to be able to speak.

"I've told you all who I am."

"Don't fucking lie to me. I'm not my son." His hand flexed against my neck, and his gaze was reckless as he searched my face. "How does Faris know you?"

"I lived in the palace my entire life." It was the truth.

Give him truths.

"And the princess?" Both hands pressed harder, and a whimper I tried to stop slipped past my lips.

"What about her?" Blood was coating my fingers.

"We need to find the princess."

"You heard him. That is asking for death."

The hand on my neck tightened, and he jerked my head until the back of my skull slammed into the bark. My vision blurred, and I fought for air once again as I felt him move even closer to me.

Wren was yelling, but I could no longer make out what she was saying.

I felt the shadow of Davian's beard scratch against my cheek, and I wanted to push him away, to draw my dagger from my vest as Dacre had been trying to teach me, but I couldn't focus on anything other than blinking away the dark smoke that seemed to cloud my mind.

"Traitors have no place in this rebellion." His mouth was so close to my ear that I could feel his lips move as he spoke only to me. "You know more than you're telling. You will help us find the princess, or you will die trying."

I had no air. My eyelids were heavy, and that dark smoke was reaching every corner of my vision. I blinked again, attempting to wash it away, but its lure was too intoxicating.

Davian's grip fell from me, and as the air rushed back into my lungs, my legs gave out beneath me. I crashed to the ground, and I was thankful for the thick moss that softened my fall, even as tears escaped my eyes when the throbbing pain of my arm intensified.

Davian took another step back from me, and Wren was at my side instantly.

"Shit," she cursed under her breath, and when I looked up at her eyes that were like warm honey mixed with a sea of green, I could see her own fear staring back at me.

"Get your trainee back underground, Wren," her father spat, not sparing me another glance. "We have damage control to do now that you've killed our informant."

He turned his back to us, and Wren's trembling hands ran over my cheeks. "Nyra, I'm going to need you to help me get you to your feet."

Nyra.

Gods, I missed her.

I tried to remember the sound of her voice, the look on her face when she would laugh, but it all felt hollow.

I missed her so damn much, and I could hardly remember her.

"Nyra, look at me."

I blinked up at her, desperately wishing I could tell her my real name. I wished I could tell Wren everything.

"It's okay," she whispered with a nod. "Let me help you."

"Let's go, Mal," Davian called, and I looked to my right to see Mal kneeled beside me, tying a thin white bandage around my arm.

She didn't meet my eyes as she worked. "I'm coming," she called behind her, but moved her head closer to Wren's.

"Get her back underground," she demanded. "Get her to Dacre."

CHAPTER 16
DACRE

I could barely concentrate on anything Kai was saying.

My head was fucking pounding.

"I'm worried about what they'll do if they don't find anything soon. They are restless, and impatience can be the death of a rebellion."

"I'd say they're more than restless." I crossed my arms as I looked out over the current recruits as they trained. "My father has been bloodthirsty since the moment we left the palace without my mother."

Far before then, actually.

Kai nodded, and I could see the same ghosts that haunted me clouding his gaze. His father had been lost in the same siege that took my mother.

It was a fool's mission, and we had all paid the price for it.

"Where's my sister?" I looked around the training grounds and avoided asking the question I actually wanted to know.

Where was Nyra?

I had gone too far last night, been too rough, but I couldn't bring myself to regret it. Because even though I hated Nyra, I desperately wanted to touch her again.

She had been so pliable under my hands, so eager for my touch when I was sure she was going to push me away.

And even if she looked at me with nothing but disgust on her face when she had walked away with Eiran, all I could do was smile.

Because she wanted me as badly as I had wanted her.

"I haven't seen her." Kai's voice interrupted my thoughts, and I looked back to my friend as he chuckled. "Are you worried about your sister or her new little tagalong?"

"I couldn't care less about Nyra besides the fact that her ass isn't here training. She's liable to get one of us killed with how bad her combat is."

"Right." Kai rubbed his hand along his mouth that was lifted in a knowing smile. "That's why everyone at breakfast this morning couldn't stop talking about you and her and apparently the ass you made of yourself last night."

Frustration crawled through me at the thought of anyone talking about me and her at all. "I didn't make an ass out of myself. I was an ass. There's a difference." I watched the two men in front of me and made a mental note to correct the stance of the one on the right whenever they finally stopped.

"If you say so." He chuckled again before a rash "Fuck" left his lips.

"What?" I looked back to him.

Kai's gaze was fixed ahead of us, near the back of the

cave, and when I turned to look there, blood rushed in my ears.

"Nyra." I cursed under my breath as I shot forward in their direction.

Nyra was leaning heavily on Wren for support, and I could see the worry in my sister's face as her gaze bounced back and forth between Kai and me.

"What happened?" I asked as I got closer. There was a bloodied bandage on Nyra's arm that she cradled close to her body, and from the amount of dried blood that coated all the way to her fingertips, I knew she had to be in pain.

"Just a bit farther," my sister spoke calmly to Nyra, but I had yet to see her face.

"This isn't good," Kai practically growled, and I watched as Nyra lifted her head and met his gaze before she finally turned to look at me.

Anger clouded my vision like thick ice over a black pond, and I clenched my fists until my fingers turned white.

There were yellow marks all along her delicate neck, and the unmistakable marks were already beginning to turn a deep purple along the edges.

Someone had their hand around her throat.

"What the fuck happened?" My voice boomed, but I couldn't control my anger.

"I'm fine." Nyra's eyes didn't leave mine, but I could see the desperation she was trying to hide beneath the depths. "I just need to sit down for a second."

She was lying.

I shifted forward and clenched and unclenched my fist

before I took Nyra's body weight against my own and helped her sit on a large boulder at the edge of the cave.

"I'm not going to ask again, Wren. What the fuck happened?"

Wren's hands shook as she fidgeted with the hilt of one of her daggers, her eyes darting back and forth between me and Kai.

"Our father took us up." Wren spoke so quietly that I almost didn't hear her, but her words hit into me as if she had screamed them.

My hands stilled on Nyra as I stared at her injured arm. "Excuse me?"

"Davian."

"I know who our father is," I snapped, and Nyra bristled and finally turned to look at me.

"Don't be an ass to her." The marks on her neck were darkening with every second she sat in front of me, and here she was defending my sister against...me.

"I'm not being an ass."

"Yes. You are." She huffed and turned back to Wren who started talking again.

"He was looking for you, and when I told him that you weren't feeling well, he wanted me on the field with him. He didn't care that Nyra only had a few days of training. He wanted her there too."

Guilt coursed through me. Fuck. If I had been here, this would have never happened. He wouldn't have taken Nyra, let alone Wren up there with him. He already knew how I felt about him putting Wren in unnecessary danger.

But her life wasn't important to him. She was just another soldier.

We all were.

"And then what happened?" I said much more calmly, even though I could barely contain my rage as I gently unwrapped the soiled gauze from Nyra's arm to check the wound beneath.

Wren opened her mouth to speak, but then she looked to Nyra. Whatever it was, it was either bad or they didn't want me to know.

"What happened?" I repeated as I pulled away the gauze from Nyra's wound and she winced as some dried blood pulled away with it.

I examined Nyra's injured arm. The wound was deep but clean as if a blade sliced through it easily.

I gently ran my thumb over the dried blood to see the wound better and Nyra whimpered.

"Davian was meeting with an informant," Wren spoke, but I didn't look up at her.

"Who?" I knew almost all of my father's informants. I was the one who had obtained them for him.

"Faris," Nyra answered before Wren could.

"And Faris did this?" I asked, nodding to Nyra's arm.

She nodded as Wren spoke again. "He kept talking about the princess and how the king has gone feral that she's missing."

"She's missing?"

"According to Faris. But the way he made it sound wasn't like the king wanted his daughter back. He wants his heir. It's like he wanted her dead."

Nyra tensed in my hold and tried to pull her arm away, but I held firm.

I searched the side of her face that she was allowing me to see, but she was giving nothing away.

"Okay?"

"And then he saw me and Nyra," Wren whispered and moved a step closer to us as did Kai. "He threw his blade at me before I even had time to react. It would have hit me in the chest if Nyra didn't jerk me behind her."

My heart pounded in my chest as I listened to Wren's words. My sister had almost been killed, and it hadn't been my father who had saved her. It was the little traitor in front of me.

She had been one of them her entire life, and still, she saved my sister.

"And her neck?" I nodded toward the darkening bruises on her skin.

"That was Dad." Wren glanced away from me and toward where they had just came as if he might appear.

My hand on Nyra's arm stilled, and I searched my sister's face. "What?"

"He was furious after I killed Faris. He was so angry that Faris knew Nyra." Wren's gaze bounced around the room. "He did that to her while he demanded answers from her she couldn't give."

My grip on Nyra's arm tightened involuntarily. "He fucking choked her?"

Without thinking, my other hand moved to cup her chin, gently turning it toward me so that I could fully see the marks my father had left on her. Her warm blue eyes met mine and where I expected there to be pain and fear, it was determination staring back at me.

"Where is he?"

"He said he was going to do damage control." Wren crossed her arms and there was fear in my sister's gaze. "Mal told me to get Nyra to you."

"Mal was there?"

Nyra made the smallest whine, and I drew my gaze back to hers and loosened my grip on her arm. *I was hurting her.*

"We need to get this wound cleaned up."

And I needed to get away from her before I did something stupid. The memories of touching her last night, of the things I had said to her, had been haunting me since the moment she walked away with Eiran, and seeing my father's mark on her now, made me feel possessive over her when she wasn't mine.

But I wanted to make sure that everyone in this entire damn rebellion knew that she was.

"If he doesn't find something soon..." Wren stopped and chewed on her bottom lip before the next words passed through them. "I'm worried about him."

"Wren, take her to see the healers, then to the springs." I stood to my full height and ran my hands over my chest, cataloging my weapons mindlessly. "I need to have a talk with our father."

I was worried about him too. Worried about the man he was becoming ever since we lost my mother. He wasn't the father I once knew.

He had become a man I didn't want to know.

My gaze met Kai's, and I started to turn away. I needed to get out of here before I lost my shit, but Nyra's hand clung to mine.

Her touch was a whisper against my skin, but she didn't

meet my eyes as she pulled her touch away and spoke. "I don't want to go to the healers."

"Nyra, you have to get your arm looked at." Wren spoke softly as she took a step closer to Nyra. "And your neck."

Nyra shook her head, and I hated the way she looked so lost. "I don't want them to touch me. I don't trust them to touch me."

"We have to get you healed."

I watched Nyra's every movement, the way her eyes darted to my face before she quickly looked away. "Dacre can heal me."

I felt both Wren's and Kai's eyes on me, but I refused to look away from Nyra.

"Dacre doesn't heal," Wren spoke in almost a whisper as if her words would upset me.

She wasn't wrong. I didn't heal. Not anymore. Not since the power I had inherited from our mother had failed me when I needed it most.

My mother had more healing powers than any other soldier in the warrior unit, as did I, but it hadn't mattered when the magic that was used to take her life had been too strong to fight.

I had tried over and over to save her while my father screamed at me to do so. I could still feel her blood coating my hands as I tried to push as much of my magic into her as I could.

But it hadn't been enough.

And I hadn't healed anyone since.

Not until Nyra.

Nyra's brows scrunched as she finally looked up and searched my face. "He's healed me before."

"What?" The sound of Wren's voice was enough to wreck me, and I needed to get out of here.

"Come on." I motioned to Nyra before reaching out my hands to help her stand. "Let's go get this wound cleaned up so I can get a better look."

"Okay." She glanced back and forth between me and Wren, but she didn't hesitate to take my hands.

"Kai, will you take Wren to get checked out? I want to make sure she doesn't have any injuries."

"I'm fine," Wren argued, and the way she was watching me made me uncomfortable.

"Just give me the peace of mind." I helped Nyra to her feet and pulled her in close to my body. "And let me know as soon as either of you hear of Father's return."

My arm pulsed with a deep, unrelenting ache that felt like it was reaching down to my bones, but I refused to look at it. I couldn't bear to see the extent of the damage.

My eyes followed Dacre's hurried movements around the cramped, unfamiliar room. It was my first time in this building, and I felt out of place as he rummaged through an old wooden cabinet.

The once grand building now stood in ruins, a stark contrast to the colorful stained windows that had somehow survived the years of neglect. Inside, makeshift beds lined the walls, and the sharp scent of antiseptic lingered in the air. Warriors littered the space, about a dozen in total, as Dacre guided me toward a private area. A healer was tending to various injuries, some more severe than others.

"Couldn't we have done this at the springs?" I pressed the palms of my hands against the makeshift bed where I sat and let my fingers curl around the rough edge.

More pain sliced through my arm.

This place reminded me too much of home. It brought back memories of the dozens of times I had to visit my mother in a similar room when she had failed again and again to produce my father a rightful heir.

It was where I had watched her familiar face wither away.

It was the same damn room I had visited her cold, hard body in before my father had found someone new to replace her.

Dacre was moving a bottle of clear liquid and some clean gauze to a small table beside the bed. "Your wound needs to be cleaned first. My magic will only go so far, the last thing we need is for you to have an infection before I close the wound."

I nodded silently, my teeth clenched as I watched him pull the stopper from the bottle. The sharp smell of alcohol stung my nose, and I winced, imagining its harsh touch on my skin. The words Wren said about him no longer healing lingered in my mind, but I held back from asking him.

Even though I was desperate to know if it was the truth.

I was desperate to know *why*.

I bit down harder on my lip to keep any questions from escaping.

My thoughts were a jumbled mess as I stared at him. The lingering sensation of his hands on my skin from the night before taunted me, and I hated that he had avoided me at our morning training session. But I could also still feel his father's hand wrapped around my throat, cutting off my air supply. I could feel the panic rising in my chest.

He was threatening me because he didn't trust me, and he was right to do so.

They had no reason to trust me, but the memory of his threats made me feel completely exposed and vulnerable in front of Dacre.

I was a traitor.

A traitor to my family, a traitor to my kingdom, and he would despise me when I became an even bigger traitor to him.

I was the true heir to my father's throne, and despite how he was touching me last night, I knew that he would raise a dagger to my neck if he knew.

I was the advantage to this war that they needed.

And I was allowing them to suffer as I hid who I was.

But I couldn't ask him any of the questions that were haunting me, so instead I asked, "Is this going to hurt?"

Dacre placed himself directly in front of me, the stool scraping against the rough stone floor. He paused before speaking, his eyes flickering with hesitation before he spoke. "It might sting a bit, but it can't be worse than the pain you're already feeling." He gestured to the supplies at his side and said, "Once we clean it up, I'll get you healed the best I can. Then Wren can take you to the springs."

I tilted my head slightly, a silent agreement as he spoke. He avoided making eye contact with me and instead focused on the bottle in his hand. My stomach churned with shame as I remembered his touch from the night before.

I had been desperate for him. I had begged him.

And now he couldn't even look at me.

With sure hands, Dacre squeezed the dropper and carefully placed several drops of liquid onto the clean gauze.

He then raised my arm, exposing the angry, red wound. I clenched my jaw in anticipation as the cold liquid hit my skin, sending sharp stinging sensations through my body. I struggled to keep a stoic expression, not wanting to show Dacre how much it hurt. My breaths came out in short gasps as I fought to control the pain.

"Breathe, Nyra." He pressed the gauze deeper into the wound, and I cried out. "The wound is deep, but it's a clean cut. We just need to get any dirt and dried blood off your arm before I can heal it."

I opened my mouth and swallowed down an audible breath as I tried to nod. My mind raced with memories of his cruel words cutting through me like knives the night before. But I couldn't seem to hold on to the anger, and I felt a familiar pull toward him, my body responding to his closeness despite my better judgment.

"Where were you this morning?" My gaze fell to the floor as I mustered up the courage to ask the question.

Dacre's calloused fingers paused on my arm briefly, then resumed their meticulous movements over my skin. My heart pounded in my chest as I waited for his answer, afraid of what it might be.

"My father won't do this again. Don't worry," he said sternly, setting the soiled gauze down on the table before grabbing another.

"That's not what I meant."

Dacre rubbed his lips together as he continued to work without looking at me. "What did you mean then?"

"Were you avoiding me after…" I couldn't force myself to say the words out loud.

"After what?" Dacre glanced up from his work, the

piercing intensity of his dark gaze freezing me in place as I fumbled for an answer to his question.

My voice trembled as I spoke, barely above a whisper. "You know what," I said, trying to mask the vulnerability in my words. But deep down, I hated how weak and small it made me feel.

"Say it, Nyra. After what?" Dacre's hands carefully ran the gauze along the skin outside the wound, and I dug my fingernails into the bed.

"After you..." My voice quivered as I spoke. "After you did that," I said, my eyes fixed on the ground. The weight of the memories flooded back, and I couldn't stop the shame I felt.

Dacre carelessly tossed the soiled gauze onto the table and then leaned in close to me. His breath was hot on my face, and I instinctively leaned back, but he pressed closer. "When I made you come on my fingers while Eiran was frantically searching for you?"

I stared up at him in shock, the rawness of his tone contrasting with the gentle touch of his fingers as he ran them over the edge of my elbow. It was as if he was punishing me for my desires, for succumbing to the forbidden pleasure he had offered me.

His words lingered in the air, heavy with the weight of what I had done.

"Dacre," I began. I swallowed hard, trying to regain some semblance of composure. "It's not..."

"Not what?" he murmured, his voice laced with temptation. "It's not like you begged me for everything I gave you?"

His words sent a rush of desire through me, battling

against the pain and shame that still clung to me like a second skin. My heart pounded in my chest as I struggled to find my voice.

My arm was tingling where he was touching me, but I couldn't look away from his eyes. I took a deep breath, inhaling the intoxicating scent of his body mixed with the hint of the sterile alcohol. The room seemed to shrink around us as I clenched my fists at my sides, desperately trying to regain control over myself as the sensation in my arm got stronger.

"Dacre," I said, my voice rough. I turned to look at my injured arm, but Dacre's fingers met my chin and brought my gaze back to meet his.

"What are you…"

"It's almost over." Dacre's voice was low and filled with a mixture of intensity and concern. His eyes bore into mine, searching for something beyond the physical pain.

My muscles clenched and spasmed as his hands moved over my body, channeling powerful magic that stitched me back together. With each surge of energy, a wave of intense adrenaline shot through my veins, making my heart race and my skin tingle with electricity. It was both exhilarating and agonizing to feel his power in such an intimate way.

I could almost taste the electricity in the air, a subtle metallic tang that reminded me of a late summer storm.

I gasped, my body arching involuntarily at the burst of energy. This was different than when he had healed me before. That injury hadn't taken this much of his power.

His magic was familiar, yet unlike anything I had ever experienced before, a blend of pain and pleasure that felt like it would leave me craving his touch whenever he stopped.

His gaze never wavered from mine, his eyes filled with a mixture of desire and torment. His eyes were darker than I had ever seen them, and it was impossible not to be affected by him.

As the intensity of his magic subsided, Dacre slowly withdrew his hands from my body. He took a small step back, and the air around us crackled. Remnants of his touch lingered on my skin.

My body trembled, unsure of how to process the conflicting emotions that swirled within me.

I ran my trembling fingers over my arm. There was still a dull ache that remained there, but the sharp pain from before was gone, and my skin was stitched back together as if the gash had never been there at all.

Dacre's voice was husky and filled with emotions he refused to give away as he took another step back. "Meet Wren at the springs." He ran his hand over one of his daggers. "You need to let that finish healing so you can get back to training tomorrow."

Training.

Was that really all he cared about?

"Of course." My cheeks burned as I dropped my hands to my sides and balled them into fists to stop myself from reaching out for him. I was still reeling from the intoxication of his magic, but his words were sobering.

"Tomorrow we are training with a bow and arrow." He turned his back to me, and I stiffened.

"What? Why?" I quickly climbed off the table and stepped toward him. I had never even held a bow and arrow, and gods only knew that I would be worse with that than I was a dagger.

He barely glanced at me over his shoulder. "Because apparently you can't dodge a dagger or pull your own in time to protect yourself." He spat the words, and every bit of the buzz I had been feeling only a moment ago bled from my body. "Maybe you'll be better with a bow in your hand."

"Wren can teach me." I crossed my arms as I moved past him and toward the door.

"Wren is shit with a bow," he said dismissively.

"Then I'll find someone else." I pulled the door open, and the sound of the warriors milling about the healing quarters flooded the room.

"Over my dead body, Nyra." He spoke so casually as I walked away from him. "You're with me."

CHAPTER 18
NYRA

The heavy thuds reverberated through the walls, making my head ache. I groaned and grabbed a pillow, pressing it over my ears in a futile attempt to drown out the noise.

I had barely slept the night before, my mind racing with thoughts of Dacre and the conflicting emotions that surged within me.

I was more irritated by the fact that I somehow continued to forget how much of a jerk he was until he proved it to me over and over.

But when I closed my eyes, it was his father I saw with his hand still wrapped around my neck, so I forced them open and let my thoughts linger back to him.

They always found their way back to him.

"Wren," I called her name, but she didn't move an inch at the sound.

The knocking hadn't stopped.

I tossed my pillow aside and swung my legs over the

side of the bed. The room was dimly lit by the single fire-light lantern outside our window, casting eerie shadows on the walls.

I wrapped my arms around myself to stave off the cold air as chill bumps formed on my skin.

I stumbled toward the door and jerked it open to stop the insistent knocking.

Dacre's hand was held in midair, and I scowled. It was far too early in the morning to be dealing with him.

I leaned against the doorframe and caught his stormy eyes taking in my wrinkled shirt all the way down to my bare feet. He raised an eyebrow in disapproval. "Do you always answer your door like this?"

"What?" I breathed out and motioned toward the window. "I'm going to assume that the sun hasn't yet risen since the firelight is still dim. I'm sorry I didn't have time to fix my hair before answering the door."

"I'm not talking about your hair." His gaze fell to my legs and lingered there for far too long.

Heat flushed my cheeks, and I dropped my hands and tugged at the edge of my shirt that barely reached mid-thigh. "Well, I wasn't expecting visitors," I snapped, my irritation getting the best of me.

When he didn't answer and his gaze still hadn't left my bare thighs, I huffed. "Is there something you need, or can I go back to bed?"

"You don't get the luxury of sleeping in when your training is going so poorly."

"You're such an ass."

His gaze finally snapped up to meet mine. "So you've told me."

"I believe I also told you that I will find someone else to train me."

He braced himself against the doorframe, but he didn't let his gaze waver from me. "And how is that going for you?"

"Wren's going to train me."

"No. She isn't." His voice was low and dangerously calm, an ominous tone that sent a shiver down my spine. "Get dressed and meet me on the training grounds. We're starting in ten."

He didn't wait for me to respond. He simply turned away and headed down the hall as if I wouldn't dare disobey him.

I watched him walk away, my fists clenched at my sides as he did so. The audacity of him, thinking he could control every aspect of my life.

I had already lived that life with my father, and I had escaped it.

While Dacre hadn't shown me the same cruelty as my father, I was still caged here. I was still under someone else's control.

I closed the door and soundlessly dressed as my anger continued to build. Wren didn't so much as change her breathing as I tugged on my boots and slid my dagger into its sheath.

When I reached the training room, Dacre was already there in the dimly lit room, his arms crossed and a bored look on his face. My blood boiled at the sight of him, but instead of letting my anger consume me, I took a deep breath and forced myself to remain calm.

"Finally." His voice dripped with arrogance as he pushed off the wall.

"There's no one else here." I arched an eyebrow, not bothering to hide my annoyance. "It's still dark."

"We're not training here," he replied without looking at me.

He moved farther into the cave where an assortment of weapons were stacked against the wall, and I followed him.

"What?"

Dacre grabbed a bow and held it out in my direction. I took it before I could think better of it.

"You're too slow with a dagger and hand to hand. If you're going to benefit this rebellion in any way, then I need to give you a fighting chance."

If I was going to benefit the rebellion. Not survive it.

My neck was still sore from his father's hand, and I knew that he couldn't see past the bruises when he looked at me.

"Take off the vest and tuck your dagger into your waistband."

"What?" I looked at him and for the first time noticed that he wasn't wearing his vest or the usual array of weapons that he normally kept on him.

He looked so *normal*.

"Can you just do what I ask for once without questioning me?" he grumbled as he continued to look through the weapons.

"Of course." I slid my vest over my head before pulling out my dagger and tucking it into the back of my trousers as he instructed. I felt bare without the now familiar weight of my vest on my chest, but I pulled the bow over my shoulder, the string stretching to my hip, and took a deep breath.

The weight of the weapon felt foreign against my back, but I met Dacre's intense gaze head-on.

Dacre walked over to a stack of arrows and selected one, examining it carefully before placing it inside the quiver with several more. "The bow requires patience and precision, but it can buy you time more than almost any other weapon."

I nodded even though I was sure I would be as terrible with a bow as I was a dagger. I ran my fingers across the thick string at my chest. It seemed so simple yet so intricate.

Dacre lifted the quiver over his shoulder before he waved me forward, deeper into the cave. It was the same direction his father had taken us the day before.

The memory made a chill run down my spine. I felt more secure down here. I felt safer in the hidden city of my enemy than I did up on the land I had known my entire life.

"Have you ever shot before?" Dacre asked, breaking me out of my reverie.

"I've never even held a bow before," I admitted, feeling a flicker of embarrassment wash over me.

He sighed heavily, as if my answer was an inconvenience to him.

The air grew colder and more damp as we descended into the depths, the sound of our footsteps echoing off the walls. Dacre led me to a secluded area, where a single beam of light filtered in through a crack in the ceiling, casting a soft glow on the ground.

"Are we going up?" I asked, and I couldn't hide the shakiness of my voice.

"We are." Dacre turned to face me, his expression unreadable. "We can get much better practice up there than we can down here."

He climbed up onto a large rock before reaching his hand out for me. I ignored it, and instead, tucked my fingers into the groove where I had just seen him do moments before.

I hoisted myself up onto the rock and there was a twinge of pain in my arm. Dacre had healed it to the point that the injury was almost completely unnoticeable, but there was still a soft ache that wouldn't let me forget what happened yesterday.

It had put a steady fear in my chest I couldn't get to go away.

As I climbed up next to him, I couldn't help but feel the weight of everything pressing down on me. I took a deep breath, trying to clear my mind, and focused on Dacre's instructions as he pushed open the rock in the ceiling and pulled himself up.

I tried to do exactly as he just did, but my body wouldn't allow me the strength to do so. Dacre reached down, careful of my injuries, and pulled me up. I blinked over and over as the light of the rising sun blinded me.

Dacre moved the rock back in place before making sure it was covered once again with moss and leaves until it was almost impossible to spot.

We were at the edge of the forest, and I could smell the deep saltiness of the sea just beyond us.

My heart raced as I stood in the sunlight, taking in our surroundings. We were so close to the kingdom, and I couldn't help but feel a sense of urgency to move.

"Where are we going?" I asked as I toyed with the string of the bow that was still strapped over my back.

"Here." He lifted a dark cloak and tossed it in my direction, which I barely managed to catch. "We need to head to the bridge first, then we're going to the coast."

"The bridge?" I squeaked out as anxiety soared inside me.

I hadn't been back there since the day I was caught.

"Yes." He nodded as he lifted his own cloak and quickly pulled it on. "It's the only way to get to the coast, and I have something that needs to be delivered." He patted his chest absently.

I quickly pulled on the cloak, tucking my hair beneath the fabric as I tried to quell the nausea that rolled through my stomach.

"Let's go." He pulled his cloak tighter around him, and I followed closely behind him.

He easily guided us through the forest, even as I tripped over roots, and the sound of sticks snapping under my feet echoed around us.

Dacre's gaze swept over the forest as we moved, never relaxing for even a moment, and my legs felt weak.

By the time we made it just outside the city, the sun was sitting high in the sky.

We climbed up the hill that kept the city separated from

everything beyond, and every step felt worse than the one before.

I shouldn't do this.

We stepped into one of the alleys, and I let my gaze roam over the people who milled about. Some of them familiar, while others looked like complete strangers.

Dacre navigated the side streets effortlessly, and it only took us a few moments before I could see the palace looming in the distance.

I could see the girl I had once been. I looked up at the castle, and I could still hear my mother's voice as she told me tales of our kingdom from my bedroom window.

They hadn't let me go to the bridge then. I hadn't been able to leave the castle grounds at all, and I used to imagine exactly what the bridge would be like.

My mother's stories had been the only thing I had.

But her stories were nothing but fables that she told to a girl who was desperate for freedom.

I forced myself to take a deep breath, reminding myself of what was at stake as we approached the bridge. Clutching my bow string tightly, I took a step forward, and my foot landed on the first paver.

The hustle and bustle of the bridge was loud and imposing, but we walked in silence as Dacre maneuvered us through the merchants and finely dressed members of the kingdom who had risen with the early morning sun to make their deals.

The roar of the waterfall was almost deafening, and oddly, it brought me a sense of peace.

I couldn't help but glance over at Dacre, trying to read

his expression, but he was staring forward, his gaze scanning the crowd for whoever he was looking for.

We made our way through the throngs of people, each step harder than the last as we passed the front gate of the castle. There were four guards stationed out front, and Dacre avoided going anywhere near them as we crossed their path.

My heart thudded in my chest as I noticed the tension in Dacre's shoulders. He clearly didn't like being this close to the palace either.

As we weaved our way through the crowd, I couldn't help but notice the faces of the people around us. Some of them I recognized from my time on the bridge, others from the palace itself. I tightened my hold on my cloak and pulled it around me.

"Are you okay?" Dacre asked so quietly I barely heard him, but there was concern etching the lines around his eyes.

"I'm fine," I replied with the lie. I was so far from fine.

I glanced around nervously, trying to keep my tension from showing as Dacre navigated us toward the other side of the bridge.

We walked toward a merchant who had a plethora of pastries and warm breads on his cart, and my mouth watered. I recognized the man because he had been one that I had stolen from a few times.

He was one who let me get away when I knew I wasn't a good enough thief to do so.

"Two peach pastries, please." Dacre spoke before he reached into his pocket and pulled out a coin and a folded-up piece of parchment.

He reached forward, sliding both into the merchant's hand. The merchant's eyes didn't widen, and his hand didn't stutter as he pocketed both items.

He was expecting us.

"Of course," he muttered, looking to Dacre and then to me. He reached for the pastries, wrapping them tightly in paper before he handed one to each of us.

I hesitantly took it, holding it close to my chest, as I noticed Dacre's fingers mess with the paper on the back of his pastry and almost unnoticeably pull another piece of parchment from beneath.

"Thank you, sir." Dacre nodded once before leading us away.

We continued down the bridge as if nothing had happened. A young boy ran past Dacre, something cradled between his hands, and his shoulder slammed into mine as he passed.

The collision knocked the breath from my lungs, and I stumbled backward. Dacre didn't even flinch as he reached out and steadied me.

"Sorry!" the boy yelled, his eyes wide as he rushed through the crowd.

Dacre's hold on me tightened, and he pulled me behind him as two guards passed by us quickly. They were searching the crowd, no doubt on the hunt for the boy who had just stolen something, but that boy had disappeared into the shadows as if he had never been there.

That was what a life of hunger gave you.

Dacre kept my hand in his as he pulled us through the crowd until we reached the far end of the bridge. As we reached it, I could feel the harsh breeze coming off the waterfall beneath.

The stones changed from the rich pavers of the bridge to the old dusty cobblestone that ran through the streets. We were just about to step over that threshold when Dacre stopped so suddenly that my chest slammed into his back.

"What are you doing?" I whisper-shouted at him, but he didn't turn to look at me. Instead, he was staring straight ahead at the two guards that were talking and laughing at the edge of the bridge.

They didn't seem to notice our presence at first, but Dacre still wasn't moving. He was just staring ahead at them, only a couple feet from us, and he looked like he had seen a ghost.

"Dacre," I whispered his name and dug my fingers into his arm, but he still didn't move.

Both of the guards seemed to notice us then, when people moving about the bridge had to shift around us, and the alertness that crept up their faces reminded me of a snake waiting to strike.

"Papers." One of the guards, the bulky one whose uniform was wrinkled and soiled down the front from whatever he had been eating, stepped forward and held his hand out in our direction.

But Dacre didn't look away from the second guard.

He was wearing the same uniform as his partner, a uniform that represented their king, my father, but his was unblemished and immaculate, as though he had just left the castle gates.

He stood up straighter when Dacre refused to look

away from him and answer the guard who was speaking to us.

"Do you have your papers?" the guard demanded again, and I moved to Dacre's side, tucking myself beneath his cloak and wrapping my hands around his middle.

I was invading his space, but I couldn't bring myself to care in that moment.

I dug my fingers into his shirt, trying to pull his attention to me, but he was frozen. His jaw bulged, the muscles taut beneath his skin, and his dark eyes looked hollow.

"Dacre." I lifted my right hand and pressed it against his cheek, my fingers tucking around the back of his neck, and I pulled his head down until he was forced to look at me.

He blinked rapidly when his gaze hit mine as if he had just realized that I was standing beside him, that I was this close. "Do you have our papers?" I asked cautiously, and my pulse hammered so hard that I was certain he could see the movement in my neck.

He blinked again, and I watched his throat as he swallowed. "Of course."

He reached into his pocket, and I started to back away from him slightly, but his other arm shot out around my waist and his fingers latched on to my hip as he pulled me impossibly closer to him.

I pressed my hand against his chest as I tried to hold myself steady.

Dacre handed two pieces of folded documents over to the bulky guard, and as soon as he opened them, I instantly recognized the black Great Seal of the Crown.

It was almost impossible to replicate the details of the seal, which meant that these documents were stolen.

"Mr. and Mrs. Harlow," the guard read from the papers, then glanced up at us. "Where are you headed?" He seemed to take us in fully then, his gaze roaming over our clothing along with our faces, and my stomach clenched violently.

If he knew who I was, they would take me back.

Dacre would have no chance of protecting me. Not this close to the bridge.

Even if he dared.

My hands began to tremble, and Dacre reached for my hand that was resting on his chest and lifted it to his mouth for a brief kiss before he spoke.

He kept my hand in his, no doubt, to keep the guard from seeing how nervous I was.

"We're heading down to the sea." Dacre pulled a fishing net from behind his back that I hadn't noticed before. It was tucked into the belt of his trousers, and it looked well used. "I have the papers for my license to fish as well, if you need those."

The guard held up his hand to stop Dacre as he started rummaging through his pocket. "That won't be necessary. Get on your way and stop blocking the bridge."

"Yes, sir." Dacre took the papers back from the guard before I noticed his gaze slip back to the other guard for only a second. His body was completely rigid against me, ready for a fight, and I gripped his hand tightly in mine as I began leading us forward.

We made our way off the bridge, and I sighed in relief as I felt the rough cobblestones beneath my feet. Dacre's grip on my hand didn't falter as we moved through the crowded street and neither did the stiffness in his body.

"Are you alright?" I whispered when we were far enough away from the bridge, trying not to attract attention.

He nodded, but the movement was rigid and his jaw was clenched so tightly I worried that his teeth had to ache.

We continued along the cobblestone streets, the wind from the waterfall growing weaker the farther we got from the bridge. Dacre turned us down side streets and small alleyways until we reached the back of an older home that was built of red bricks and covered in years of dirt and overgrown weeds.

The home which I had slept behind for months with my friend.

"What are we doing?" I tried to pull my hand from his as my unease seemed to creep higher, but he held firm. I looked around, searching for any signs of Micah.

But there were none.

"One more stop." He lifted his other hand and knocked against the back door three times.

The door opened almost instantly, and a woman with white hair and a deeply lined face stood there staring at us.

"You brought them," she said, her voice giving nothing away.

Dacre let go of my hand and stepped forward. "I didn't have a choice."

She nodded, stepping aside to let us in. "Neither did she."

As we stepped into the dark hallway, the smell of musty old books and stale air hit me, making me feel claustrophobic. I looked back at Dacre as he closed the door behind us, his eyes still fixed on the old woman.

I wanted to ask him where we were, my body was begging me to run from this place, but there was something that stopped me. Dacre had looked over at me and his gaze held mine, unwavering and intense, silently begging me to trust him. Something he would never say with his words, and I hated that I did so, so easily.

As we stepped deeper into the dimly lit house, the walls seemed to close in on us, and I couldn't shake the chill that was running up my spine. The air grew warmer, and the scent of decaying wood and dust overwhelmed my senses.

We were led into a small room with a single window that looked out onto the overgrown garden outside. The woman seated herself at a rickety wooden table, where a candle burned weakly, casting eerie shadows on the dusty, cluttered surroundings.

Dacre released a deep sigh and followed suit, but I remained standing by the window. I pressed my hand against the small of my back, feeling the dagger there, and the deep grooves of the handle brought me the tiniest bit of comfort that I needed.

The woman was watching Dacre carefully, almost reverently, and I glanced away as I felt like I was intruding. There were so many things to look at throughout the room. The small bookshelves were chock full of trinkets, books, and photos. But there was one frame at the very top of the shelf that drew my attention.

It was a photo of a young girl, black hair blowing around her face as she laughed, but it was her eyes that caught my attention. She had the exact same eyes as Dacre.

"You look familiar to me, girl," the crone said from across the table, and when I turned back to look at her, she was assessing me with narrowed eyes.

I swallowed, searching for a response, but none came.

"She's one of the new recruits," Dacre answered as he leaned back in his chair, a loud creak echoing throughout the room.

The woman's eyes scanned my entire body, her gaze seeing right through my disguise that I wore so carefully. I felt exposed and vulnerable as she watched me.

"What's your name?" she asked, and there was no smile on her face as she studied me.

Dacre shifted in his chair, but he didn't turn to face me.

"Nyra," I answered her and crossed my arms over my chest.

"Like the former queen?" she asked, and her eyes only seemed to narrow further.

No one ever called my mother by her name.

"Exactly. I was named after her. My mother was quite fond of the former queen."

Lies. Lies piled on top of more lies.

She nodded her head slowly, but his gaze lingered on me.

"Nyra used to work in the palace." Dacre pulled another piece of parchment from his pocket, and for a moment, I wondered how he was able to keep them all straight.

"And how did you get out?" She cocked her head, studying me even more carefully than before.

"I ran." I shifted on my feet. "I ran during the chaos of the raid." I was honest, and that honesty cost me as memories of that day flooded me.

Dacre's shoulders stiffened as I spoke.

"Were you hurt that day?" she asked, and even though the woman didn't trust me, there was concern clouding her eyes.

Was I hurt? Gods, I couldn't think of that day without pain slicing through my chest.

"It doesn't matter." I shook my head and let my gaze flick back to the photo of the woman. "All I cared about was getting out of that palace."

"Well, Nyra." She said my name as if it didn't belong to me. "I'm glad that you made it out alive. Many don't."

I nodded, and more memories flooded me. Memories that I couldn't allow.

"I'm glad you made it to this one." She nodded her head toward Dacre. "My grandson will rule this entire kingdom one day."

She said the statement with such confidence, and when I turned back to face her, I didn't see a shred of doubt in her gaze.

Dacre's face twisted into something between pain and honor at her words, and his hand clenched around the parchment, crumpling it slightly.

"Were you able to get the information we need?" Dacre's tone was serious and cut to the point of why he was here.

A point that I had been left out of completely.

"I got what I could." His grandmother turned around, her chair creaking under her small frame, and she opened a drawer from the wooden hutch behind her.

"Remember, my boy," she said with a sternness in her voice that made my eyes widen. "Davian isn't to see."

My attention snapped to her at her words, but Dacre simply nodded as he tucked the papers into his pocket.

He was doing something behind his father's back?

"What happened to your neck?" She pointed a finger at me, but I was still thinking about what she had just said.

"I'm not very good in a fight."

She studied me far too intensely before she replied, "I don't think that's true."

I shifted uncomfortably under her penetrating gaze.

Dacre cleared his throat, breaking the intensity of the moment. "We should get going," he said, his voice strained. "We don't have much time."

"You remind me of her." She nodded to the woman in the picture frame. "My Camilla."

Dacre went rigid at the mention of her name. His eyes flickered with a mix of pain and longing as he turned and stared at the photograph.

"She made many sacrifices for the people she loved. Like you."

"I've not made any sacrifices."

"Haven't you?"

She stood and groaned as she held on to the table for support. She moved next to me and looked out her back window.

"The boy you used to stay with." She nodded to the back of her house. "I haven't seen him in days."

"What?" I whipped my head around so quickly to face her.

"He was still staying there after you'd gone, but it's been days since his return."

"What do you mean he hasn't returned?" I demanded, my voice trembling with worry.

The woman's gaze remained fixed on the garden outside. "Did he know?"

"Know what?" I swallowed, my mouth suddenly dry.

She turned to look at me, her dark eyes staring into mine for a long moment. She didn't say anything. She just stared, and I felt completely bare before her.

Did she know who I was?

My fingers felt numb as I clenched them at my sides. I didn't dare look at Dacre, but I could feel him watching us.

I gave my head the tiniest shake, and I didn't know why I did it. I didn't know this woman; I didn't owe her anything.

But by the way she was staring at me, I felt like she knew me.

The real me.

The lost princess of Marmoris.

Micah told me that was what they had called the princess for years as no one in the kingdom had seen her since she was little—seen me.

And I guessed I had been lost.

I slid my gaze over to Dacre and sucked in a ragged breath. He was watching me carefully, too carefully, and I was suffocating under their scrutiny.

"We need to go. We've risked too much time here already."

I nodded, my heart pounding in my chest. Dacre was right. We couldn't afford to stay any longer.

I forced myself to tear my gaze away from Dacre and

focus on the woman once more. Her eyes were still fixed on me, eyes narrowed as she cocked her head.

"If he returns, will you tell him that I'm alright?" I didn't want to think about him not returning. Was he arrested for thieving? Was he killed?

Dread washed over me, threatening to consume me whole.

"I will tell him that I saw you, but I don't know that you're alright." Her gaze trailed down to my neck, and I swallowed.

"Then lie," I demanded of her, and a small smile formed on her lips.

"As you wish." She suddenly dipped her head into a bow, her hair falling in her face, and I couldn't help but be taken aback by the unexpected motion.

I jerked backward, my back hitting the bookshelf behind me, and I looked to Dacre.

"We should go."

He nodded, moving forward and placing a brief kiss to his grandmother's head before he led me from the room.

I glanced back at the woman who was still watching me carefully.

"Be careful, Dacre. More now than ever." He huffed out a response, but the woman's gaze was still glued to me. "And, Nyra, stay with my grandson."

CHAPTER 19
DACRE

We made our way through the winding streets of the city, our pace quickening with each step.

Nyra's gaze was darting around the slums we now walked through, searching for someone.

Searching for him.

And I couldn't stop the irrational envy that coursed through me.

As we walked through the narrow alleyways, the pungent stench of garbage and piss filled my nose. But as we neared the edge of the city, a salty breeze brought relief, and I could almost taste the ocean on my tongue.

I started to reach for Nyra's hand as we began the descent down the sharp rocky hillside that bled into sand but thought better of it.

I had already let her get too close, even with my lack of trust, and it was foolish.

I wanted to kill my father for what he had done to her. I had threatened to do so last night.

My own fucking father.

His eyes had narrowed on me, suspicion coating every inch of his face, but I couldn't look at her neck and not be reminded of what he did. Even if she had it mostly covered with the cloak she now wore, the memory of those marks was branded into my mind.

As we reached the bottom of the hill, the crashing waves drowned out the sounds of the city behind us. The salty air whipped at our hair and clothes, filling our lungs.

The sea stretched out before us; its vastness mirrored in her eyes.

There were half a dozen ships lining the beach and the pier, and the shouts of the men getting on and off them echoed around us.

One of my informants leaned against the edge of the pier as he stared over at me, and I should have gone to him. He could have information, or better, supplies, but my attention was drawn back to Nyra.

I had already put her in danger today by bringing her with me, but I refused to leave her anywhere near my father when I wasn't there.

His words from the night before kept echoing in my mind.

Don't lose your head in the body of a traitor.

He trusted her far less than I did, and his distrust was only growing.

A surge of protectiveness washed over me as I watched her close her eyes and breathe in the salty air as if she had never been allowed the simple pleasure before.

I looked back to the sailor. He was smoking a pipe,

watching me carefully, but I turned my back to him and went to her.

"Do you ever wish you could just get on a ship and leave?" Her question caught me off guard as she opened her eyes, and the vulnerability in them made my chest feel heavy.

"The rebellion?"

"All of it." Her answer was immediate. "I used to look down here from the windows of the palace, and I would make up little stories in my head about stepping onto one of those ships and leaving."

She laughed softly and pushed the hood of her cloak from her head.

"I imagined being a sailor and living for nothing but the sea. But after a week, I think I'd get tired of the fish."

I smiled at her. The thought had never crossed my mind.

But as I looked out at the expanse of the sea, I allowed myself to feel the kind of longing she spoke of. It was not for a life of adventure at sea but rather for a life free from the pressure of my responsibilities.

A life of freedom.

"I've never really thought about it," I replied, my voice laced with a hint of weariness. "I've always known what my life would be."

Nyra turned to face me, her eyes searching mine. "Is it worth it?"

Her question caught me off guard once again. I hesitated, unsure how to answer. The weight of my duty pressed down upon me and a heavy sigh escaped my lips.

"Sometimes, I'm not sure," I admitted quietly before nodding down the beach.

She began walking with me without question.

"There are days when the burden feels unbearable, but then I remember why I fight, why I endure." My mother's face flashed into my mind as I said it, and I made myself remember the life she had been forced to live before she ran from the city.

Nyra's gaze softened, filled with understanding. "How are we supposed to train out here?"

"Over there." I pointed farther down the beach where the steep cliff wall loomed ahead.

We walked in silence until we reached the cliff and the secluded cove hidden from prying eyes, smooth with sand and a few scattered rocks. The waves crashed against the shore in a rhythmic symphony, drowning out any other sounds.

I pulled the cloak from my back, dropping it to the sand before I slid the quiver off and leaned it against the rock wall.

"We'll practice here for a bit before we head back." I looked over at her, and she was already pulling the bow from her back.

Nyra's hands shook slightly as she held the bow, her fingers brushing against the smooth wood. "How do you know about this place?"

My mother. But I couldn't think about her anymore today.

So instead of answering, I asked her the question that had been burning in my head ever since we left my grandmother's. "Who was the guy my grandmother was asking you about?"

Nyra jolted back, and her gaze dropped to the sand. "No one."

More lies.

I didn't know how she could keep them straight at this point.

"You do realize that I heard you talking about him, right?" I let the anger force its way into me. I much preferred it over the emotions that overwhelmed me when thinking about my mom.

"You do realize that you're not privileged to every bit of information about me, right?"

I choked on a laugh at her words. "Considering I know nothing about you, I think that point is crystal clear."

She took a deep breath, her eyes fixed on an imaginary target ahead.

Her grip on the bow tightened, her knuckles turning white. Her voice was strained as she spoke. "His name is Micah. He's my friend."

I stayed silent, studying her face for any signs of deception. A tumultuous mix of emotions swirled within me, battling against reason and instinct. I wanted to press further, to demand answers and unravel the secrets she held so tightly.

I reached for the quiver of arrows and moved closer to her. I took one arrow in my hand as I lined myself up behind her.

I pulled the bow from her hand before lining it up correctly and notching the bow with my other. Her back was pressed against my chest, and my arms were wrapped around her body as I tried to set her up.

"Did he ever touch you?"

"What?" she stuttered.

"Micah." I practically spit out his name. "Did he ever touch you?"

Her body tensed against mine, but she made no move to pull away. I could feel the rapid thud of her heartbeat against my chest, mirroring my own. The warmth of her body enveloped me, distracting me from the task at hand. "No. He didn't."

Because she was mine.

That thought was ridiculous. I hadn't even known her then, but I couldn't stop the jealousy that raged through me at the thought of anyone else touching her.

"Good." I gritted my teeth as I tried to tamp down my possessiveness. I had never felt like this before.

"You can't be serious, Dacre." She huffed, and I breathed in her scent.

"Focus on your breathing," I whispered, my breath tickling her ear. I could sense the hesitation in her grip as I gently adjusted her fingers on the bowstring. "This is all about control."

Nyra's breath hitched as she leaned into my touch.

Closing my eyes, I relied on muscle memory and years of training to guide my hands. In a swift motion, I released the arrow and watched it soar through the air, hitting the sand at the very far end of the cove.

Nyra gasped, and she turned to face me over her shoulder. "Teach me."

And so we began.

We spent hours honing her skills, correcting her posture, and improving her aim until the sun was starting to dip in the sky.

Nyra had done well, but she was starting to grow frustrated.

"You're getting ahead of yourself," I barked at her when one of her arrows landed nowhere near where she was aiming. "Focus on your breathing and let your instincts guide you."

"My instincts are guiding me to aim this arrow at your head right now."

I chuckled and leaned back against the wall. "I would be worried if you had any aim at all."

She cursed under her breath and notched another arrow. When she let this one fly, it landed even farther than the last.

"You're angry."

"You noticed?" she snapped and moved through the cove to collect her arrows.

"You're letting your anger take control instead of you." I rubbed at my chin. "You'll never be able to shoot if you can't keep yourself calm."

Nyra shot me a glare as she retrieved her arrows, her frustration evident in every step. "Well, it's hard to keep my shit together when you keep pushing my buttons," she retorted, her voice laced with sarcasm.

I couldn't help but smirk at her response. "That's what training is for. Take a moment to…"

She pointed the arrow in her hand in my direction as she cut me off. "If you say breathe, I swear to the gods, I will do my very best to aim this at you."

"Testy." I held my hands up in surrender. "Would you like me to take the edge off for you? Help you relax?"

She rolled her eyes, but I watched as she pressed her legs together. "Don't you dare touch me."

I pushed off the wall and took the smallest step in her direction. "Pick up your bow and stop me then."

She surveyed the distance between us, her eyes flicking back and forth as her chest rose and fell rapidly. The tension crackled in the air, thick and palpable.

And gods, I didn't want her to stop me.

I watched as she hesitated for a moment, her fingers clenching around the bow before she lifted it along with the arrow. The determination in her eyes matched the fire that burned in my chest.

"I don't need your help," she declared, but even as she spoke those words, her expression softened, and her eyes searched mine with a longing that reflected in their depths.

Without breaking eye contact, I took small steps toward her, closing the gap that separated us. The anticipation hung between us, thick enough to taste.

"I haven't stopped thinking about that night."

She let her eyes fall closed for only the briefest moment before they shot back in my direction. They were glazed over with lust and defiance. Her grip on the bow tightened, and I smiled as she notched the arrow.

"I've been trying to forget." Her voice quivered.

More of her lies.

"Which part?" I cocked my head as I studied her. "When you begged me or when your pussy dripped down my fingers with how badly you wanted me?"

She released the arrow so quickly that I wasn't

expecting it. It whizzed past me and dug deep into the sand about three feet to my right.

"Did I hit a nerve?" My eyes widened as I chuckled and ran a hand over my chest.

Gods, I wanted her.

We still stood several feet apart, but I could see her hand trembling and her eyes flashing with a mix of anger and arousal that made my cock harden painfully against my trousers.

"Don't come any closer," she warned, but her eyes begged me to.

"You've done nothing to keep me away." I looked back at the arrow that had been nowhere near me. "I already crave you, even though I know you're keeping things from me. You think an ill-shot arrow will be the thing to stop me?"

The heat between us was so intense the wind seemed to hush in our presence.

Her eyes never left mine as I took another step closer and she staggered back, the bow slipping from her fingers.

"That was a mistake." I smirked and took another step, closing the distance between us even more. "Now, what will protect you?" My voice was low and filled with my want for her. I wanted to push her buttons further.

I wanted the girl to fight.

Her breathing had become ragged, and her chest heaved with the effort. Her lips were parted slightly as I took yet another slow step, closing the gap between us, and she stumbled back another.

"Fine. You win." The air crackled around us, and I could feel it coiling around my insides.

"That's not how this works." I shook my head. "An enemy isn't going to let you call a truce."

As I closed in on her, I could feel the air around us grow thick and heavy, like a storm brewing on the horizon. It was as if the very fabric of our reality was being stretched and twisted, bending to our will.

"Is that what you are?" She planted her feet in the sand and stepped away from me. "My enemy?"

"If that's what you want me to be."

The air around us shimmered as if caught between two worlds. Her gaze flickered toward her bow that lay in the sand, then back to me.

I lunged forward, crouching low and reaching for the bow. But before my fingers even touched the cool wood, a forceful blow knocked the wind out of me and I stumbled backward, my chest on fire from the impact.

I gasped for air, rubbing my chest where the pain was most intense. Nyra's blue eyes were wide with shock as she stared at me.

"What…what was that?" I wheezed, struggling to regain my breath.

"I don't know," she retorted, but her gaze was glued to her hands. "I don't know what happened."

Nyra stumbled backward, her eyes growing wider with each passing moment.

The air crackled with an electric intensity, sending shivers down my spine, and for the first time since I had laid eyes on her in that cell, I could feel her power.

"Nyra."

Her eyes darted to me, and there was so much fear swimming in their depths. "What just happened?" Her voice trembled like a leaf caught in a gust of wind. "I…I didn't mean to do that."

I extended a cautious hand toward her, but as my fingertips grazed her skin, a burst of energy erupted from her core into my skin.

"You said you didn't have any magic."

"I don't." She quickly shook her head. "I've never…"

Her words trailed off as she clenched her fists, her body trembling with the force of her own power.

I reached out to her again, not with caution this time, and I took one of her elbows in my hands. Her power thrummed beneath my fingers.

I wanted to believe her, but everything in my gut was telling me not to. "It would appear you do now."

I could see the panic rising within her, threatening to engulf her entirely.

"Or that you're a better liar than I've given you credit for."

She tried to pull away from my touch, but I held on to her. Her eyes searched mine, desperate for some reassurance. But I had none to give her.

Not when I felt like such a damn fool. Not when I desperately wanted to believe her, but I couldn't.

"Dacre."

"We should get back." I reached down and grabbed one of the arrows from the sand. "It isn't safe for us traitors to be traveling the bridge after dark."

"Traitors?" She questioned the word.

"I'm a traitor of the crown." I pointed to my chest before grabbing my cloak. "I have no idea who it is you're betraying."

CHAPTER 20
NYRA

I should have gone to sleep, but adrenaline coursed through my body.

I could still feel my *power*.

The city slumbered as I quickly moved through the quiet pathways and made my way to the training grounds.

I had my bow and quiver strapped to my back, and even though my fingers ached with the hours of practice we had been doing, I felt desperate to wrap my hand around the grip.

I hadn't been good at it, but it gave me a sense of control that I hadn't had before.

I quickened my pace as I crossed the old wooden bridge, avoiding looking down at the murky water below. The rickety boards creaked and swayed under my feet, making me feel unsteady as I moved toward the other side.

The streets were quiet, but I could hear the echoes of footsteps somewhere in the distance as I made my way to the training grounds. A constant blanket of darkness cast over the deserted grounds, and there was only a faint flicker of firelight lighting the path.

With the others gone for the night, a sense of eerie stillness settled in the air.

But I still continued forward and leaned my quiver against the far wall as I pulled my bow off my back and ran my fingers along the taut string.

The night air was cool against my still buzzing skin as I took an arrow from the quiver and moved several paces in front of a makeshift target on the wall. I held the bow in my hand at my side as I stared at it.

Traitor.

The word ran over and over in my head, and I couldn't stop thinking about it no matter how hard I tried.

Dacre had barely spoken to me after we left that cove. He thought I was a liar, and I was, but not about this.

Not about my power.

My power.

Each syllable felt like a stranger in my mind, but the lingering warmth of magic still coursed through my veins. It was hard to accept the reality of what had happened.

A sharp, searing pain radiated in my chest as memories of my father's relentless attempts to pull power from me flooded my mind.

Guilt slammed into me as I thought of my mother. Tears threatened to spill over as I thought about what could have been, if only I had been stronger.

She would still be queen.

She would still be alive.

My hands, once steady, now shook uncontrollably. I stared down at them, desperate to summon the power that

Dacre had forced from me. But despite my efforts, my palms remained empty and powerless.

I didn't know what was wrong with me.

"You do realize that staring at the target doesn't actually do anything, right?"

I jumped at the sudden sound of Dacre's voice, my eyes scanning the dimly lit training grounds. My heart rate jumped as I saw him sitting against the wall, his form illuminated by a flickering flame nearby. One leg was bent in front of him while he leaned his head against his arm, exhaustion evident in every line of his body.

"What are you doing here?" My fingers clenched around the smooth, polished wood of my bow, and I shoved both hands behind my back.

His eyes narrowed as he leaned in closer, his gaze fixated on me. "I should be the one asking you that," he said, his voice low and predatory. "It's late."

"I couldn't sleep." I swallowed and looked back to the target for only a moment before looking back to him.

He ignored my words completely and squinted his eyes for a moment as he assessed me. "You should leave."

I scoffed at the absurdity of him. "No. You should leave." I pointed the tip of my arrow in his direction.

"Not tonight, Nyra." His voice was cold and harsh as he spoke, each word laced with venom. My skin prickled in response to the malice radiating from him. "I'm not in the mood to deal with you tonight."

"You're never in the mood to deal with me." My heart raced, sending waves of heat through my body. "You're always in a bad mood."

He was silent for a long moment, but his gaze didn't

waver from me for even a moment. "I am." He nodded as he ran his hand slowly over his jaw. "But tonight, I might take it out on you."

My heart hammered against my rib cage, echoing in my ears as I locked eyes with him, and the surge of power that had been fueling me earlier now felt like a raging storm inside me. An ache started low in my belly, and I struggled to keep my breathing steady.

"And what if that's what I want?"

He swallowed hard, and I watched as his Adam's apple bobbed in his throat. "You don't."

"You don't know that." My voice trembled, but all I could think about was the way he had touched me before and the way he had acted as if he regretted it ever since.

I couldn't get his words from earlier out of my head. The memory of him standing before me with fire in his eyes as he accused me of betrayal played on repeat. Even the set of his jaw and the clenched fists at his sides conveyed his conviction.

He had called me a traitor before, but this time, every part of him believed it.

Dacre's eyes narrowed, a dangerous glint flickering in the dark depths. I could still see his anger in his gaze, but there was also an undeniable hunger that boiled just beneath the surface.

"Tell me what you want, little traitor," he demanded, his voice low and menacing, and my stomach ached as the last word slipped from his lips.

I swallowed, trying to keep my nerves in check. This was a dangerous game, but I couldn't stop myself from playing. I didn't want to stop. "Don't call me that."

"I'm not in the mood to take orders from you." He leaned his head back against the wall as if he needed to get a better look at me. "Tell me what you want."

"I don't know," I whispered, feeling the lie in my voice even as I said it. "But I can't stop thinking about it."

He let out a low laugh, the sound echoing through the empty training grounds. He turned away from me, letting the flickering firelight cast shadows over his face as he clenched and released his jaw.

"What do you want?" I asked, my voice barely audible.

He turned his head, a glint in his dark eyes as they raked over my features with a predatory intensity. His lip curled into a sly smirk, and I couldn't help but feel a shiver run down my spine.

"Drop that bow and get on your knees." He ran his tongue over his bottom lip, and I almost fell to them at that one movement. "Then I want you to crawl to me and beg."

I didn't know what I was doing, but I felt my hand instinctively tighten around the bow's grip as if it were the only thing keeping me anchored to reality. My other hand moved, and my fingers trembled as they wrapped around the string, the cold wood a stark contrast to the heat that was surging through me.

"You can't just order me around like that." My voice trembled, and he smirked at the sound.

"Yes. I can." He ran his hand over his knee, and I felt mesmerized by watching him. "And you want to do it."

The way he said the words made my spine snap straight and my core tighten.

"Don't you?"

He was right. I couldn't deny the desire that was pooling in my core and threatening to consume me.

But I also hated that he knew it. With a simple look, he knew what he was doing to me.

I started to shake my head to deny the truth that we both knew, but he wouldn't allow it.

"On your knees, Nyra. Don't make me tell you again."

"I…" I trailed off, unable to form the words. My heart was pounding in my chest, and I could feel the unfamiliar magic coursing through my veins. I wanted to do what he said, and there was something about the way he was commanding me to do so that made me want it even more.

Even though I knew I should have left and gone straight back to my room.

I should have been running from this place altogether.

But it wasn't what I found myself doing as I gently laid my bow and arrow on the ground at my side and dropped to my knees before him.

The searing heat of the firelight flickered and danced in the darkness, its light casting eerie shadows across Dacre's cold, hard features as he watched me without making a single move. I felt as though I were being devoured by his eyes, consumed by the darkness that threatened to swallow me whole.

"Good girl," he purred, a sinister smile curling his lips as he watched me with anticipation.

I swallowed, the ache in my belly intensifying as I stared at him.

"Come here." He lifted a hand, and he gave a subtle curl of his fingers, beckoning me forward.

My hands trembled as I leaned forward and pressed

them into the cold, hard ground. I dropped my head as my chest heaved, trying to swallow breath after breath.

"Look at me."

My head snapped up at his command.

"I want to see you as you crawl to me." Dacre ran his hand down the front of his trousers, and my breath hitched at the bulge I saw there.

For a moment, I was frozen in place, my heart racing at his command. But then, against every ounce of willpower I had left, I pushed myself forward, crawling slowly toward him. The hard ground was rough against my knees, and I could feel the gritty dirt sticking to my palms.

As I reached the edge of his boot, I stopped, still on my hands and knees, but looking up at him with wide eyes.

"Closer," he hissed. His eyes were dark, almost black, with a glint of hunger that made me feel alive. They seemed to devour me, like two deep pools of obsidian that held a hint of fire within.

I took a deep breath as he widened his legs, making room for me to come even closer. I began to crawl again, pulling myself toward him inch by excruciating inch.

The intense warmth emanating from his body enveloped me. It was intoxicating.

Dacre reached forward as I stopped, his finger lifting my chin higher until I had nowhere to look but at him. His thumb ran over my bottom lip roughly, and I felt powerless under his touch.

In spite of my magic surfacing, he still managed to make me feel weak.

"You look so fucking beautiful like this," he groaned as he dropped his hand to run over the length of my neck. He toyed with my hair, his touch gentle, almost tender. And yet, there was a fierce intensity behind it, a promise of something more.

He leaned closer to me until his lips brushed against the skin of my throat. I gasped, a shiver running down my spine as I felt moisture pool between my shaky thighs. Dacre was dangerous, but the ache in my core only grew stronger with each passing second, my need for him becoming almost unbearable.

"Please," I whispered, my voice barely audible.

"I love hearing you beg," he murmured against my skin, and I couldn't stop the small whine that passed through my lips. "You like it too, don't you?" He groaned and his tongue ran over the skin where my neck and shoulder met.

My hands trembled against the ground, and I desperately wanted to reach out for him. To touch him in ways I had been imagining for days.

"Fucking beg me, little traitor," he commanded before his teeth grazed against my skin.

The moan that left my mouth was loud enough to make my cheeks flush with embarrassment. I pressed my thighs together and desperately wanted to reach between them with my fingers and ease the ache that was threatening to consume me.

Instead, I dug my fingers into the ground and begged the gods for Dacre to do something.

For him to do *anything*.

"Gods, you do love it." He pulled back and his hand moved to the back of my neck. He gripped my hair roughly in his hand before he forced my head back farther, and the edge of pain made my body tighten even more. His mouth ran over mine, not in a kiss, more of a caress as he spoke against my mouth. "Let's see how much you love to beg while I taste you."

He let go of my hair abruptly, and I rocked forward without his touch. He moved out from in front of me, and I tried to watch him as he stood and moved behind me.

My breath caught in my throat as I forced myself to remain still on my knees, my eyes drawn to the ground as I tried to calm my racing heart. I could hear the rustle of his clothes as he moved, and my hands trembled against the ground as anticipation raced through me.

His hand lazily grazed over my lower back, and I let out a small whimper. His touch was so light, I would have thought I imagined it if it hadn't been for the electricity that was sending shivers down my spine.

I tried to focus on that feeling, to revel in the heat of his touch, but my mind was clouded by the need for more.

His hand skated over my lower back until he reached my ass, and I surged forward as he slowly ran his hand over the curve until he reached the edge of my thighs. It didn't matter that I was fully clothed. I felt completely bare before him.

I turned and glanced over my shoulder to see his hungry gaze taking in every curve of my body. Self-consciousness crept into me, but he quickly snuffed it out as his hands pressed more firmly against my thighs and a ragged groan left his mouth.

He dropped to his knees behind me, and my chest heaved as my core tightened.

His hands moved in a lazy path over my thighs, gently

grazing against my core, and I arched my back in a desperate attempt to get closer to him.

"Such a needy little thing." He laughed, but the sound held no humor as his hands moved to my hips and gripped just above the hem of my trousers.

His thumbs slid just beneath the fabric, only enough that there was nothing between us, but my skin burned as if he were branding me.

Dacre leaned forward, his breath hot against my neck as his body curved over mine. "You look so perfect like this," he whispered hoarsely. His fingers dug possessively into my hips, making my muscles clench involuntarily.

His hands slowly moved down the sides of my thighs, and I could feel the rough fabric of his trousers that did little to hide his want for me. His hand moved around my body, and I jerked forward as his fingers roughly pushed against my sex through my trousers.

"Are you ready to beg yet?" His lips were against my ear, and I gasped as his teeth nipped against my sensitive earlobe.

"Please," I begged, my voice rough with want.

His fingers pressed harder against me, and pleasure lashed through me as he began to stroke me through the fabric of my trousers.

"Please what, little traitor?"

"Please touch me, Dacre." I was too needy to be embarrassed by my words. I knew I would most likely regret them tomorrow, but right then, I had no room for shame.

Not when I wanted him so badly.

Not when I felt so raw from everything that happened today.

His laugh was dark and seductive, and I shivered at the sound. "You're not begging me properly, little traitor." His hand pressed hard against me, and I could feel my clit throbbing beneath his touch. "I think I need to give you more motivation to plead for it."

I didn't answer him, and I didn't need to. He pulled his hand away from me, and a whimper passed my lips before I could stop it. He was making me feel crazy, but I didn't care.

His hand skated up my abdomen until his finger dipped into my belly button through my shirt. My hands and knees were beginning to ache, but I couldn't think about that when he slowly lowered his hand again, but this time slipping it beneath my trousers. His warm skin pressed against mine as he moved his hand against me at an achingly slow pace.

"Are you wet for me?" His opposite hand pressed against my chest and lifted me until my back was leaning on his chest.

I nodded my head, and he ran his nose along the length of my neck as his fingers gently drummed against the top of my sex, making me more than aware of how desperately I needed him to lower them.

"Use your words, Nyra."

Nyra. Gods. For the first time since I arrived, I regretted not giving him my real name. He would hate me for who I really was, but I wanted to hear him call out *my* name; I wanted to hear how desperately it would roll off his tongue.

"Please, Dacre," I breathed, my voice laced with my want. "I'm so wet for you."

His groan was deep, and I could feel the vibrations travel through my body and echo in my core. "I think I should make sure of that."

His hand slowly lowered, and I reached behind me, gripping onto his thigh for support. I dug my nails into his trousers as his fingers found the wetness that was waiting there for him, and I arched back against him.

His cock pressed firmly against my ass, and I ground down against it as his fingers skimmed over my clit.

"Fuck." He groaned against the back of my neck as his fingers slid through me easily. "Is this all for me?"

He spread the wetness around as he toyed with me, his two fingers sliding up and down my pussy as if he was trying to memorize every inch.

"Please." I ground harder against him and whimpered at the feel of him behind me. He was everywhere, yet he felt just out of my grasp all at once. "Dacre, please."

His fingers paused just over my clit before he pressed down roughly, and my hips shot forward at the sudden change.

"Oh gods."

His fingers began to move in small circles, the movement concentrated exactly where I needed him, and I chased the feeling with my hips.

I was so busy focusing on those two fingers that I missed the way his other hand crept up my chest and pressed against my jaw. He forced my head toward him, giving me no choice but to face him, and his dark eyes narrowed as if he couldn't decide if he wanted to fuck me or destroy me.

In that moment, I would let him do anything he wanted.

Looking up into his stormy eyes while he played my body so easily was too much, and I whimpered as I closed my eyes and tried to focus on nothing but the feeling he was giving me.

"Look at me." The command in his voice forced me to snap my eyes back open, and I watched as he licked his lips just as his hand tightened on my jaw. "You're such a needy little traitor."

His thumb grazed across my bottom lip, and I was desperate for him to kiss me. I wanted it more than anything. I nipped my teeth against the tip of his thumb before he could pull it away, and his gaze somehow darkened even further.

"So fucking greedy." His words sounded like a plea before he jerked my chin toward him and slammed his mouth down against mine. The kiss had none of the delicacy of his fingers. It was as if something had snapped inside him, some need that he wasn't able to control, and my kiss was the only cure.

His lips were harsh against mine, his tongue begging for entrance, and when I gave in, his teeth nipped, and he kissed me as if he worried he would never taste me again.

His fingers slid lower until he pushed them both inside me, and I groaned against his mouth at the fullness of him.

"Gods, look how well you take me," he murmured against my lips as he curled his fingers in and out of me and pressed his palm against my clit. "When I can't sleep at night, it's because I can think of nothing but the way you would look beneath me with my cock sliding in and out of this tight little pussy."

His words sent shivers through my body, and I arched

back into him in response. It was too much for me to handle, the feel of him, his words, and the heat between us that threatened to burn me alive.

The way my power seemed to thrum inside me with him being so close.

"Please," I begged again, my voice raw and pleading. My hips bucked against his fingers as I desperately tried to find some relief.

He groaned against me, his breath hot against my cheek.

"You want more?" He withdrew his fingers from me, and I groaned in protest.

I looked at him, searching his face for some clue as to what he was thinking, but he wasn't looking at me. He was staring down at his hand as he pulled it from my trousers and lifted it before us. I could see my wetness coating his fingers, and a flush crept up my face at the sight.

"You've had the pleasure of tasting this, but I haven't." He moved his hand closer to us until he held it directly between our mouths. "It's another thing that keeps me up at night. Imagining exactly what you'll taste like."

I whimpered, and he slid his fingers between his lips as his gaze held mine. He didn't lap at them gently. Instead, he made a show of rolling his tongue over every inch of his fingers that were coated with me.

He pulled his fingers from his mouth and ran them over my lips before they fell to my neck. "It's even better than I could have dreamed."

His hand tightened on my neck, and he moved closer to me until his mouth was pressed against mine. "Now I won't be able to sleep until I taste it from your skin." He nipped my bottom lip between his and sucked it into his mouth. "I think we should fix that."

Dacre pulled away from me, but his dark gaze lingered on my mouth. My body shook with need as I tried to calculate his next move.

"On your feet, Nyra."

My pulse hammered in my chest, and I tried to calm my shaking hands. He was going to taste me, put his mouth on my body, and even though I had never wanted anything more, fear raced through me.

"What if that's not what I want?" My voice trembled with need and betrayed my words.

He smiled at me, the move sinister and lacking warmth, as he reached out and cupped me directly between my thighs. "We both know it is. You want it, and you're going to take it."

His hand pressed firmly against me, and my thighs trembled with how badly I needed him.

"Stand up. Don't make me tell you again."

I hesitated for only a second before I pushed myself to my feet. Dacre lifted higher on his knees before me, and his hands trailed over my thighs before settling on my hips.

He pulled at the edge of my trousers, lowering the leather down an inch before he stared up at me. "If this isn't what you want, you need to leave." His voice was lethal. "I'm not lying when I tell you that I will take whatever I want from you, and you will not leave this cave until the sound of my name is the only thing you can taste on your tongue."

He watched me with a hungry gaze, his eyes dark and

intense as I made no move to leave, and we both knew that he held all the power in this moment.

I felt a strange sense of relief wash over me, accepting that I was at his mercy. I didn't want to fight what I so desperately wanted any longer.

He slowly pulled my trousers lower and lower, taking my undergarments with them until I was bare before him. I swallowed down a shaky breath as I fought the urge to cover myself.

"So beautiful," he murmured so quietly that I barely heard him.

He leaned forward until he was lined up directly in front of my pussy, and I looked to the ceiling as I felt him press a kiss to the inside of my thigh before he brushed his nose against my center.

"Look at me." His voice was low and commanding, sending a surge of desire through me as I obeyed.

His hands ran up the length of my thighs, and they trembled beneath his touch.

"I want you to watch me as I taste what's mine for the first time."

"It's not yours." I somehow managed to find my voice long enough to say the one thing I shouldn't have.

His hands paused at the apex of my thighs, and he grinned before quickly moving them to my pussy and spreading me open with his thumbs. "Let's see exactly how long you can hold on to that resolve, little traitor."

I opened my mouth to argue back with him, but he leaned forward, and his tongue ran up the length of my pussy and threatened to bring me to my knees. I gripped my fingers into his hair, holding on to him as I tried to breathe, but it was no use.

He sucked my clit between his lips, and I cried out.

And I couldn't look away from him.

There wasn't an ounce of tenderness in his touch, and as his teeth raked against my sensitive flesh, my moan could be heard throughout the entire cave. My fingers raked through his hair, tangling in the strands and pulling him impossibly closer to me.

I had never felt such pleasure, such overwhelming, consuming want. Dacre's mouth feasted on me, exploring my body in ways I didn't know were possible, as his hands gripped my thighs so tightly that I bit down on my lip at the sting of pain.

He hummed against me, the sound vibrating through me, and then, finally, he lifted his hand and thrust two fingers inside me.

I arched my back, meeting his hungry mouth, my body feeling so greedy for more. My stomach tightened and my breath hitched as he moved his fingers in and out of me in perfect rhythm with his tongue. I could hardly spread my legs, and the position made me feel so incredibly full of him.

"You're so tight," he murmured against my skin. "So wet."

His words were like fuel to my already raging desire, and I couldn't help but beg for more. "Please, Dacre...please..."

I gripped his hair tighter in my hands, and he looked up at me. The wickedness in his eyes reflected the desire I could feel rippling through me. "You want to come?"

"Please." The way I begged him felt so foreign on my tongue, but it also felt so right.

He chuckled, the vibrations spreading through my sensitive flesh. "Tell me who this pussy belongs to." He plunged his fingers deeper inside me, making me cry out at the mixture of pleasure and pain.

I bit down on my tongue because the smirk on his face made the defiance inside me flare. But I knew that he was going to get exactly what he wanted. I would tell him anything to finally give me the feeling I was chasing so desperately.

"Fucking tell me it's mine, little traitor." He curled his fingers deep inside me before he sucked my clit back into his mouth, his tongue flicking over the sensitive bud in a rhythm that would make me tell him anything.

"It's yours," I managed to choke out. The admission felt like a knife twisting in my chest, but I couldn't deny the truth. He was the last person I should have been saying it to, but he was the only one I wanted.

Dacre pulled back with a smirk, his eyes glinting wickedly as he released my clit from between his lips. I was trembling on my feet, my mind a whirlwind of emotions and sensations. I felt humiliated, aching, and yet so alive.

"That's right." His fingers moved in and out of me at a pace that was driving me crazy. "This is mine, little traitor. You are this fucking wet for *me*. No one else."

He leaned forward and nipped his teeth on my inner thigh. "You're mine." The growl that ripped through his chest was almost enough to push me over the edge.

He continued to lick and suck at my clit, his fingers still

pounding inside me until I felt like I was going to lose my mind. My fingers squeezed in his hair, and I could feel tears prick behind my eyes.

"Mine."

I cried out as he thrust his fingers in and out of me, the vibration of his claim pushing me over the edge. My body shook uncontrollably as I came, my orgasm rippling through me like a current.

His other hand wrapped around my back, holding me steady as he milked every bit of my orgasm from my body.

"That's it." I could feel him watching me, but I didn't care.

My pussy was clenching around his fingers in a desperate need for more, and I never wanted to come down from the high he had given me.

Dacre didn't let up as he continued to slowly fuck me with his fingers, prolonging the pleasure, making me cry out his name again and again until my body went limp against him.

Dacre pulled his fingers out of me, slowly withdrawing his hand from my wetness.

I looked down at him and felt a strange mix of relief and shame course through me.

He climbed to his feet, licking his fingers clean, a satisfied grin on his face, before he reached forward and helped me pull my trousers back in place.

I looked down and saw how hard he was beneath his trousers, and despite the shame that I couldn't deny, I wanted to touch him. I wanted to have the same power over him that he had over me.

I ran my hand over the length of him, and he groaned

low and guttural as his hand slipped into my hair. He tugged back, forcing me to look up at him, and the desire that was staring back at me was almost enough to make me come again.

"I want to touch you," I whispered, and his gaze seemed to become impossibly darker.

"Nyra." His growl was a warning, but it did nothing but send a thrill through me.

"I want to taste you."

His hand tightened in my hair to the point that I cried out in pain, but still, I wanted more. I wasn't sure there would ever be a moment when I didn't want more from him, and that thought scared me.

I could feel the heat in his eyes as he studied me, the intensity of it making my heart race.

"Do you want me to get on my knees for you?" I reached out and pressed my hand against his chest.

"Little traitor." The words were a plea on his lips.

"Dacre." The deep voice echoed through the space, and my spine stiffened.

Dacre dropped his hold from me and stepped back quickly as if he had been caught with the traitor that he thought I was.

That he *knew* I was.

His gaze flickered to the towering figure in the entrance to the cave, his eyes blazing with fury.

"Father." Dacre's voice faltered for only a second before he straightened and looked every bit of the leader that they had forced him to be.

My stomach ached, and my body screamed for me to

run. I hadn't seen Dacre's father since he choked me while looking for answers I had refused to give.

"We just got word," his father said, his gaze flickering back and forth between me and his son, even though Dacre had his back turned to me. "We're leaving within the hour."

I brushed my hand through my hair, pushing it out of my face, even though I was sure I still looked completely disheveled from what we had just done.

"I'm ready." Dacre nodded, stepped forward, and leaned down until he grabbed my discarded bow and arrow in his hand.

"Do you need to escort Nyra back to the quarters?"

"No." Dacre's answer was swift and firm. "She can find her own way back."

It was a dismissal. He had just been as desperate for me as I had been him, and now he was dismissing me as if I was nothing.

His father looked at me, and there was nothing but distrust staring back at me. It made me feel sick to my stomach. Yet, Dacre just stood there.

"I'm more than capable." I stepped forward and jerked my bow from Dacre's hand before quickly moving back to the target and grabbing my quiver from where I left it.

I could feel Dacre watching me, but I didn't give him the satisfaction of turning back around.

CHAPTER 21

NYRA

The wine burned my throat as I took another drink.

"Maybe you should slow down." Wren was watching me carefully, and she hadn't stopped ever since I told her what happened.

She was the only one I had told about my power.

If that was what you could even call it. I could hardly feel it anymore. I knew it was still there, but it felt like it was hiding from me now.

I held my hand. palm up, in front of me, and I attempted to call it forward. But there was nothing.

It had disappeared as easily as Dacre had two days ago.

Two days and not a single word. Not a single trace of power, and I wasn't sure which angered me more.

I had been desperate for some trace of power my entire life, but still, all I could think about was him.

"I'm good." I held the bottle close to my chest as I stared at the fireplace, watching the flames lick up the sides of the stones.

Wren sat beside me, refusing to leave my side, but Eiran was pressed in on the other side and I had barely paid him any attention since he placed the bottle in my hand.

"Training was good today." He nudged my shoulder, and I glanced over at him. "As much as I hate to admit it, Dacre was right about the bow."

Dacre.

Why did he have to say his name?

My stomach clenched at the memories of the other day. Every thought more confusing than the last. The cove, my power, the way he had touched me, the way he *dismissed* me.

My mind was a chaotic battlefield of thoughts, all centered around him and the overwhelming emotions he stirred within me.

I took another swig of the wine, trying to drown out thoughts of him that were threatening to overwhelm me.

The alcohol was clouding my head, and even though I was angry with Dacre, I couldn't ignore the burning desire I felt whenever I thought of him.

"Nyra, are you alright?" Wren's voice cut through my thoughts, and when I looked over, my chest ached at the concern in her eyes.

"Yes, I'm fine," I lied, taking another sip of the wine.

Eiran was observing me carefully, as he did all day today during our training, and I just wanted it to stop.

Without thinking, I blurted out the question that had been nagging at me all day. "Actually, have you seen your brother?"

Wren's eyes widened, and her body stiffened as she slowly turned to face me.

"He's been busy with my dad," Wren said slowly, her tone gentle but distant. "But I saw him and Kai come back earlier."

I shook my head, taking another gulp of wine to ease my nerves. "Is he in his room?"

Wren's eyes softened. "You've had a lot to drink tonight. Maybe we should head up."

I knew that she was just trying to look out for me, trying to make sure that I didn't end up hurt, but it still pissed me off.

I didn't want to be protected from her brother.

"Okay." I nodded and climbed to my feet, still clenching the wine in my hand. "Night, Eiran." I saluted him with the bottle as I swayed slightly, and his gaze jumped to Wren.

"I've got her." She wrapped her arm in mine and led me from the room and up the stairs. I stumbled a little, but she kept me steady, her brows scrunched as we walked.

"Why did you say that your brother doesn't heal?"

"What?" Her eyes widened as she clung to me. We had barely made it halfway up the stairs, but I was desperate for her answer.

"Before, when I was hurt, you said Dacre didn't heal." I couldn't stop thinking about it, obsessing over what she meant.

"You should ask Dacre about that." She looked away from me and up the staircase.

"I'm asking you, Wren." I wrapped my hand around her forearm and squeezed. "Please."

She glanced back at me, and her face softened. "Dacre used to heal." She swallowed, and I could feel the slight tremble of her fingers against me. "But he hasn't healed anyone since he couldn't save my mother."

I sucked in a sharp breath that made my head swim, and Wren kept going. "He tried to heal her as the other's continued to fight. He kept trying as they lifted her limp body and brought her back home." Wren's voice shook as she spoke. "They had to pull him away from her cold body because he refused to stop trying. But the magic used against her was too much."

"I didn't know." I held onto more tightly, both of us clinging to the other for support. "I'm sorry."

"I haven't seen him heal anyone since that night. Healing magic is rare, and most healers are taken to the capital as soon as their magic is discovered. We only have a few healers here, but still Dacre refuses."

She searched my eyes for a long moment before she spoke again.

"He inherited his healing abilities from my mother, and he feels like he failed her."

"He didn't..." I shook my head as I tried to wrap my head around what she had just told me.

"I know that." She tightened her hand around my arm before leading me up a step. "But it doesn't matter what I think. Dacre hasn't been the same since we lost our mother. He will never forgive my father, never forgive himself."

"He's healed me twice." I admitted out loud even though I felt like I was simply reminding myself of that fact. My heart raced in my chest as I tried to work out what that meant in my alcohol-clouded mind. "Why?"

My stomach tightened as I asked the question. I didn't know if I was ready to admit the answer to myself or why I desperately hoped there was only one reason for him to do so.

I wanted Dacre to care for me as I had begun to care for him.

"Come on." Wren led me up the last few steps. "You've had too much to drink, and we both need our sleep."

"Thank you for taking care of me."

She chuckled and pulled me against her side. "It's what friend's do."

When we made it to our room, Wren reached for the handle, but I slipped my arm from her hold. I moved before she could stop me, and I pounded my fist against Dacre's door.

"Nyra, it's late," Wren hissed even though there was humor in her voice, and she tried to pull me back to her. But not before I pounded one more time. "Dear gods."

She laughed, and I couldn't stop the giggles that bubbled up my own throat.

Neither one of us could stop, the hall echoing with the sound of our hysterics, and Dacre ripped open his door and stood before us, his face contorted in anger.

I couldn't control my laughter as he glared at us with a mixture of annoyance and frustration.

I couldn't stop the thought from plaguing my mind. *Does he care for me?*

"What time is it?" His voice was rough with sleep, and his hair was mussed from his bed.

I desperately wanted to run my hands through it.

"Midnight," Wren said, still giggling.

Dacre's eyes narrowed on us, but I was too busy staring at his bare chest. "What are you two doing?"

"Where have you been?" I crossed my arms, still clinging to the bottle of wine, and studied every inch of him. "I haven't seen you in days."

"I didn't realize you were keeping tabs on me." His gruff retort slammed into me, and my gaze shot up to meet his.

Heat rose in my cheeks, but I refused to let him win. "No tabs." I held up my hands in surrender. "I just found it odd that I trained with Eiran today after you said... What was it?" I tapped my finger against my chin. "Oh, yes. I was yours."

"Oh shit." Wren laughed under her breath, and Dacre's eyes narrowed on me. "We should head back to our room."

"Are you drunk?" His voice was laced with a hint of warning.

"Why?" I cocked my head to the side and studied him. "Are you keeping tabs on me?"

"Wren, you can head back to your room. I've got Nyra." There was irritation lacing his words as his sister looked back and forth between us. A threat in his eyes that made me press my thighs together.

"I don't know if that's a good idea."

"It's okay, Wren." I nodded. "I'll be fine."

She took a step back, the wood floors creaking softly beneath her feet, but neither Dacre nor I looked away from the other.

"I'll kill you, Dacre." She spoke just as I heard her open the door to our room, and I smiled. "Don't you dare hurt her."

The door closed behind her, and Dacre crossed his arms

as he leaned against his doorframe. "What are you doing here, Nyra?"

I wanted to see you.

I couldn't tell him the truth, so I resorted to another lie. "I just wanted to make sure you were okay. People were talking about a lot of commotion up there."

That wasn't a complete lie. I had overheard some warriors in the training room talking about Davian and the supposed intel he had been getting.

"And who said that? Eiran?"

"No." I shook my head and pushed off the wall behind me. "Eiran's focus was elsewhere."

That made the muscles in his jaw tic. "I'm sure it was. Didn't I tell you that I didn't want you training with him again?"

"You've told me so many things." I waved my hand dramatically. "It's hard to keep track of all your commands."

I closed the distance between us, and he tensed. "You should go to your room."

"You..." I pressed a finger against his chest. "Should stop ordering me around."

I let my hand drop an inch and splayed my fingers out over his bare skin.

Dacre's breath hitched, and I could see the desire in his eyes mirroring my own. His gaze flicked to my lips, and I couldn't help but lean in.

"What are you doing, Nyra?" he finally demanded, his tone low and dangerous.

"I told you I wanted to touch you," I whispered, leaning in closer as I lowered my hand. His hand moved quickly, snatching my wrist before I could get to where I wanted. "To taste you."

"That's not happening tonight." His eyes narrowed dangerously, and his grip on my wrist tightened, pulling me even closer.

I felt a surge of determination and frustration, my heart pounding in my chest. Our eyes met, and I could see the conflict in his gaze. His hand, still holding my wrist, shook slightly. I knew he was torn between desire and duty, just as he was torn over who he believed me to be.

"But I'm wet." I ran my tongue over my lips, and he looked mesmerized by the movement. "I trained with Eiran today, but all I could think about was you."

He scowled down at me, his eyes burning with black flames. "You're drunk."

"And I'm going to make myself come whether you're with me or not." My words were much bolder than I felt, but I didn't regret them.

"Fuck," he swore under his breath before he grabbed the front of my shirt and pulled me into his room.

The door slammed shut behind us, and my skin buzzed with more than just the alcohol. It was anticipation. It was my *power*.

It purred in his presence, waking in a way I hadn't been able to get it to do on my own.

"You know others can hear you out there in that hall, right?" He ran his hand through his hair, and he looked so frustrated with me.

"You don't want them to know that I make myself come while thinking about you?"

I could see the tension in his face as he processed my

words, his eyes narrowing dangerously. But to my surprise, he didn't let go of my wrist. Instead, he pulled me closer, our bodies pressed together. I felt the hardness of his erection against my thigh, and my breath hitched.

"You're playing with fire, Nyra," he warned, his voice low and gruff.

"Let me touch you," I whispered, my voice shaky with lust and a desperation I wished I could control.

He hesitated for a moment, his grip tightening on my wrist before he backed me up until the backs of my knees hit the bed.

"You're drunk." He reiterated his words from earlier.

I opened my mouth to argue, but he pressed a finger against my lips to stop me. He kept pushing until I fell backward, my ass hitting his mattress, and he leaned into my space.

"I'm not going to fuck your mouth for the first time when I'm not even sure you'll remember it."

I pressed my thighs together, trying to ease the ache there, but it was no use.

He jerked the bottle of wine from my hand, bringing the alcohol to his lips, and he drank as he pulled a chair from the corner of his room and set it directly in front of me.

He dropped into the chair, letting the bottle of wine rest on his thigh, as he stared at me.

"Go ahead." He nodded toward me, and my stomach sank.

"What?"

He smirked, watching me carefully as I tried to figure out what he wanted. "Touch yourself." He settled back in the chair. "You said you were going make yourself come. Show me."

"I…" My voice shook as I gasped for words.

"You heard me." He arched a brow before taking another drink of the wine. "Go on. I want to watch you."

I couldn't catch my breath as I stared at him, the alcohol mixed with my power pounding in my veins.

I reached for the top of my trousers, undoing the ties there, and he tsked.

"Take off the shirt. I want to see you."

I should have told him no. I should have gone back to my room, but I didn't do either of those things. Instead, I grabbed the hem of my shirt, and with trembling hands, I pulled it over my head.

Dacre's gaze darkened, narrowing on my midsection, and I tossed my shirt on his mattress.

"Nyra."

"Yes?" I pushed down the top of my trousers, lifting my hips slightly as I shoved them past my hips, but Dacre wasn't moving.

"Who the fuck did that to you?"

I followed the direction of his gaze, and I winced at the scar that wrapped around my back and over the edge of my stomach. I quickly put my hand there, covering the mark.

"It's nothing."

His gaze darkened, but he still hadn't pulled his eyes away from my midsection.

I sat there, feeling exposed and vulnerable, but I knew he wasn't going to let this go.

"You didn't answer my question." Dacre growled, unmoving. "Who hurt you?"

"It was a long time ago."

His gaze slammed into mine, and I was shocked by the amount of venom I saw there.

"Who?"

"My father." It was the only truth I could give him.

Dacre ran his hand over the back of his neck, and I could feel him pulling away from me, retreating into his anger where he was comfortable.

"It was a long time ago, Dacre. It doesn't matter."

"Doesn't matter." He laughed, and the sound startled me. "You think that anyone could get away with hurting you and that it wouldn't matter?" He shook his head.

"I don't want to talk about this." I leaned back on my elbow and trailed my hand along my chest as he watched. "I didn't come in here to talk at all."

"Nyra." He growled my name, and I let it fuel me as I cupped my breast in my hand and squeezed my nipple.

"Yes, Dacre?" I whimpered his name and blocked everything out of my mind except for me and him.

Nothing else mattered in that moment. Not my past, not his.

Not our loyalties.

It was just me and him, wrapped up in a web of lust and unspoken emotions.

He watched me, his eyes burning with a mix of desire and fury, his jaw tense as he tried to control himself.

But I didn't care. I wanted him, needed him.

I let my fingers trail down my stomach, feeling the scar that served as a reminder of my past, and then continued down to my waistband. I hooked my finger in the edge of my trousers and slowly pulled them down, revealing the juncture between my thighs.

My hands trembled, but I didn't stop.

"Spread your legs. Use your fingers to spread your pussy open for me so I can see," he commanded, his voice low and demanding.

Dacre's eyes never wavered, never blinked, as I reached between my legs and slipped my fingers inside, feeling the moisture there.

I moaned softly as my fingers sank into my wetness, my hips bucking slightly at the contact. Dacre's eyes darkened further, his breaths coming in ragged gasps as he watched me.

"Fuck, Nyra," he growled, his voice a husky rasp that made shivers race through me. "You're going to make me come just from watching."

He shifted his hips in the chair, pulling his cock from his shorts, and I gasped as I watched him run his hand up and down the length of it.

Dacre's eyes blazed with hunger and need as he watched me touch myself, and he matched my movement, stroking himself harder and faster. I could see the tension in his muscles, the way his jaw clenched, and I knew that he was as close to losing control as I was.

I slipped another finger inside my pussy, stretching myself open and moaning at the fullness I felt. My hips bucked again, chasing the pleasure that was building inside me.

"Please, Dacre," I begged, my voice barely more than a whisper. "Touch me."

He glanced down at my hand, still buried between my

legs, and then back up to my eyes. For a moment, I thought he might refuse, but then he stood, still stroking himself as he stared down at me.

"You look so perfect." He dropped to his knees before me and jerked my pants farther down my legs before tossing them on the floor.

I moaned, dropping my head backward, and I jumped, my hips surging forward as I felt cool liquid drip down my pussy.

My eyes shot open, and I watched as Dacre held the wine bottle above me, letting the wine drip down my body and between my thighs.

"Dacre," I whimpered his name, and he looked up at me.

"I don't think I've had enough." He leaned his head down, and he lapped at the wine from my pussy.

My hips bucked, and I gasped as his tongue moved lower, flicking at my clit before dipping into my wetness. My hands fisted in the sheets, and I moaned loudly, my body arching off the bed as he continued to pleasure me with his mouth.

"So sweet." He let more wine fall from the bottle, and he licked every drop of it up from my skin, his eyes never leaving mine.

His fingers trailed up my legs, spreading me open, before he pressed them against my clit, rubbing them in time with his tongue.

"Dacre, please," I begged, my voice high and needy. "I need more."

He groaned, long and loud, before he moved until he was kneeling on the bed between my thighs. His cock looked so huge as he continued to run his hand up and down the length of it, and for a moment, I thought he was going to fuck me.

And the realization hit me that I desperately wanted him to.

I wanted to be claimed by Dacre in every way possible.

"Where do you want my cum, little traitor?"

My gaze snapped open, and I watched him as he pressed the head of his cock against my clit. My back arched off the bed, and I whimpered as he moved, sliding up and down my wetness before pushing into my clit once again.

"Inside me," I answered and felt his cock twitch as he ran it back through the length of me. He pushed the head of his cock into my entrance, only slightly, before he pulled back out.

Shivers ran through my body, and I was ready to beg him.

"You want me to fuck you?" he asked and pressed against my clit once more.

I was so close. So damn close.

"Yes," I whispered, my voice trembling with anticipation.

He looked down at me, his eyes dark and hungry, filled with desire and so much possession. "You are mine, Nyra."

"Yes," I breathed and moved my hips, trying to catch the high he was dangling in front of me. "I'm yours."

"That's a good fucking girl." He pumped his cock, his hand hitting me, pressing hard against my clit, and I almost came out of my skin.

"Oh, gods." I kneaded my breasts in my hands and listened to him groan as he watched.

"I'm going to cum all over you, little traitor. Mark this body in a way that your fake rebellion mark never could."

My legs clenched around him, trying to close, but he refused to allow it.

"Let me have it, Nyra." He growled and his movements became more frantic and forceful, and I couldn't hold on any longer. "Give me what's mine."

My body was strung like a bow, taut with tension, and the moment it snapped, there was no holding it back.

I cried out, my hips bucking against his hand, just before I felt his own pleasure release.

"Fuck," he grunted, his voice hoarse as he pumped his hand harder and his cum hit my clit.

I jerked forward and watched as he came against my pussy, coating me in his cum and letting it drip down my thighs as the wine had done only a few moments before.

"Dacre," I said his name like a plea, but I didn't know what I was asking. My body was still reeling from what we had just done, my heart slamming into my chest.

His gaze met mine, and his eyes were almost solid black as he ran a finger through my pussy and lifted it between us.

I sucked in a breath, feeling suddenly self-conscious. I tried once again to close my legs, but he was still between them, forcing me to remain exposed to him.

"Taste." He lifted his finger to my mouth, and I let him run his finger along my tongue. "You look so pretty covered in my cum."

CHAPTER 22
DACRE

Nyra released the string, and the arrow shot through the air, narrowly missing her target.

She was getting better.

"Watch your breathing," I said as she reached for another arrow. "Steady it."

She nodded and notched another.

In my peripheral vision, I caught a glimpse of movement. Kai was walking toward us, his expression so dark that I could almost see the black swirls of his magic trailing behind him.

"What's wrong?"

He nodded his head to the side, clearly not wanting Nyra to overhear whatever it was he had to say.

I glanced at her, but she was busy staring at the target.

"Davian intercepted a missive. It's from your grandmother."

"What?" I pushed off the wall and faced him fully.

"I have no idea how, but he's asking for you." Kai

looked over his shoulder and my stomach tensed. "He's demanding your presence."

I straightened and checked over my daggers instinctively. "Take Nyra back to her room."

He nodded and looked back over at her.

"Keep her with Wren."

"What's going on?" Nyra asked, holding her bow loosely in her hands.

"Nothing." I shook my head. "I need to meet with my father. Kai's going to take you back to your room."

"I'm capable of getting there myself. I think I've finally figured out parts of this city." She smiled and my chest ached.

"Just do me a favor this once and let him take you."

Her shoulders straightened at my words, but she nodded once as she slipped her bow onto her back.

I had no idea what my father could have intercepted from my grandmother, but I knew it couldn't be good. My grandmother never sent word to me.

I came to her.

That was our agreement.

I had been doing it for years behind my father's back and dread filled my stomach at the thought of him knowing.

"I'll be back."

"He's at his house." Kai winced as he spoke the words. He knew how much I hated going back there.

I nodded once, and I didn't wait for either of them to say goodbye. I turned on my heel and stormed out of the training grounds, my mind racing with a million different thoughts.

Whatever my father found, I couldn't let it escalate into something that could threaten my allegiance to the rebellion or my allegiance to my father.

Unfortunately, those two things weren't the same.

My power slithered through my veins, and I could feel its restless energy, yearning to be unleashed.

My feet dragged along the pavement, each step heavier than the last as I neared our house. My heart raced, knowing the confrontation that awaited me. It had been a long time since I truly feared my father, but I could feel that familiar apprehension creeping into me now.

The orange glow of flames danced on the window, casting eerie shadows in the dimly lit room. I took a deep breath to calm my nerves and raised my hand to knock on the heavy wooden door. My fist tapped gently against the surface, but my heart was beating so loud, I was sure he could hear it from inside.

"Come in." The sound of his voice, deep and familiar, echoed through the door. I hesitated for a moment before finally pushing it open and stepping inside.

The scent of bourbon and old books filled the air as I crossed the threshold.

As I stood in the living room, dust particles swirled around me in the firelight. The floorboards creaked beneath my feet, and the faint smell of my father's soap still lingered in the air. This house had once been filled with laughter and love, but now it felt empty and haunting. Avoiding the family photos on the mantel, I faced my father.

It was just me and him, surrounded by the ghosts of our pasts we both tried to avoid.

He lounged in a worn leather armchair, his long legs crossed and one ankle resting on the opposite knee. A crystal tumbler filled with dark amber liquid dangled from his fingertips as he took a slow sip.

He gestured toward the cluttered kitchen table, where an unfolded parchment sat among half-empty mugs and scattered papers. "I have something for you," he said, his eyes locked on mine.

The delicate handwriting on the parchment was a familiar sight to me, and my heart raced as I looked away from it and back to my father.

"What's that?" I asked, trying to keep my voice steady.

"That's what I want to know too." His weathered hands, covered in calluses and scars, gently traced the rim of the glass as he spoke. "But it's not addressed to me. It's addressed to my son."

His eyes narrowed, following my every breath, and I could practically see the wheels turning in his head as he carefully observed me.

"What does it say?" I asked carefully.

He gestured with the glass on the table as he spoke, the dark liquid swirling inside. "You should read it," he said, his voice low and hesitant. "I don't think I can do it justice."

Something was wrong, very wrong.

I knew my grandmother wouldn't have sent a missive unless she felt it was dire, and now it was in the hands of my father.

With cautious steps, I made my way to the table, keeping a careful eye on my father's stern expression. As I reached for the parchment, I willed my fingers not to tremble.

The words, written in my grandmother's delicate cursive, were short and to the point. But their impact was like a heavy blow to my chest, crushing everything inside me.

My vision blurred as I read and reread each line, trying to make sense of what she was saying.

The king's soldiers are scouring every inch of the city, searching for her.

She is no longer hiding in the safety of the castle walls.

We both know who she is, Dacre, and you must protect her.

Protect her at all costs.

Everything inside me recoiled at her words.

Nyra.

I scanned over her words once more. She had to be wrong. Nyra wasn't the princess of Marmoris.

She was a girl who barely had power; she had been locked in the dungeons under the palace itself; she had been on the run.

Everything came to a halt as the truth crashed into me, stealing my breath.

She was a liar.

Nyra had been hiding in the streets since the raid. She had said that she hadn't been able to get out before then.

I remembered her from the raid. I had seen her even though I couldn't completely place her through all the chaos.

She had lived her life in the palace because that was her home.

The truths started tumbling out before me. Clicking into place.

The lack of her power, the way she feared going on the bridge more than I'd ever seen another, the scars that stretched so far over her back that they wrapped around her stomach.

She told me that it had been her father.

What she didn't say was that it was the king.

I tore my gaze away from the page in front of me and looked up at my father. His eyes were fixed on me, but he tried to appear nonchalant as he leaned back against the chair. I could feel his silent scrutiny weighing on me. "What is this?"

My father's gaze didn't falter. "That, my son, is a letter from your grandmother," he said, his voice low and steady. "Care to let me in on who she's referring to?"

I stared at the parchment, feeling a heavy weight settling onto my chest. "I have no idea."

"You're a great leader, Dacre." My father stood and set his glass down on the table before me. "You'll make a great commander of this rebellion one day or of this kingdom if we ever defeat the king. Read that parchment again. I think you'll find the truth lying in its pages."

I pressed my lips together as I studied him. "Which is?"

"Don't be daft, Dacre." He ran his hand along his sword that sat on the table before us. "You think I wasn't aware that you've had communications with your grandmother even though I forbid it? Do you really think I didn't have eyes on you when you took that girl there who you've spent more time training in your bed than you have in combat?"

My heart pounded in my chest as I felt a wave of betrayal wash over me. He had been watching me.

"She's all we have left of Mom," I retorted, my voice shaking with anger and confusion. "You can thank her for half of that intel I deliver to you."

My father's expression remained impassive, like stone. "That's the part I can accept. I've made up my own excuses for you in my head." He tapped his fingers against his temple. "But the princess?"

I shook my head as I searched his eyes. "I had no idea who she was."

His eyes narrowed, studying me carefully. "You were never suspicious of her?"

"I was." I was honest as my heart raced. "But the thought of her being the princess never crossed my mind. I thought she was a traitor, just using our rebellion as an escape from a life she didn't want."

I hesitated, my mind racing as I tried to find the right words as I tried to find the truth.

"It would appear you were right about that. The little bitch is a traitor indeed." My father's face curled into a sneer. "She's been living in our city. You brought her here when you should have left her behind to rot in that dungeon, and now the daughter of that wicked king knows things that we have been protecting most of our lives."

He walked over to the mantle and picked up a framed photo of my mother, his fingers tracing over the glass.

"Bring her to me."

A chill ran down my spine as I watched my father's eyes narrow on my mother's photo.

"What are you going to do to her?"

There was a flicker of anger in his eyes as he brought them to meet mine. "Don't make me repeat myself, son. Bring her to me now."

I swallowed hard, feeling the weight of the truth pressing down on me. I owed my father loyalty, but all I could think about was Nyra.

Fuck. That wasn't even her real name.

"Tonight, Dacre." He moved toward me, and with a firm grip on the back of my neck, he pulled me close until our foreheads touched. "She is the key to it all."

I nodded once, and without another word, I left in search of the princess.

CHAPTER 23
NYRA

I sat gingerly on the edge of Dacre's neatly made bed, careful not to disturb the stack of books next to it. I picked up the one on top, its pages yellowed with age and marked with creases. As I flipped through, small puffs of dust floated up into the firelight streaming in from the window. My eyes scanned over the words, but my mind was elsewhere, too preoccupied by the unsettling feeling that something wasn't right.

I heard the sound of voices in the hall, and I quickly closed the book, returning it to its place, and stood.

The door creaked open, and Dacre slipped inside, carefully shutting it behind him. He stood with his back to me, hunched over slightly, hands clenched at his sides. The room seemed to tremble with the tension that rolled through him.

"Are you okay?" I asked and took the smallest step toward him.

His back went rigid, and I felt a shiver run down my spine as I inched closer.

"I'm fine." He slowly turned toward me, but he didn't look fine. His dark gaze looked *haunted.*

"Are you sure?"

"Can we not talk about it?" He shook his head and let out a humorless laugh. "I don't even want to think about my father anymore tonight."

"Okay," I said hesitantly as he closed the gap between us.

"What are you doing in here?" His gaze flicked from his bed and back to me.

My stomach dipped, and suddenly, I was questioning coming in here at all.

"I was waiting for you. You looked upset about whatever Kai was saying."

Dacre's long strides brought him across the room in seconds. Before I could catch my breath, his hand was tangled in my hair, pulling me closer. He pressed his lips against mine with a fierce urgency, and I responded eagerly, kissing him back with just as much need.

Dacre's grip tightened in my hair, and desire coursed through me. His lips were warm and demanding, consuming me in a firestorm of emotions. I wrapped my arms around his neck, pulling him closer, feeling his heartbeat thundering against my chest.

Just as suddenly, Dacre broke the kiss, staring into my eyes with a desperate intensity. "I need you," he whispered hoarsely. His voice was raw, filled with a longing that left me breathless.

Gods, I needed him too.

I nodded, not trusting myself to speak. Dacre's gaze never left mine as he kicked off his boots. His hands shook slightly, but he didn't seem to notice.

I slid my own boots off my feet before tugging my trousers down my hips.

"Gods, you're beautiful." Dacre closed the gap between us, tucking his fingers into my pants and pulling them the rest of the way down my legs.

There were no delicate or teasing touches. It was all urgency, and I was thankful for it.

I felt desperate and crazed, and I wanted him to feel the same loss of control when it came to me.

Dacre's hands were everywhere—tracing my back, sliding down my sides, exploring every inch of my skin. My heart pounded against my chest as I felt his fingers delve into my pussy.

"Already so wet." He growled and nipped at the sensitive skin of my neck.

"Yes." I nodded and pulled at his shirt until he lifted it over his head and let it fall to the floor.

I wanted all of him, completely bare.

There were a million secrets between us, but I didn't want them here tonight.

I just wanted him and me.

Not a rebel and a princess.

He pulled me closer, his lips finding their way to my neck, sending shocks straight to my core. I moaned softly, my head falling back in pleasure.

Tonight, I wasn't a princess or anything else that I pretended to be.

I was his.

No matter what happens.

I was his.

Dacre's hands shook as they undid his trousers with haste. I followed suit, eagerly shedding the remainder of my clothes until I stood completely bare before him.

The room filled with our hushed breaths and the steady rhythm of his heart. He lowered me gently onto the bed, his eyes never leaving mine. There was a raw hunger in his gaze, a longing that matched my own.

I reached up, running my fingers through his disheveled hair, feeling the warmth of his skin. I wanted this. I needed this. I wanted to be completely lost in the moment, in him, and forget about everything else.

He lowered his head, his lips brushing against mine, and I felt the world around me melt away. His tongue flicked against mine as his hands roamed my every curve.

I moaned softly, my breath catching in my throat as he traced the sensitive skin on my throat and chest. As our kiss deepened, I felt his erection press against my thigh, and I pressed them together to stave off the ache.

"I want you," I whispered, my voice low and husky.

He kissed his way down my body, his hands trailing over my skin. My heart was pounding in my chest as I felt his lips graze the sensitive skin of my stomach, moving lower and lower until they reached the juncture of my thighs.

He glanced up at me, his eyes dark and intense. "Are you sure?"

"Yes," I breathed, my breath coming in short, sharp gasps.

He pressed a kiss to my pussy, a chaste touch of his lips

that had me squirming beneath him before he stood back to his full height and gripped his cock in his hand.

He rubbed the head through me, spreading the moisture, and I lifted my hips, silently begging him for more.

"Please," I begged him, the desperation in my voice matching the ache between my legs.

Dacre met my gaze, his eyes filled with a hunger that matched my own. He positioned himself at my entrance, and I gasped as he slowly pushed inside me.

The sensation of him filling me was overwhelming, and I lifted my hips upward, trying to adjust. His hands were on my waist, holding me steady as he pushed deeper inside me inch by inch.

"Are you okay?"

I nodded even though I wasn't sure I was telling the truth. He was so big, and it hurt, but all I knew was that I didn't want him to stop.

I never wanted him to stop.

Our eyes locked as he began to move, his thrusts slow and deep. The bed creaked beneath us with each move-ment, filling the room with a low, steady moan.

I ran my fingers through his hair, pulling him closer, our lips brushing against each other's with every motion.

"Gods, you're so tight," Dacre groaned, his voice hoarse against my mouth.

I moaned, the pleasure of being filled by him over-whelming me. Dacre's eyes were locked on mine, his breathing uneven as he continued to thrust into me.

"More," I gasped, feeling the desire building within me.

Dacre's expression changed, his eyes darkening as he complied with my request. He increased his pace, his thrusts more fierce, more demanding. My head fell back, lost in the sensation of his cock sliding in and out of me, the pain mixing with pleasure as it coursed through my body.

My hands clawed at the sheets, my hips meeting his every movement. I could hear him grunting, his breath ragged as he fought to maintain control.

He slid his arm around my back and lifted me. I wrapped my legs around his waist, my hands holding on to his shoulders, as he moved to the head of the bed and sat with me straddling him.

"Ride me." He groaned, and I pulled my knees beneath me.

I lowered myself onto him as far as I could and whimpered. This position felt far deeper than before. Far more intimate.

I began to ride him as he'd instructed, my hips moving in a steady rhythm that matched his thrusts. The bed was now a mixture of moans, gasps, and the slap of his skin against mine.

I leaned forward, resting my hands on Dacre's chest, my breasts brushing against him with each movement. His hands gripped my hips, helping me rise and fall against him as he thrust up into me.

"Harder," I urged, my voice low and breathy. Dacre responded, his thrusts growing more pronounced, his hips snapping up to meet each downward stroke.

My head fell back, my hair cascading around me as I arched, and Dacre's fingers moved against my clit until my entire body trembled against him.

"Tell me you're mine." His voice was more demanding

than I had ever heard before, and I gave him exactly what he wanted.

"I'm yours."

He held the back of my neck, cradling me against him as our bodies slammed together. It was overwhelming and all-consuming, and I found myself never wanting to leave this moment.

It was just him and me, and nothing else mattered.

"I'll make you fucking forget anyone who ever came before me."

I snapped my eyes open to meet his and told him the truth. "There's only ever been you."

His breath hitched, and every part of his body stiffened. "This pussy belongs to me. You belong to me."

I nodded frantically as I cried out.

"I'm so close, Dacre," I cried and dug my fingers into his hair as I rode him.

Our chests were slick with sweat as they heaved against one another. His thumb rubbed rapid circles against my clit, and I couldn't hold back any longer.

Pleasure coaxed me from every direction, and I clamped down around his cock as I cried out.

"That's it, princess." His words slammed into me, and I fought to catch my breath as I opened my eyes and searched his.

What did he just say?

He wrapped an arm around my back, helping my body lift and fall against his as I rode out my orgasm.

"Come for me, Verena."

I instantly recoiled from him, but his grip was unrelenting. He held me against him, his black eyes boring into mine, and I couldn't stop the pleasure still coursing through my body even as it mixed with fear.

As his body pressed into mine, I felt my muscles contract and release in rhythm with his movements, even as I shoved at his shoulders. He finally released his grip on me and I collapsed onto his bed, watching as he stroked himself to completion, his chest rising and falling with each heavy breath as he spilled his release onto his stomach.

We stared at one another, neither one of us daring to move, but his next words were like a shock to my system.

"For such a filthy fucking traitor, you opened your legs for a rebel so easily."

"Dacre." I grabbed the blanket from his bed and held it against my chest, trying to cover as much of my body as I could. Fear, cold and ruthless, shot through my veins as I watched him.

"You should leave." He stood from his bed, reaching down for my clothes that were on the floor, and tossed them in my direction. "My father knows who you are."

He headed toward his bathroom without looking at me, but he paused with his hand on the doorframe as I shoved my shirt over my head as quickly as I could. My hands were shaking as I tried to wrap my mind around what was happening. I had just given my virginity to him, all the while he was fucking me for revenge.

"He wants you brought to him."

I rolled off the bed and scrambled to pull on my wrinkled trousers. I jammed my feet into my boots, almost tripping over the laces.

My heart hammered against my rib cage and a wave of panic washed over me as Dacre slowly turned to look at me. Our eyes locked for a fleeting moment before he turned away again, but it felt like an eternity as my chest constricted with fear, with longing.

"Run, Verena." His voice was cold. "Before he sends me on the hunt."

On the hunt.

I wanted to beg him to stop, to choose me in a way that no one ever had before.

In a way that I would have chosen him.

But his loyalty didn't lay with the girl he just fucked. It lay with the rebellion that would rather see me dead.

His bathroom door closed with a sharp click, and there was only one thing for me to do.

So, I ran.

READY FOR MORE FROM THE VEILED KINGDOM SERIES?

**The Hunted Heir is coming
July 23rd**

Preorder now!

MORE FROM HOLLY RENEE

Stars and Shadows Series:

A Kingdom of Stars and Shadows

A Kingdom of Blood and Betrayal

A Kingdom of Venom and Vows

A Kingdom of Fire and Fate

The Good Girls Series:

Where Good Girls Go to Die

Where Bad Girls Go to Fall

Where Bad Boys are Ruined

The Boys of Clermont Bay Series:

The Touch of a Villain

The Fall of a God

The Taste of an Enemy

The Deceit of a Devil

The Seduction of Pretty Lies

The Temptation of Dirty Secrets

The Rock Bottom Series:

Trouble with the Guy Next Door

Trouble with the Hotshot Boss

Trouble with the Fake Boyfriend

THANK YOU

Thank you so much for reading The Veiled Kingdom! I hope you loved this world as much as I did creating it.

Ready to fall in love with another world that I have created? A Kingdom of Stars and Shadows is a sexy, enemies-to-lovers fantasy romance that will have you begging for more!

I would love for you to join my reader group, Hollywood, so we can connect and talk about all of your thoughts on The Veiled Kingdom! This group is the first place to find out about cover reveals, book news, and new releases!

Xo,

Holly Renee
www.authorhollyrenee.com

Before You Go
Please consider leaving an honest review.

ACKNOWLEDGMENTS

Thank you to all the readers for taking a chance on this book. Dacre and Nyra/Verena are so special to me, and I hope that you loved the beginning of their story as much as I did.

Thank you to my husband, Hubie. No one will ever support or love me more than you. Thank you for always proving to me that true love exists.

Thank you to my circle of authors who constantly cheer me on when I'm having a hard time believing in myself.

Thank you to my entire team who I couldn't do this without. Lauren, Regan, Savannah, Ellie, Rumi, Cynthia, Becca, Rebecca, Katie, and Sarah: thank you, thank you, thank you.